destination unknown

destination unknown

Amy Clipston

We want to hear from you. Please send your comments about this book to us in care of zreview@zondervan.com. Thank you.

ZONDERVAN

Destination Unknown
Copyright © 2014 by Amy Clipston

This title is also available as a Zondervan ebook. Visit www.zondervan.com/ebooks.

Requests for information should be addressed to:
Zondervan, Grand Rapids, Michigan 49546

ISBN 978-0-310-73669-1

All Scripture quotations, unless otherwise indicated, are taken from The Holy Bible, *New International Version®*, NIV®. Copyright © 1973, 1978, 1984, 2011 by Biblica, Inc.® Used by permission. All rights reserved worldwide.

Any Internet addresses (websites, blogs, etc.) and telephone numbers in this book are offered as a resource. They are not intended in any way to be or imply an endorsement by Zondervan, nor does Zondervan vouch for the content of these sites and numbers for the life of this book.

Cover design: Gayle Raymer
Cover photography: Les and Dave Jacobs
Back cover photograph: Shutterstock

Printed in the United States of America

14 15 16 17 18 19 20 /DCI/ 21 20 19 18 17 16 15 14 13 12 11 10 9 8 7 6 5 4 3 2 1

For Janet Pecorella—
Your friendship is a blessing!

chapter one

W hitney!" My best friend, Kristin Bailey, rushed across the school parking lot toward me. She balanced her backpack over her shoulder, a small pink gift bag in her hand and a large brown teddy bear on her hip.

"Hey, Kristin." I waited for her to catch up.

"I've been looking all over for you." She nodded toward the large bear grinning at me from her hip. "Look at what Doug gave me." Then she pushed the gift bag toward me, and the rich aroma of milk chocolate filled my senses. "Chocolate hearts. Isn't that romantic?"

"Yeah, that's great. Very romantic." I forced a smile and adjusted the heavy backpack on my shoulder. "Thanks for the candy grams you sent me in homeroom."

"Thanks for the ones you sent me too. What did Brett give you?"

"Nothing yet. I haven't seen him all day." I shrugged to give the impression that it wasn't a big deal, even though it was a huge deal to me. In fact, I got the overwhelming suspicion he was avoiding me when he didn't show up in the cafeteria at lunch. Not a good sign for our first Valentine's Day together.

"Nothing at all?" Kristin's eyebrows pinched together above her nose. "He didn't even send you a chocolate candy gram in homeroom?"

"Nope. I only received candy grams from you, Tiffany, and Emily."

"And you haven't seen him at all today?"

I shook my head. Wasn't Kristin listening? She was showered with gifts while I got *nada. Zip. Zero. Zilch.*

Despite my humiliation, Kristin's eyes rounded with excitement. "I bet he's going to do something huge! Maybe he's planning a romantic dinner at a very exclusive restaurant."

I raised an eyebrow. "I doubt it, Kristin. The most romantic dinner I've had with Brett was spaghetti and meatballs with my parents and my little brother at my house."

"I know he's going to make it up to you." Kristin bumped my arm with her elbow. "I bet he's at the mall buying you expensive jewelry right now."

I opened my mouth to protest her generous assessment of my boyfriend but was interrupted by another friend's voice.

"Girls!" Tiffany Liu approached, her face beaming. "I have big news!"

"What's going on?" I asked.

"Oh my goodness." Tiffany looked from Kristin to me while taking a deep, dramatic breath. "I'm still reeling from the excitement."

She then clamped her hands on my wrists with such force that I yelped.

"Tiff!" I cried. "You're hurting me."

"I'm sorry." Tiffany pushed her long dark hair behind her shoulders and then held up her left hand, palm down. "Just look at what Spencer gave me today."

I peered down at a gold ring with a tiny diamond displayed between two intertwined hearts. I looked up into Tiffany's wide, almond-shaped eyes. "Wow. Does that mean you're ... ?"

"You're ... you-re ... you're *engaged*?" Kristin stammered.

"Well, kind of." Tiffany waved her hand around. "Spencer

said it's a promise ring, so we're actually engaged to be engaged. We're going to get officially engaged our senior year in college. That way we can get married after we graduate."

Kristin dropped her teddy bear and bag on the ground and then hugged Tiffany. "Congratulations, Tiff! That's so exciting."

I stared at them, wondering how logical it was for Tiffany to bind herself to Spencer during her senior year of high school. Sure, he was a nice guy, he treated her well, and he was even good looking. Yet I wondered how she could be certain he was the man she wanted to spend the rest of her life with after dating him less than six months. Who knew if they'd even be together when prom rolled around in May? Besides that, our lives were about to change with graduation only four months away. We needed to be thinking about college, not marriage. But I knew I had to be supportive. After all, that was my job as one of her best friends.

"Oh, wow, Tiff. I'm so happy for you." I squeezed her arm. "That's a beautiful ring."

"We have to celebrate," Kristin said. "After all, this is our senior year, and we have to celebrate every holiday together before we all leave for college. It's our last Valentine's Day together."

"You're right, Kristin." Tiffany beamed. "Let's have a party at my house tomorrow night."

"Perfect!" Kristin picked up her teddy bear and bag as she began listing the food items she planned to bring for the big celebration.

I agreed to bring chips and dip, along with soda.

Once the party was planned, Tiffany eyed the teddy bear balanced on Kristin's hip. "What did Doug get you?"

Kristin displayed the smiling teddy bear and bag of chocolates while Tiffany oohed and aahed with approval.

"What about you, Whitney?" Tiffany turned her brown eyes to me. "What did Brett get you?"

"I haven't seen him." I glanced toward my orange Jeep Compass sitting patiently on the other side of the parking lot. The urge to flee from my friends' stares tempted me.

"You haven't seen him?" Tiffany tilted her head. "Not at all today?"

"Nope, but it's no biggie, right? Valentine's Day is just a holiday created by the greeting-card industry to boost sales." I couldn't believe I had just quoted my eleven-year-old brother, Logan. Was I losing my mind?

"I bet he's planning something big for her." Kristin nodded with emphasis. "I'm certain he's going to surprise her with a romantic dinner, roses, and jewelry."

"Oh yeah." Tiffany's expression brightened. "Absolutely. I think Brett is romantic under that tough football-player exterior."

"Sure he is." *And I'm the queen of Sheba.* I gazed toward my Jeep. "Well, I need to get home. I'll see you tomorrow night."

Tiffany and Kristin waved as I made my way across the parking lot. A cool breeze pushed my long blonde hair back from my shoulders. I shivered while hugging my Cameronville High cheer-team hoodie closer to my body. Once again my mother was right. I should've listened to her and grabbed my jacket, but I thought I'd be warm in the sun. I hit the Unlock button on my key fob and then yanked open the driver's-side door.

"Whitney!" Brett appeared behind me. "Hey." At five foot ten he stood eye level with me. I never seemed to attract guys who were taller than I, which made things awkward when I wore heels. Not that I wore heels every day, but dances were somewhat comical when I was taller than my football-player boyfriend on the dance floor.

"Oh, hey, Brett." I tossed my backpack onto the passenger's seat and then eyed him with suspicion. "Have you been hiding from me today?"

"No, no." He jammed his hands into the pockets of his jeans. "I was looking for you."

"You were trying to find me so you could wish me a happy Valentine's Day, right?"

"Right. Happy Valentine's Day." He opened his backpack and fished out a small pink box of candy with "Happy V-Day" printed across the top. "This is for you."

"Thanks." I set the box of candy on the front seat of my Jeep. I briefly wondered if he'd somehow forgotten today was the most romantic holiday of the year and had run to the nearby pharmacy to quickly buy something during lunch. "Did you get the candy gram I sent you in homeroom?"

"Yeah. Thanks." He looked down at my front tire as if it were the most interesting item on the planet. He was avoiding my stare, and I was getting more and more aggravated by the second.

The awkward silence grew between us like a great chasm.

"I'm glad you liked the chocolate." I motioned toward my steering wheel. "I guess I'll see you later. I have to get home."

"Wait." He touched my arm and then pulled his hand back as if my hoodie had shocked him with a bolt of electricity. "I wanted to talk to you."

"Oh?" I closed my fingers around my keys. "What did you want to talk about?"

"Us." He motioned between us. "What we're doing here."

"What do you mean?"

"I like you, Whitney. You're nice and you're pretty."

Oh no. I bit back a groan as a familiar break-up speech echoed through my mind. My ex-boyfriend, Chad, had broken up with me by using similar words on Halloween during our junior year.

"Let me guess what you're going to say, Brett. This has been fun, but you just want to be friends, right?" I spat the words at him. "I'm a nice girl, but you just don't think of me *that* way. You want to break up but stay good friends. It will be as if nothing has really changed, though. Did I get it right, Brett? Is that what you wanted to say?"

He snapped his fingers. "Exactly. I'm so glad you understand." He tapped my arm. "Thanks, Whitney. You made this so much easier than I thought it would be. I'll see you around. Happy Valentine's Day."

He jogged off toward the other side of the parking lot while I stared after him, taken aback by his callousness. He'd handed me a cheap box of candy and then broke up with me. To make the situation even worse, somehow I helped him break up with me by guessing what lame excuses he'd give for ending our six-month relationship. And he dropped the break-up bomb on Valentine's Day, which was supposed to be the most romantic day of the year.

I climbed into the driver's seat and then glanced over to where Brett approached a group of his football buddies. He traded high fives and then fell into step with them as they moved toward the far end of the parking lot. Today was just another day to Brett.

I jammed the key into the ignition and then cranked the engine while contemplating this strange day. In a matter of minutes, Tiffany revealed she was "sort of" engaged, and I broke up with my boyfriend.

The strangest part was that I wasn't as heartbroken as I thought I'd be over losing Brett. Yes, the rejection hurt, and I was offended he'd chosen today of all days, as well as frustrated I'd given him an easy way out by explaining why he was breaking up with me. But instead of feeling dejected, I felt some sense of … relief.

I contemplated Brett as I steered through the Cameronville High School parking lot and merged onto Main Street. Our relationship had been nothing more than a perception at school. Kristin had told me I was lucky when Brett asked me to the homecoming dance. In the beginning of our relationship, I was honored he wanted me to be his girlfriend. After all, he was handsome, with his light-brown hair and pale-blue eyes. I heard people whisper about how we would be the next prom king and queen.

So much for that prediction.

I merged onto Glen Avenue and headed toward my neighborhood. Deep in my heart I knew my relationship with Brett wouldn't last. There was no spark. When we were together, he always seemed to be distracted, as if I were only part of the background. I wondered if the only reason he was dating me was the same reason I was dating him—because we were expected to be together, since he was the captain of the football team and I was the captain of the cheerleaders. We were *supposed* to be in love, but it was forced instead of genuine. It was as if we were *supposed* to hang out at school and at parties. We were *meant* to go to the homecoming dance together last fall. And, of course, we were *expected* to go to prom together in May.

I steered past the large brick signs welcoming me into Castleton, the neighborhood I'd known since birth. Brett was good looking, but he was exhausting to be with. I felt as if I had to always be on guard. I had to look perfect and keep the conversation going, even when a comfortable silence was what I craved. I never found a comfortable silence when I was with him. In fact, he never made me feel comfortable.

I turned onto my street and pulled into the horseshoe driveway in front of my family's dark-red brick colonial, which was similar to the other brick colonials in Castleton. The two-story house featured huge windows, an attached three-car garage, a wraparound porch, and a detached three-car garage at the back of the property.

I parked at the top of the driveway and climbed out of the Jeep. A cool breeze sliced through my clothes as I hoisted my heavy backpack onto my shoulder and retrieved the small box of candy. My thoughts moved to last summer as I glanced at the Olympic-sized, in-ground pool and the cabana enclosed inside the wrought-iron fence behind my house. I longed for the warmth and ease of summer as I started toward the back door. Things seemed so easy when I was volunteering as a tutor for summer school, teaching cheerleading at the summer recreation camp, and spending time with friends around the pool before senior year had started. Now I was facing my high school graduation and an unknown future.

I moved past my mother's shiny Mercedes SUV (an almost replica of my father's) and climbed the deck steps leading into the kitchen. I pushed the sliding-glass door open and stepped inside.

"Hello! I'm home." I dropped my backpack onto a kitchen chair, set the candy on the table, and crossed to the refrigerator to pull out the container of my favorite iced tea. I poured a glass and then swiped an apple from the fruit bowl in the middle of the island. I was settling onto a kitchen chair with my snack when my mother appeared scowling in the doorway.

"Whitney Jean." My mother's voice was disapproving, and I immediately felt my eyes widen at the mention of my full name.

"Hi, Mom. How was your day?" I bit into the apple, hoping her disapproval was caused by something other than me.

"Not good at all. Well, my day actually was good until I got home from my meeting at the club and found this in the mailbox." She stepped into the kitchen and waved around a piece of paper that appeared to be a letter. She was dressed in a pair of khaki slacks and a white shirt with a yellow collar, which tipped me off that she'd been at the country club for one of her women's-group meetings, since that's her usual club attire. Only collared shirts and slacks (no jeans!) were permitted at the Cameronville Country Club.

Mom sank into the seat across from me, her platinum-blonde bob bouncing with the movement. She slapped the piece of paper onto the table in front of me, and her brown eyes narrowed. "What's this?"

I peered over at the letter, and the words *"progress report"* jumped out at me. At first I thought perhaps my brother bombed another test, but my shoulders stiffened when I read my full name next to the word *"student."*

"I got a progress report?" I studied the document with confusion. "I've never had a progress report in my life. How's that possible?"

"A D on a test will earn you a progress report, Whitney Jean." My mother crossed her arms over her chest. "How do you expect to keep your admission into Kentwood University if you flunk calculus?"

The apple suddenly tasted sour. "I'm not flunking, Mom. I got a D on one test, but I'll do better next time." I sipped my iced tea, hoping to drown my agitation.

"A D means you're not doing well at all." She pointed toward the big, red D next to the word *calculus* on the letter. "This is going to ruin your 4.0 grade point average. This is serious. Only the best get into Kentwood University. You can't blow this."

"KU is *your* top choice, not mine." I wrapped the apple core in a napkin and placed it on the table.

"Don't be silly." She shook her head. "Only the best go to my alma mater, and you're the best. You've maintained a 4.0 since middle school. You belong at my alma mater. I can see you now walking across campus with my sorority letters emblazoned across your hoodie."

I squelched a rude reply as I stared at her. I'd heard this speech repeatedly since I was in middle school. It was my mother's dream for me to go to her alma mater and join her sorority as a legacy. Note: *her* dream, not mine.

"I'll be fine, Mom. I only messed up one test. I'll do better next time." I sipped my iced tea and hoped my mother would drop the subject.

"No, this won't do. You could lose your admission, and I can't stand for that. It's unacceptable. I was able to get into KU due to my good grades and scholarships. I don't want you to miss this chance, Whitney. I only want the best for you. Your father and I vowed to give you and Logan the best opportunities we could, and KU is one of them." She studied the letter with renewed focus. "I've already spoken to Mrs. Jenkins about it."

"You called my guidance counselor?" I asked with disgust.

"Yes, I did." Mom sat up taller. "It's my responsibility to make certain you do your best. Your guidance counselor and I agree that you need a tutor."

"*No.*" I enunciated the word. "I don't need any help. I can figure it out myself."

"Don't you talk back to me, Whitney Jean." My mother pointed a well-manicured finger at me. "I know what's best for you, and you need a tutor. Mrs. Jenkins is going to speak with your math teacher and set up something through the peer mentoring program. That's the end of it."

"This is humiliating!" I stood and flailed my arms with renewed irritation. "I'm a part of the peer mentoring program. I've mentored kids in English and Spanish for four years. I can't possibly have a tutor when I *am* a tutor."

My mother tilted her head and squinted, peering at me as if I'd just declared myself an alien visiting from the planet Jupiter. "Why can't peer mentors tutor other mentors? Is that in the rule book somewhere?"

"No," I mumbled. I tossed my apple core into the trash, grabbed my backpack, and started toward the stairs. "I'm going to my room." I pointed toward the box of candy on the table. "Logan can have that candy. I don't want it."

"Wait a minute." My mother stood. "Don't think you're going to get a progress report and not be punished for it."

I spun toward her. "Isn't being forced to get a tutor punishment enough?"

"Needing a tutor isn't punishment. It's a good idea to admit when you need help. Don't act like it's the end of the world." Mom jammed her hand on her hip. "You're grounded for two weeks. You'll only leave this house to go to school and church. No social gatherings."

"But Tiffany's throwing a party tomorrow night."

"I don't care. You need to take your grades seriously, Whitney."

"I do take them seriously, Mom. You already know I do my best, which is why this is my first grade below a B."

"Graduation is coming fast."

"I know." I started toward the stairs again. "Not fast enough," I muttered while climbing to the second floor.

I moved past my younger brother's room and spotted him holding a video-game controller and wearing a headset while yelling at the television. I assumed he was playing an online video game with one of his Xbox buddies. I wondered how he'd managed to play video games instead of doing his homework. I pushed the thought away, knowing he was constantly in trouble with Mom about his grades. Perhaps it was my turn to carry the burden so he could enjoy a break from Mom today.

My steps slowed as I approached the guest room where my cousin, Emily, had stayed when she and her father lived with us for eighteen months. Emily and Uncle Brad had moved to Castleton to rebuild their lives after my aunt Claire died of cancer and my uncle lost his business.

I'd felt a mixture of happiness and regret when Emily moved out of our house shortly before Christmas. Although I was happy she and Uncle Brad were financially able to find a place to rent, I knew I'd miss our late-night girl talks. I could've used one of those girl talks today after breaking up with Brett and coming home to a mortifying progress report and subsequent lecture from my mom. Emily would've listened and understood, whereas my mother was so focused on my grades being perfect that she didn't even ask how my day was. I didn't get the opportunity to tell Mom about Brett and his lousy idea of Valentine's Day.

I stepped into my room, which still had the same light-pink walls and white furniture I'd begged for in elementary school. I dropped my backpack on the floor in front of my walk-in closet and then flopped onto my bed. The whole day felt like a dream that had gone from bad to worse. The rumor of my failed relationship with Brett would spread like wildfire at Tiffany's party tomorrow night.

Although I knew in my heart that Brett wasn't the right guy

for me, I felt as if he and I were friends. We hung out with the same people, and we spent time together both at school and on weekends. I'd hoped that maybe someday we'd feel more like a couple. We weren't the best match, but it made sense that we would date, since Tiffany and Kristin were dating his two best friends, Spencer and Doug. Now our friend group wouldn't be the same. Things would be awkward when the six of us were together. I imagined the dream of the six of us heading to prom together in a limousine disappearing in a puff of smoke. After all, Brett certainly wouldn't be my prom date if we were no longer a couple, and I knew I'd rather go alone than with him.

Prom, however, wasn't the only issue haunting my thoughts. Deep down it hurt that he'd broken up with me. I'd never imagined that he'd reject me, especially in the parking lot after school on Valentine's Day. Brett rejected me, and then I arrived home only to find out my grade point average was shot. And now I was destined to miss Tiffany's party. It seemed things couldn't possibly get any worse.

I groaned when I thought of the party. I rolled to my side and spotted my iPhone peeking out from the side pocket of my powder-blue backpack across the room. I needed to text Tiffany and Kristin to tell them I wouldn't make it to the party tomorrow night, but I needed to first come up with a good excuse for not attending. How could I admit that I, Whitney Richards, aka Miss Straight As, needed help with calculus?

A number of fibs rolled through my mind as I fetched my phone. I could tell my friends I had to babysit my brother while my parents went out, but my brother was eleven and hadn't required a babysitter for a couple of years now. I considered inventing a fake church or family event, but both would require colorful backstories and details. Finally, I decided to feign a twenty-four-hour stomach flu, which would begin tomorrow morning and end Sunday night. That seemed the easiest and less embarrassing excuse for missing the party.

I placed the phone on the bedside table and stared up at the white ceiling as humiliation coursed through me. I'd been certain I understood the calculus concepts prior to the test, and seeing the D on my test paper last week had knocked the wind out of me. I never imagined Mr. Turner would send out a progress report to my parents and completely crush both my confidence and self-esteem. I thought I'd have a chance to rebound and bring my grade up to at least a B-plus without my parents ever knowing about my flubbed test.

An idea hit me, and I sat up straight on the bed. If I studied all weekend, I could ask Mr. Turner to give me a retest. And if all went as planned, I would bring up my grade, which would make my mother happy and prevent the embarrassment of having a tutor.

I popped up from the bed, grabbed my book, and then sat at my desk. As I turned to the current chapter in the book, I closed my eyes and sent up a quick prayer, begging God to help me understand calculus. I then set about proving I didn't need anyone to help me pass calculus. I could do it on my own.

chapter two

Kristin climbed into my Jeep Monday morning and slammed the door with emphasis. "What's going on with you? I've been worried about you. You never answered my texts all weekend."

"Oh, I'm sorry. I was really sick until last night, and I didn't look at my phone after I texted you and Tiff." I backed out of her driveway and steered through the neighborhood, hoping I sounded convincing. I'd texted Kristin and Tiffany Saturday afternoon and told them I was suffering from stomach flu, and then I'd avoided their text messages the rest of the weekend. While pretending to be sick, I'd spent all weekend studying calculus and trying my hardest to make sense out of the confusing concepts.

"How are you feeling now?" She turned to me looking concerned.

"Fine." I kept my eyes on the road ahead. Avoiding eye contact was my best option for seeming genuine. "It was a twenty-four-hour thing, so I'm all better now. Tell me about the party."

"You missed the most awesome party Saturday night." She sat up straight in the seat as if to brace herself for quite a story. "It turns out Monica Barnes and Paul Jefferson have been cheating on each other. It all came to a head in the middle of Tiffany's family room around midnight."

Kristin launched into a complicated story I didn't really care to hear while we drove through Castleton and merged onto the main road.

"It was quite a scene," Kristin said, concluding the story. "Monica left in a huff, and Paul tried to stop her."

"Wow." I felt her eyes studying me, and I cleared my throat. "It sounds like they put on a show."

"Were you really sick?"

I gave her a sideways glance. "Why would you ask that?"

"Well ..." Kristin touched my shoulder. "Brett told us you broke up on Friday. I'm so sorry. Why didn't you tell me? I could've been there for you."

"Oh. That." I shrugged. "It's no big deal. I think it was sort of a mutual thing even though he initiated it." And I was telling her the truth. I'd awakened Saturday completely fine. The hurt was gone and replaced with relief. I no longer felt obligated to be his girlfriend, and I wasn't worried about how the breakup would affect our clique. Instead, I was more focused on calculus and worried about ruining my nearly-perfect GPA.

Kristin looked unconvinced. "I thought you guys were happy."

Is she serious? I bit back a sarcastic remark. "I think we were just sort of biding our time until graduation."

"I just wish you'd told me. You didn't have to stay home from the party because of being embarrassed. I mean, everyone goes through a breakup now and then. We could've drowned your sorrows in chocolate together."

"I'm doing okay. Really, I am."

She studied me again. "So you really were sick over the weekend?"

"Yeah." *Sick of calculus.* "But I'm fine now."

"Oh, good. Well, let me tell you more about the party. Tiffany looked spectacular. She and Spencer are so happy." Her expression transformed into a scowl. "But things won't be the same now that you and Brett broke up. We won't be able to do things together as couples. Tiffany and I were talking about that Saturday night. We're going to really miss that."

"It's okay. Really, it is." I found myself consoling her over my breakup, and it was weird. It was even stranger that I was over the heartbreak. Yet my friends seemed more upset about the fact that Brett and I seemed like the perfect couple than the fact that my heart was supposedly crushed. I pondered that notion while Kristin kept talking.

"I wish the three of us could be happy with our boyfriends again, but you'll find someone before prom, Whitney. I'm sure of it."

"Yeah, I'm sure of it too." I shook my head, thinking that there was definitely more to life than finding my true love at the age of eighteen.

Kristin talked on about the party while I drove the rest of the way to school. I parked in my usual spot near the front of the lot, and then we made our way toward a group of friends waiting by the door. I greeted my friends and made small talk about the weekend. When the bell rang, I went over the speech I'd prepared for calculus class. I was determined to prove to Mr. Turner and my mom that I didn't need a tutor. I could pass calculus with flying colors on my own.

Mr. Turner was in the middle of explaining our homework when the bell rang at the end of calculus. "Whitney," he said, making eye contact with me. "Please stay so I can talk to you for a few minutes."

I nodded, trying to ignore the curious stares around me.

While the other students filed out of the classroom, I lingered behind, pretending to organize my books in my backpack. After the last student left, I made my way through the sea of desks to Mr. Turner's at the front of the room.

"You wanted to talk to me." I fingered the zipper on my CHS cheer Windbreaker, hoping to appear more confident than I felt.

"Whitney." Mr. Turner pulled off his glasses and gave me an overly sweet and encouraging expression. "Your mother called Mrs. Jenkins to say she was very upset when she received your progress report."

"I know." I closed my hand around the strap on my backpack. "Believe me, I know."

"Mrs. Jenkins asked that we find you a tutor." He pointed at me with his glasses. "I have a fantastic tutor in mind. He's all but taught my classes. I'm certain the kid is a genius. I know he can—"

"Wait." I held up my hand. "Excuse me for interrupting, but I have a better idea. I studied all weekend long, and I think I can retake the test and do better. You know I always work hard. If you just let me retake the unit test and do some extra credit, I'm certain I can get at least a B."

Mr. Turner's expression clouded, and my hope sank. "Whitney, I'm sorry. There are plenty of kids struggling, and I can't give you any special privileges."

"Oh, no, no. I didn't mean I wanted special privileges or an advantage." Heat crept up from the base of my neck, and my mind raced. Why couldn't I remember the speech I'd prepared? I babbled, saying anything that came to mind. "I know I can do better. I just need more time. I promise I'll study extra hard. I know I can do this on my own, Mr. Turner. I know I can."

"I think the tutor will give you the extra help you need. He's good. I've recommended him to a few of my other students, and they quickly brought failing grades up to a C."

"A C?" Panic surged through me. He had to be kidding me. I couldn't bear the thought of not getting at least a B-plus!

Mr. Turner chuckled. "Not everyone gets As all the time, Whitney. Every once in a while you might struggle a bit, but that's a part of life." He put his glasses back on and picked up a notepad and pen. "I'll talk to Mrs. Jenkins today and arrange for a tutor to start this week. I think a session once a week would work for you. Once you get the concepts down, you'll be fine. I'll have it all set up by tomorrow, and the tutor will contact you."

"Okay. Thanks." I started toward the door, and my shoulders hunched as I accepted my fate. Maybe just one session would work for me. I'd pass the next test, and everything would be just fine.

After school I stood in the parking lot flanked by Tiffany, Kristin, Doug, and Spencer. I greeted a few students who walked by, and they responded with waves. Although I was standing with my best friends, I felt out of place without Brett by my side until I remembered I wasn't dating him anymore. I didn't exactly miss being his girlfriend, but I suddenly felt like I didn't belong.

"So, how about a movie tonight, Kristin?" Tiffany elbowed Kristin in her side. "Spencer and I are going, and we'd love you and Doug to join us." She glanced toward me. "Oh, and you can come too, Whitney."

"Thanks, but I can't. I have a ton of homework." Not only did I dread being a fifth wheel, but I also could never admit I was grounded for a bad grade. My friends used to call me Whitney "Ruin the Curve" Richards. I couldn't stand the humiliation if they started calling me Whitney "Progress Report" Richards instead.

"You study too much." Spencer stood behind Tiffany, wound his arms around her waist, and pulled her to his chest. "All work and no play makes Whitney a dull girl."

I glared at him. "You expect me to listen to advice from a straight-C student?"

"Burn!" Doug laughed and punched Spencer in the shoulder. "She got you, Spence!"

Brett jogged up to the group and grinned at his fellow football players. "What's so funny?"

Although I felt like a fifth wheel without Brett, I didn't want to hang out with him either. I waved and stepped away from the group. "I have to go. See you all tomorrow."

"Wait." Brett jammed his hands in his pockets. "You don't need to go because of me. We're still friends, right?"

I forced my sweetest smile. "Don't flatter yourself, Brett. I'm leaving because I have to go, not because of you."

"Wow. She's on a roll, huh? She told Spencer off, and now Brett." Doug looped his arm around Kristin's shoulders. "You're getting mouthy, Whitney. What's going on?"

"Nothing." I adjusted my backpack on my shoulder. "I just need to get home. That's all. I have to study for a ..."

"Whitney!" a voice called from behind me.

I turned and spotted Taylor Martinez waving toward me as he stood near the bike rack.

"Is Martinez talking to you?" Kristin asked.

"I don't know." I studied Taylor, and he waved again.

"Yes, I'm calling you, Whitney Richards," Taylor said. "Can I talk to you for a minute?"

"What does Taylor Martinez want with you?" Brett sneered. "Charity?"

"Hey," I snapped at Brett. "That's not funny and not cool."

Doug snickered, and I swallowed the urge to yell at him as I walked toward Taylor, who was dressed in tight blue jeans and a faded-green army jacket that reminded me of one my uncle Brad said he bought at Goodwill. Taylor lifted a helmet off the motorcycle behind him.

As I approached him, I wondered how he had gotten so tall. I'd know Taylor since kindergarten when I was the tallest kid in the class. In fact, I was the tallest student until middle school. However, I hadn't noticed that Taylor had shot up in height and was now a few inches taller than I was. My eyes were drawn to his face, which had transformed from a chubby elementary student's face to a thin young man's face. I'd never before noted that he had a pouty mouth, with full lips, or that his hair was so thick, dark, and curly.

He looked sullen and serious, and I wondered what he wanted to discuss with me. From what I remembered, Taylor and I hadn't spoken since we had shared our lunchtime desserts in elementary school.

"Hi, Taylor." I stopped in front of him and fingered a tie on my Windbreaker as I looked up at him. "What did you need?"

He stepped closer to me and lowered his voice. "Mr. Turner said you need some help with calculus."

"You're a tutor?" The words escaped my lips before I could stop them, and I immediately wanted to slap myself for being rude.

"I imagine you find it hard to believe that someone like me could actually understand calculus, huh?" He raised an eyebrow but didn't smile. I felt myself drawn into his deep-brown eyes. I wondered if his eyes had always been so dark and bottomless.

They were innocent and worldly all at the same time. Had they magically transformed when he shot up to nearly six foot two?

"I'm sorry. That was rude, and I didn't mean to say it." I felt the tips of my ears burn with embarrassment. "I won't take up a lot of your time. I don't need much help."

"You only need a little help, right? I hear that a lot, until the students actually get into calculus. When they realize just how difficult it is, they wind up spending a whole lot of time with me." He hugged the black helmet to his chest, and his expression remained dark but confident. "How's tomorrow at twelve thirty?"

"That works." I nodded. "I have a free period after lunch."

"I'll wait for you in conference room number two in the library. I'm tutoring someone in geometry during my lunch period, so I'll be there already." He took a step back toward the motorcycle. "Bring your book and your last test."

"Okay." I studied him and wondered how long he'd been mentoring students. Why hadn't I seen him at any of the peer mentoring meetings? Was it because he only tutored math, while I helped students with Spanish and English?

He pulled the helmet over his head and fastened the strap before straddling the motorcycle next to him.

"Is that your bike?" I pointed toward the motorcycle and wondered what it would be like to ride on one. Was it as exciting and liberating as it looked in the movies?

"No, I'm stealing it." His response was muffled through the helmet. "See you tomorrow, Whitney."

Before I could respond, the bike roared to life. It choked and went silent before he revved it again and then sped off through the parking lot. I, meanwhile, just stood there, watching him disappear around the corner. I'd never imagined that Taylor Martinez was a math tutor and rode a motorcycle. He'd transformed from the quiet boy who shared his chocolate-chip cookies with me during lunch in fourth grade to a tall, arrogant senior who was a math whiz.

"What did Martinez want?"

I spun around and found Tiffany, Kristin, Brett, Doug, and Spencer watching me.

"Whitney, I'm talking to you. What did he want?" Kristin asked again.

"Oh. You mean Taylor?" I searched for an excuse for my conversation with him. I couldn't bring myself to admit that Taylor was going to be my calculus tutor. "He and I have a project we need to work on together for class. We're going to meet tomorrow to talk about it during my free period."

"What class are you and Taylor in together?" Kristin asked.

"Calculus." It wasn't exactly a lie. Taylor was going to help me with calculus, so that qualified as a project. My friends couldn't dispute it, since none of them were taking that subject.

"Did you know Taylor's dad left him, his mom, and his sister years go?" Tiffany blurted. "I think he was six. I can't imagine growing up without a father, can you?"

"No, I can't. It's got to be really hard," Kristin agreed. "I heard his mom has to work two jobs to get by. That's why they live over in Great Oaks. They have a tiny little house, but it's better than no house at all."

"Don't gossip." I looked around at my friends. "My cousin lives over in Great Oaks, and her place is nice enough. You can't judge people by where they live."

"Get real, Whitney." Doug crossed his arms over his varsity jacket. "Taylor is a loser. He doesn't hang with our crowd, and he's never at any of our parties. Whenever I see him, he's always studying alone in the library." He pointed toward where Taylor's motorcycle had been parked. "Did you check out that rat bike?"

Brett grinned. "Yeah, man. What a loser. I almost laughed when it didn't start. I was wondering if he was going to walk it home."

"What's a rat bike?" I asked.

"It means it was pieced together with odd parts," Doug said. "I'd be too ashamed to ride that thing."

"You're so shallow, Doug." I wondered why Kristin liked him so much. I'd never realized until that moment that he was such a jerk. I regarded Doug and Brett with disgust and then turned toward my Jeep. "I need to get home. I'll see you all later." I headed across the parking lot.

As I drove home, I sent up a prayer:

I'm so confused and stressed out. I've always gotten straight As in school and tutored other kids, and now my grades in calculus are so bad, I need a tutor myself. It's embarrassing and humiliating. Please help me understand calculus so I can bring my grades up. But what I'm most confused about is my friends—my best friends since elementary school. Suddenly I don't feel like I belong in their group anymore. I don't really know why, but everything feels different now. Are they changing or am I? I just know I'm really confused and don't know what to do. Please help me, God.

chapter three

The following afternoon I stepped into the library conference room and found Taylor scowling while sitting at the table.

"You're late." His lips formed a thin line illustrating his discontentment. He was wearing an unbuttoned, well-worn, red-plaid flannel shirt with a plain black shirt underneath. "I figured you weren't going to show up, since you said you really didn't need my help anyway."

"Well, I did, and I'm here now." I sat across from him and wondered if he was always so outspoken. "I lost track of time while I was eating lunch. I'm sorry." I pulled out my notebook, found my infamous calculus test with the big, red D in the upper-right corner, and placed it on the table.

"Let me see that." Taylor picked up the test paper and examined it as if it were a specimen he was about to cut open and study. He began explaining problems and concepts, and I tuned him out while staring down at my notebook and wondering how I could blow off this tutoring session and convince Mr. Turner I didn't need any help.

"Whitney? Are you listening to me?" Taylor sounded irritated.

My eyes snapped to his. "Yeah, I'm listening. I'm sorry."

Taylor drummed his pencil on the table and studied me, causing me to feel self-conscious and wonder if I had salad stuck in my teeth. "If I'm wasting my time here, then let me know. I can think of better things to do with an hour before I have to go to class."

"You're not wasting my time or yours. Let's just get it over and done with. I have better things to do too." I sat up straight and studied his deep-brown eyes while he talked on about calculus concepts.

"Did what I said make any sense at all?" His question broke through my thoughts and caught me off guard.

"Yes, it does."

"So you think you could recreate this problem here and get the right answer?" He pointed toward the first problem I'd messed up on the test.

I shrugged. "Sure."

"All right. I'd like to see you do that." He rewrote the problem on a blank piece of paper and pushed it toward me. "Show me."

"Okay." I took the pencil from him and studied the question.

"Want me to show you how to do it again?"

I looked up at him and wondered how a guy so gruff on the outside could have such warm and captivating eyes.

He raised his eyebrows. "Why are you staring at me?"

"Why do you tutor?" The question burst from my lips before I could stop it. Why was I so blunt when I was around Taylor? His outspokenness seemed like a highly contagious disease.

"Why do *you* tutor?" He bumped the question back to me as if it were a volleyball.

"How did you know I was a tutor?"

His smile was wry. "I've seen you at the peer mentoring meetings. I guess you didn't notice me because I don't wear a varsity football jacket."

I blanched. "Not all of my friends are into sports."

"And none of them live on my side of town either." His expression challenged me to prove him wrong.

"That's not true. I know someone who lives in Great Oaks."

"Yeah. Sure you do, Whitney." He averted his gaze by looking down at the test again, and I wondered why he was so cantankerous. "Back to work."

"You never answered my question." I planted my hands on my notebook. "Why do you tutor?"

"Why do I tutor?" He rubbed his chin as if considering the question in great depth. "Let's just say not everyone has a college education handed to them on a silver platter. I have to earn the privilege of going to college through activities and good grades. Without a scholarship, I'll be working the fryer at Burger World, and I would rather put my math abilities to better use."

"Are you saying I have everything handed to me on a silver platter?" I challenged his harsh remark.

"I didn't mean that." He shrugged. "I just meant some kids have it easier than others. Did you get to choose which college you wanted to apply to without worrying about the cost?"

I paused, not knowing how to answer. The truth was my mother was more worried about prestige than cost when it came to choosing a college. She only let me apply to the local university and State because I begged until my dad finally allowed it.

"Since you can't answer the question, I would imagine you can go to any college you want to, since you get awesome grades, have participated in all of the right activities, and your father makes a lot of money."

I tapped the table for emphasis. "Let's just say I don't have as much choice as you think I do."

"You have more choices than I do. Right now I'm thankful I got a full scholarship."

"You did?" I smiled widely. "That's awesome, Taylor. Which school are you going to?"

"I got a full ride to U." His eyes narrowed. "Don't patronize me, Whitney."

"I'm not patronizing you. I think it's awesome." I felt a twinge of jealousy nip at me. University, or U as everyone called it, was where Emily planned to go, and it was where I wanted to go, since it had a fantastic teaching program. But my mother was insisting on Kentwood, so I had no choice in the matter. "Why can't you just accept a compliment?"

His expression softened a fraction. I wondered if he ever smiled, or if he was this frosty all the time. "I'm just glad I get to go to college."

"Look, Taylor, my life isn't perfect. I'm certain you have problems, but I do too. Just because my problems are different from yours doesn't make your life any harder than mine. Everyone has problems." I couldn't help but wonder why he was acting so prickly. I felt as if he was judging me because of where I lived, which was just as bad as Doug and Brett making fun of where Taylor lived. Maybe Taylor was just as socially prejudiced as they were.

Taylor snorted. "Whitney, I doubt you have any idea what it truly means to struggle in life."

Speechless, I stared at him. *Why does he have such a big chip on his shoulder?*

"Enough chitchat. Back to work." Taylor looked at his watch and then pointed toward the paper in front of me. "We don't have much time. I'd like to eat lunch before my next class. Let's see if you can figure that one out."

"Okay." I started writing down what I thought was the right answer to the problem.

"Actually, you're closer, but that's still not the answer."

I slumped in my chair and folded my arms over my chest.

"You'll get it. I promise you. I'm a good tutor." He pulled out another blank piece of paper from his notebook and began to write. Mr. Turner was right when he said Taylor was a genius, but he was an arrogant one.

He continued to discuss concepts, and I watched him, wishing I could understand the subject like he did. Why didn't calculus come as easy to me as history, science, Spanish, and English did? I couldn't comprehend why I was struggling so much. It was so unlike me to feel lost when it came to school.

Soon the bell rang, and I gathered up my notebook. "Thanks."

"So much for eating lunch today." He packed up his supplies. "Same time next week?"

"Yeah, sure." I hoisted my backpack onto my shoulder and moved through the door.

I spent all of Spanish class wondering why Taylor had been so defensive with me. Did he truly believe I was a snob who would never acknowledge him? If so, then he didn't know me at all.

While Señora Zoch prattled on about the Spanish novel we were studying, I propped by elbow on the desk and rested my chin on the palm of my hand as I considered the thought. Could Taylor possibly be right about me? Was I a snob because I hadn't noticed him at the peer mentoring meetings? The question wouldn't let me go. I'd always tried my best to be a true Christian in every sense of the word. I knew I wasn't perfect. I tried not to be the stereotypical cheerleader in the movies who thought she was better than everyone else and didn't acknowledge students who weren't a part of her exclusive group. So then why did Taylor accuse me of blowing him off and being a snob? The accusation stung me, and I couldn't get it out of my mind.

Señora Zoch moved on to our homework assignment, and I pulled out my notebook. I flipped to the problem we'd discussed during the tutoring session, and my eyes focused on Taylor's handwriting. I couldn't possibly learn anything if I spent the entire tutoring session wondering exactly why Taylor didn't like me. I had to find a new tutor. And there was only one way to get a new tutor—I needed to convince Mr. Turner that Taylor and I weren't the best match when it came to learning.

The bell rang, announcing the end of the school day, and I hurried down the hallway toward Mr. Turner's room. I stepped into the room and found him clearing his desk.

"Hey, Mr. Turner." I fingered my notebook in my hands. "Can I ask you a quick question?"

"Sure, Whitney. What's going on?" He stood.

I wracked my brain for a reason to find a new tutor. How could I possibly admit I felt uncomfortable working with someone who accused me of being a snob? "I was wondering if there's another tutor available to help me with calculus."

"Oh." Mr. Turner swiped his glasses from his face. "Taylor is the only calculus tutor we have. Isn't it working out with him?"

"It's working out fine." I hoped my voice sounded upbeat. "He's really smart." Why was I such a chicken? Why couldn't I admit Taylor made me feel uncomfortable?

"So, then, why do you want to find another tutor?" He picked up a briefcase and began to fill it with papers.

"I guess it's sort of a personality thing." I tried to smile and act causal even though I was humiliated. "I don't think he likes me."

Mr. Turner looked as if he was holding back a laugh. "I find that hard to believe." He closed the briefcase. "You said you didn't want any help. Just complete a few sessions with Taylor, and then you'll be ready for the next test."

"Right."

"Have a good evening, Whitney." He lifted the briefcase. "I'll see you tomorrow."

I made my way out to the parking lot wondering how I was going to get through the future tutoring sessions. Maybe if I was as sweet as sugar to Taylor, he would be nice to me. Grandma always said I should kill people with kindness. Perhaps Taylor was the kind of person she was referring to when she'd shared that advice.

I found my friends standing in the usual spot by the tree, and I sidled up to them.

"Hey, Whitney," Tiffany said as I approached. "How was your afternoon?"

"Good." I nodded. "Yours?"

"I have a ton of homework," Tiffany said. "I should've been reading that stupid book all along. The test is Friday, and I'm totally unprepared. I can't stand English. What's the point in reading old books anyway?"

I bit my lip to stop my smile. Tiffany would tease me if I told her I loved the classics almost as much as I loved contemporary fiction.

"I know what you mean." Kristin examined her fingernails. "I need to study for a Spanish exam, but I totally need to get a manicure." She looked at her watch. "I wonder if I run to the mall right now if I can get my nails done before I start studying."

I shook my head. If my friends worked harder at school, they too could be on the honor roll. The roar of an engine drew our eyes toward the parking space where Taylor straddled his motorcycle.

"That reminds me." Kristin turned toward me. "I meant to ask you how your project is going with Taylor."

I shrugged while watching Taylor secure his helmet. "It's going fine."

Tiffany grinned. "He's kind of hot on the back of that motorcycle, huh?"

Taylor sped through the parking lot, and I watched him until he disappeared around the corner. *Yeah, he's good looking, but he's a tad bit abrasive.*

"Definitely eye candy." Kristin smiled.

Tiffany looked at Kristin. "So, are you going to the mall to get your nails done? I'll come with you. I need a fill really bad."

I spotted Spencer, Doug, Brett, and my other ex-boyfriend, Chad, approach, and I groaned. "I have to go. See you tomorrow."

I climbed into my Jeep and steered through the parking lot while considering my day. I wondered why Taylor didn't like me, while Brett was jealous of him. I switched on my favorite radio station in an attempt to drown out my conflicted thoughts.

When I pulled into the driveway, I stared up at my house and wondered what Taylor would say if he came over for a visit. Would he sneer at the house my father had paid for with his successful banking career?

I headed toward the back door with my backpack slung over my shoulder. I couldn't figure out why Taylor didn't like me. I couldn't get past it, even though I knew I should just let the frustration go. I'd always tried to be everyone's friend. I wanted people to like me. As far as I knew, most kids at our school thought I was nice. And if that was true, then why didn't he like me?

I hoped I could grasp calculus quickly and not have to deal with Taylor Martinez for more than a few tutoring sessions.

chapter four

The following afternoon I made a detour to the mall after school. Although I was still technically grounded, I knew my mom had a meeting at the country club and wouldn't be home for about another hour and a half. I had just enough time to dash into the bookstore and see if the new Ludwig Becker mystery had made its bookstore debut. I'd been watching the author's website, and it said some exclusive bookstores would have copies today. I hoped the mall's bookstore was considered exclusive.

I steered into a parking space near the mall entrance and then hurried into the bookstore. I perused the new arrivals section, and my heart sank when I didn't find my favorite mystery author's book on the rack. I made my way to the mystery section and scanned the shelves, finding Becker's shelf. I pulled out one of his books and began to read the summary on the back, even though I'd read the book twice already.

"Can I help you find something?"

I looked back and found Taylor Martinez watching me with a couple of books in his hands. He wore a blue shirt with a nametag pinned to it, declaring him a bookstore employee.

"Taylor. Hey." I hugged the book to my chest. "I didn't know you worked here."

"I've been here a couple of years now." He pointed toward the book in my arms. "You're a Becker fan, huh?"

I glanced down at it. "Yeah. I've actually read this one a few times. I was hoping to find his new book."

He stepped over to me. "Excuse me. Let me just put these books up."

"Sure." I moved to the side, and his arm brushed mine as he placed the books on the shelves.

He moved away from the shelf and tapped the book in my hands. "So you're waiting for *Beyond the Fog* too."

"You read Becker?" I studied him, finding it interesting that he liked the same author I did.

Taylor shrugged. "Sure I do. I like a good mystery, and he knows how to write them."

"Yeah, he does. I heard it was going to be out early in a few exclusive stores. I was hoping our little bookstore would be considered exclusive, but I guess not."

He leaned against the bookshelf behind him. "No, I don't think we're exclusive." He pointed toward the front of the store. "That book's actually going to hit our new-arrivals shelves on Friday. Do you want me to snag a copy for you? We have a waiting list, but I can sneak your name in."

"Oh." I was caught off guard by his thoughtfulness. Could we actually be friends? "Sure. I'd love one."

"Okay." Taylor touched the cover of the book in my hands. "I liked *Murder in the Delta*. That was a good one, but *Sweet Revenge* was my favorite." Reaching past me, he retrieved *Sweet Revenge* from the shelf and handed it to me.

"Yeah, it was his best. I hope the new one is just as good."

"I bet it will be." He pushed an errant curl back from his forehead, and I wondered what it would be like to have naturally curly hair. I wondered if he hated his hair or appreciated it.

I reached out to place the books on the shelf, and he stepped closer to me.

"Want me to put those back on the shelf for you?"

"Thanks." I handed him the books.

"You're welcome." He pushed the books into their proper places and then faced me again. "You do realize I get paid big bucks to keep these books straight."

I laughed. "You make the big bucks, huh?"

"Absolutely. Bookstore work pays minimum wage, and don't you forget it." He grinned, and I was caught off guard by his smile, which made him even more attractive.

"Why don't you put your high salary to good use and recommend another good mystery author for me."

"I'd be happy to." He began pulling books off the shelf while telling me which authors wrote the best stories.

He handed me a few books, and his witty commentary about the stories made me laugh. Before I knew it, I was holding a stack of six books.

"These are a few of my favorites anyway. If we had all afternoon, I could give you my recommendations for all of the sections." He took the books from my hands. "Do you think you'll purchase any of them today?"

"Hmm." I pressed my finger to my lips. "Which are your top two picks?"

"That's a difficult question." He examined the books. "These two." He pulled out two from the stack.

"I'll take those, then." I took the books from him, and he put the others back on the shelf. "What time is it?"

He checked his wristwatch. "Almost four fifteen."

"Oh no." Panic washed over me. I had less than thirty minutes to get home. Mom always got home by 4:45 on her meeting days. "I have to run."

"Let's get you checked out."

I followed him to the register, where he rang up my books and I paid. "Thanks for your help," I said as I took the bag from him.

"I look forward to hearing how you like the books."

"Great." I adjusted my purse strap on my shoulder. "See ya."

I rushed to my Jeep and sped home, cutting through a nearby neighborhood to avoid driving past the country club.

When I reached the driveway, I parked in my usual spot and then ran into the house. I hid the two new books in my room, and then I ran down to the kitchen. I was spreading out my homework on the kitchen table when Logan appeared in the doorway.

He crossed his arms over his chest and smirked at me. "I thought you were grounded."

I glared at him, but he just stood there grinning like the Cheshire Cat. "Look, I ran by the bookstore on the way home. Just keep it to yourself, okay?"

The hum of an engine announced my mother's arrival home. I was arranging my schoolbooks on the table when Mom bounded through the back door.

"Hello!" She balanced a grocery bag on her hip. "Logan, would you please go get the other bag in my trunk and then lock the car?"

"Sure." Logan gave me one last smirk before taking the keys from Mom and disappearing out the door.

"Hi, Mom." I popped up from the table and started to put the groceries away. "How was your day?"

"It was good, thank you. And yours?" Mom poked her head in the refrigerator and began opening drawers.

"Fine, thanks." I placed a jar of peanut butter in the pantry.

Mom stacked lettuce, cucumber, tomatoes, green peppers, onions, radishes, and carrots on the counter and then looked at me. "Did you see your tutor today?"

"No." *Yes, I did, but he didn't tutor me.* "We only meet on Tuesdays."

"Oh, that's right." She pointed toward the pile on the counter. "Whitney, would you be a dear and start making the salad? I need to get the salmon loaf in the oven."

"Sure." I pulled out a large crystal salad bowl and began slicing and dicing the vegetables.

My mother preheated the oven and then started pulling together the ingredients for the salmon loaf. While we worked, she filled me in on her club meeting and their charity benefit plans for the coming spring. I nodded and feigned interest, but my thoughts were stuck at the bookstore. I silently pondered the new information I'd discovered about Taylor Martinez—not only did he work at the bookstore, but he also liked the same genre of books and author I did. Perhaps he and I did have something in common, and we could be friends. What a crazy notion! I had to be losing my mind.

"Whitney?" My mother studied me. "Are you okay? You seem to be on another planet."

"I'm sorry." I began to cut up an onion, hoping that the smell would pull my attention away from my thoughts of Taylor. "I was just thinking about school. I have a test in health class tomorrow."

"Oh." My mother looked concerned. "Are you prepared?"

"Yeah, I'll be fine. I just need to review the material again." I lifted the cutting board and sprinkled the onion into the bowl.

"Oh, good." She placed the salmon loaf in the oven and set the timer. "Is the calculus tutoring helping you?"

I shrugged. "Yes, I think so."

"That's good." Mom wiped her hands on a towel. "I expect at least a B on your next calculus test."

I swallowed a sigh. "Yes, Mom."

I listened to my mother talk on about her friends at the country club and church while I finished making the salad. Then Mom began washing up some larger bowls and items that wouldn't fit in the dishwasher, and I dried.

"I saw Brett's mother today at the meeting." Mom handed me a clean mixing bowl. "How's Brett doing?"

"Fine, I guess." I dried the bowl.

"Did you two have a disagreement?" My mother tilted her head with concern.

"We broke up." I turned my back to her while placing the bowl in the cabinet.

"What?" My mother's eyes were wide with surprise. "You didn't tell me."

"I haven't had a chance. We've both been busy."

"Oh, Whitney. I'm so sorry. I'm never too busy to talk to you when you need me." Mom cupped my face with her hands. "You must be devastated."

"Not really." I shrugged.

"Did he break up with you?"

"It was sort of mutual. He was starting to break up with me, but I finished his sentences for him."

"Oh dear." Mom shook her head and clicked her tongue. "When did this happen?"

I grabbed the utensils from the sink and slipped them into the dishwasher. "Valentine's Day."

"I had no idea." She touched my shoulder. "I wonder why Rhonda didn't say anything about it to me. That's simply terrible. I must say something to her about it."

"Mom!" I grabbed her arm. "Please don't say anything to Brett or his mom. I said it was *mutual*. I'm okay with it. Don't get involved." This was why I didn't want to tell my mother about the breakup. She overreacted about everything, and this wasn't something I needed her to handle for me.

"If you say so." She shook her head. "He was such a nice young man. Maybe he'll change his mind and ask you to prom. You certainly don't want to go alone."

"I'm really not worried about prom right now, Mom. It's only February. Besides, it wouldn't be the end of the world if I went to prom alone." The idea of walking into my senior prom without a date didn't thrill me, but I could handle it.

"Oh, don't say that! You have to have a date for the prom, Whitney." Mom tapped her chin. "I'll have to talk to some of my friends. I don't think Lola's son is dating anyone."

"Mom, I don't need your help finding a date for prom, okay? Just worry about your charity events for your women's group." *Don't make me your charity case.* I closed my eyes and silently counted to ten to prevent myself from saying something rude.

She nodded. "Fine. But if you want me to speak to Rhonda, I will. Maybe she can talk some sense into Brett. You two were an adorable couple."

I turned my back toward her so she couldn't see my scowl. "I'm going to go work on my homework until Dad gets home." I packed up my books and moved to the dining-room table, where I worked until I heard my father's Mercedes SUV pull into the driveway.

"Whitney!" Mom called from the kitchen. "Your father is home. Would you please set the table?"

"Yes." I closed up my notebook and headed to the cabinets to grab the dishes. I was setting them out when my father came through the back door.

"Hello, hello!" Dad placed his briefcase on the bench by the door. He was wearing an expensive Italian suit, and his graying brown hair was cut short.

"Daddy!" Even at eighteen, I was always excited when Dad got home. "How was your day?"

"It was good, pumpkin. How was yours?" He made his way into the kitchen, pulling off his tie as he walked.

"Good." I placed the dishes on the table and then fetched the utensils.

"What smells so good, Darlene?" Dad moved behind Mom and placed a kiss on her cheek, a gesture I'd witnessed every night since I was little.

"Salmon loaf." Mom motioned for him to move away from the oven. "I need to pull it out." She glanced toward the doorway. "Where's Logan? Whitney, would you please call your brother down?"

"I'm here." Logan appeared and crossed to the cabinets, stopping briefly to high-five Dad on his way. "I'll get the glasses."

I set out the utensils while Logan placed a glass at each setting and brought the pitcher of tea. Mom and I brought the meal to the table, and then we all sat in our usual spots.

My father nodded at Logan. "Say the prayer, son."

We all bowed our heads while Logan prayed out loud. Once he was finished, my father took the large crystal salad serving bowl and filled the small bowl at his place setting before passing the salad to my mother.

"Whitney," Mom said while filling her salad bowl. "Would you mind running a stack of mail over to Uncle Brad's tomorrow after school? I've been meaning to take it to him, but I keep forgetting. I have a ladies' luncheon at church tomorrow, so I won't have time." She handed the salad to me and then pointed toward the counter. "There are a few letters for your uncle. I'm not certain they're important, but I think we should take them to him right away. It's funny how he's still getting mail here. I guess it takes a while for an address change to catch up with everyone."

"Sure." I filled my salad bowl. "I'd love to see Em. I haven't run into her at school."

"Oh my gosh. The funniest thing happened at school today." Logan launched into a story about something that had happened during gym class, and my parents laughed.

I studied my parents, and I suddenly felt overwhelmed by emotion. I was truly blessed to come from a family that was still intact.

As I watched my father delight in my brother's story, I wondered what it would've been like to grow up without a father.

chapter five

After school the next day, I steered into Emily's driveway and parked behind the red Honda Accord my mom had given her last year. The car looked great since Uncle Brad worked on it. In fact, it looked much better than when it had been mine. Brad had healed up nicely after slicing his arm in a body-shop accident over a year ago, and he'd gotten back to both working as an assistant manager in the Cameronville Auto and Body shop and doing some car repairs on the side. Aside from giving the Honda a good tune-up, he'd fixed the dents I'd put in it and painted it bright red. Emily had told me more than once that she loved the car and was thankful Mom gave it to her.

I climbed from the Jeep and walked up the front path toward the small, two-bedroom, ranch-style house. The aluminum siding was beige, and the windows were accented with country-blue shutters. I walked up to the front door and knocked.

Emily opened the door and pulled me into a hug. "Hey, cousin! I was so excited when I got your text message. It's been way too long since we've talked. Come in."

She was a few inches shorter than I was and had long, naturally curly, brown hair and emerald-green eyes. I'd often told her I'd love to have her naturally curly hair, but she insisted I wouldn't like it as much if I had to deal with the constant knots and tangles. She often let her hair hang free, which drove my mother insane. When Emily lived with us, my mother constantly nagged her about straightening her mess of curls, but I always felt the hair suited my cousin just fine. She wore faded jeans and a loose T-shirt with a classic-car design on it. Her only makeup was a twinge of pink lip gloss, but that was all she needed.

"I'm so glad you're home. I heard you've been working a lot." I handed her the mail and then followed her into the small family room at the front of the house.

"Yeah, I am," she said as we walked toward the kitchen. "My dad is letting me work as many hours as I want at the shop as long as I keep my grades up. He's actually letting me work on a few cars along with doing some of the paperwork in the office." She tossed the mail onto the counter and then opened the refrigerator. "My scholarships and grants aren't going to cover all of my expenses next year, so I have to work." She pulled out two cans of Diet Coke and handed me one. "It's nice out. Want to sit outside and talk for a while?" She picked up a bowl of caramel popcorn.

"That sounds great." I grabbed a handful of popcorn as we started back to the door. "I love this stuff. My mom would flip if she saw me eating it."

"Is she still on you about your weight?" Emily pushed open the door.

"She's on me about everything." I shook my head and stepped onto the porch. "Boy, do I miss having you at my house. Don't get me wrong. I'm glad you and your dad are on your own, but I miss our talks."

"I do too." Emily lowered herself into a plastic chair on the small front porch and rested her ankle on her knee. "Have a seat. Tell me what's been going on."

I sat next to her and grabbed another handful of caramel popcorn. "So much has been going on. It's crazy. I'm actually grounded right now. The only reason I was allowed to come over here was to deliver your mail."

"What?" Emily studied me. "You haven't been grounded at all since I moved down here last year. In fact, I've never heard of you getting in trouble, ever, Whitney. What on earth did you do to get grounded?"

"I got a D on a test." I filled my palm with more popcorn and glanced toward a similar ranch-style house across the street as I spoke. "My mother flipped."

"What a minute." Emily faced me with a few frizzy curls falling past her shoulder. "You, Whitney Richards, got a D on a test. How did that happen? Was it a deliberate way of rebelling against your mother?"

I grinned. "That's a wonderfully evil plan, Em, but sadly, no, it wasn't deliberate. I'm seriously struggling in calculus."

"Yikes." Emily shook her head and then sipped her can of soda. "That's rough. I know how much your grades mean to you and how hard you work for that 4.0 GPA. I bet your mom did flip."

"She also made me get a tutor through the peer mentoring program. I can't tell you how demeaning it is to be tutored when you're a tutor yourself."

Emily scooped up more popcorn. "Oh, Whitney, I'm so sorry, but just remember you don't always have to be perfect. We all fail sometimes, but we just pick ourselves back up and keep going."

I nodded, knowing that my cousin was right. Yet at the same time, I couldn't accept my failure. It was just too painful. "How are things with you? How's Zander?"

Emily grinned. "He's doing well. He came home for the weekend for Valentine's Day." She pulled a gold locket with a cross on it out from under her T-shirt. "He gave me this and chocolate."

I was glad to hear Emily's relationship with Zander was still going strong. Their friendship shifted into a relationship when she met him while living at my house last year. Zander's parents lived next door, and Emily and Zander met through their love of working on cars. In my opinion, they were a perfect match.

"Oh, wow." I touched the little gold locket. "He's such a thoughtful guy."

"Yeah, he is." Emily fingered the necklace. "How was your Valentine's Day? I hope Brett was good to you too."

I shared the story of our parking-lot breakup.

When I finished my tale, Emily studied me, disbelief apparent on her face. "You've got to be kidding me. He broke up with you on Valentine's Day?"

I nodded.

"What a creep. I'm so sorry." She squeezed my hand. "He wasn't good enough for you. He sounds just like Chad. I'll never forget how he broke up with you on Halloween. That was terrible. We need to find you a good guy."

"Thanks. I knew you'd be supportive. I don't know what I'd do without you." I ate more popcorn while thinking about Emily and Zander. "I haven't seen Zander's Jeep at his parents' house much. I guess that's a sign he's really enjoying school."

"Oh yeah." She filled her hand with more popcorn. "He loves school. Motorsports Tech is just want he thought it would be. I'm so glad he convinced his dad to let him go."

"That's great." I grabbed another handful of popcorn.

"He said he might think about transferring to the University after he graduates from the motorsports program. He wants to continue his schooling and get a degree in business." She fingered her soda can as she spoke. "Zander keeps telling me he'd love to open a shop with my dad. You know it's my dream to run a shop with my dad like the one he ran back before my mom got sick. I'd love to see my dad, Zander, and me go into business together, but I think it would be smart for both Zander and me to get our degrees first. Dad and Zander could handle the cars, and I could work in the office until the business grew. And I'd fix a car here and there when needed, of course."

"Wow." I shook my head in amazement. "You and Zander have it all figured out."

"What does that mean?" Emily eyed me with suspicion while digging into the popcorn bowl. "I think you're pretty put together yourself. I'd kill for your grades."

I snorted. "Even the D in calculus?"

She laughed. "Well, no. You can keep the D. I just mean your other As. I was happy just to get one B-plus last semester."

"Grades aren't everything. You know what you want. You know where you want to go to school."

"Wait a minute." Emily held her hand up as if to stop me from speaking. "What are you saying? I thought you were accepted at, like, three schools. What's going on?"

"I was accepted at all three I applied to, but my mom is pressuring me to commit to her alma mater. I'd rather go to the University with you, but you know my mom. She won't listen."

"Have you tried talking to your dad?"

"I have in the past, and he's always talked to my mom and gotten her to back off." I tilted my head. "I guess it might be a good idea to talk to him again. He always knows how to calm her down and remind her that I need the chance to live my own life."

Emily shrugged. "It's worth a shot."

I contemplated trying to explain my reasons for wanting to go to the University to my dad, but my thoughts were interrupted by the sound of a loud engine approaching. I glanced down the street just as a motorcycle carrying a tall driver and a smaller passenger steered into a driveway across the street and a few houses down from Emily's house.

The driver of the motorcycle climbed off and then helped the passenger down. The smaller person turned toward Emily and me and waved.

"Hi, Vanessa!" Emily waved back.

Vanessa removed her helmet and waved again. "Hi, Emily!"

The driver removed his helmet, and when I realized it was Taylor Martinez, my eyes widened. He waved to us before putting both of the helmets on the back of the bike.

"Taylor Martinez is your neighbor?" I asked with surprise.

"Yeah. They're a really nice family." Emily nodded toward Taylor and Vanessa. "Vanessa is coming over to visit. She's in eighth grade. We chat all the time. She's like my surrogate little sister. I guess we have a lot in common, since I lost my mom and she doesn't have a dad. I love talking to her. She tells me all about her middle-school drama. I'm so glad those years are over, you know?"

"Oh yeah. I know." I began wiping popcorn crumbs off my hoodie. I had no idea why I was worried about my appearance, but I suddenly felt grungy. I touched my hair, hoping my ponytail was still intact. Across the street, I spotted Taylor moving his motorcycle into the small one-car garage attached to the house. His house looked to be the same model as Emily's, only the burgundy paint on the shutters was peeling, and the vinyl siding was a faded yellow.

"Hey!" The girl approached. "I'm Vanessa." She was about five foot six, with long, dark hair and milk-chocolate eyes that mirrored her brother's. She wasn't thin, but she wasn't fat either. She was what my mother would call "average." She stuck her hand out, and I shook it.

"Hi, Vanessa. I'm Whitney. Emily is my cousin."

"Great to meet you," Vanessa said.

"How'd you do on that earth science test?" Emily asked, clasping her hands with anticipation. I assumed they had discussed the test previously.

"I got a B-plus!" Vanessa held up her hand, and Emily gave her a high five.

"Great job! Want some caramel popcorn?" Emily held out the bowl. "I know it's your favorite."

"I shouldn't." Vanessa paused and then grinned. "You know I can't resist."

Taylor sauntered up the driveway, and I touched my hair again. I briefly wondered if I was obsessed with my appearance all the time or if this was a new trend because of him.

"Hey, neighbor." Emily greeted Taylor. "You're just in time for some caramel popcorn."

"Thanks." Taylor grabbed a handful and nodded at me. "Hi, Whitney. Fancy meeting you here in Great Oaks. I guess you actually do have a friend in this neighborhood."

I spotted Emily giving me a questioning expression out of the corner of my eye.

I knew he was making a reference to our earlier conversation, and I refused to let him see my irritation. Instead, I smiled. "I told you I knew people on this side of town. You do realize Emily is my cousin, right?"

He looked confused for a moment and then held up a finger. "Oh, right. I did forget about the family connection." He ate a piece of popcorn. "Did you start either of those books I recommended to you?"

"I did." I sipped my Diet Coke. "I started the one by Brantley Morgan. It's really good."

Taylor gave me a thumbs-up. "I told you it was. Let me know how you like it."

"What are you two talking about?" Emily looked confused.

"Books. I recommended a few authors for Whitney to try." Taylor fished another handful of popcorn from the bowl.

"Oh my gosh!" Vanessa's eyes rounded, and I was certain they might pop out of her head as she stared at my chest.

"What?" I followed her glance toward my hoodie, wondering what the excitement was. Did I have a revealing hole in my hoodie? Was there a giant spider on my chest? I shivered at the thought.

"Are you a *varsity* cheerleader?" Vanessa continued to look as if she might burst with excitement at the revelation.

"Yes, I am." I nodded slowly. "Why?"

"Vanessa ..." Taylor cautioned.

"Taylor, I have to ask her." Vanessa grabbed his sleeve. "You know what this means to me."

"What does she want to ask me?" I turned to Emily, hoping she knew the answer, but she only shrugged.

Vanessa stood up straight. "I'm going to ask her."

The sullen expression I'd seen on Taylor's face during our tutoring session returned as he stood behind his sister. I wondered if he was always this moody. His mood seemed to change so often that I couldn't keep up.

"Whitney, it's my dream to become a varsity cheerleader." She folded her hands as if to say a prayer. "Would you please help me train for spring tryouts? Please, Whitney. It would mean the world to me."

I studied her puppy-dog eyes for a moment and then looked up at Taylor, who had his eyes fixed on me while he shook his head in disapproval. It was apparent to me that Vanessa had her heart set on getting my help. And after Taylor's sarcastic comment about my having friends in his neighborhood, his disapproval only made me inclined to help her.

"Sure," I said. "When do you want to start training?"

"Yay!" Vanessa jumped up and clapped her hands. "That's awesome! Thank you so much, Whitney."

"Wait a minute." Taylor held up his hand. "We need to discuss this with Mom first. You know how Mom wants to know where we are at all times. She may not want you out training."

I wondered if Taylor was serious or only making excuses to derail my plans. "Why would your mom be upset if I came over and showed Vanessa how to do a few cheerleading moves? I can work with her at your house if you need me to."

Taylor shot me a warning glance that killed the joy I'd felt at the idea of training another prospective cheerleader. It was obvious Taylor was overprotective of his little sister and was worried about my influence over her. I wondered if his mistrust was only aimed at me or if he mistrusted everyone.

"Vanessa," he began, "I need you to go home and start supper. Mom is working late, and she'd appreciate it if we have supper done for her. Can you do that?"

Vanessa snapped her fingers with disappointment. "But I want to talk to Whitney about cheerleading. Can't you give me a few more minutes?"

"You can talk to her another time." Taylor's tone warmed a little.

"Fine." Vanessa looked disappointed. "It was nice meeting you, Whitney."

"You too, Vanessa. I'll talk to you soon."

"You keep up the great work with your science tests!" Emily called after her.

"Okay! Bye!" Vanessa turned and waved one last time and then hurried down the street.

Once Vanessa was out of earshot, Taylor turned to me. "Just drop the whole cheerleading thing, okay? Please, just let it go."

"Why? What have you got against cheering?" I challenged.

"It's not personal." He held up his hand as if to surrender. "I just don't want you to make a promise to my little sister that you can't keep. She's had enough disappointment in her life."

"What's that supposed to mean?" I sat up straight, preparing for an argument. I'd had it with his attitude and comments about cheerleaders and people like me. "If you're saying I'm going to disappoint your sister, then it *is* personal. How do you know whether I keep my promises or not? You don't even know me."

"No, I don't know you. But I know cheerleaders, and my sister isn't going to be one of them." His expression told me he meant business, and it really ticked me off.

"That doesn't even make sense, Taylor." I shook my head. "Why are you so negative about cheerleading?"

"I have to go." He nodded toward Emily. "Thanks for the popcorn. See you guys at school."

I watched him head across the street, and the frustration inside me welled. "I don't understand that guy at all. One minute he's super-nice to me and recommending books I might like, and the next he's upset with me and accusing me of disappointing his sister. What's his problem?"

"He's always been nice to me." Emily held up the bowl to offer me the last of the popcorn, and I shook my head. "I don't know why he reacted to you that way about the cheerleading. It was as if it hit a nerve with him."

"He's prejudiced against cheerleaders," I muttered into my soda can.

"You're so silly." Emily laughed and swatted me with her hand. "I doubt that. I know he's very protective of his sister, though."

"Do you think he's afraid I'll be mean to Vanessa? I do my

best to be nice to everyone, but maybe I haven't done as well as I should. Oh no." I clutched my soda can and contemplated how I'd treated him and his sister. "Do you think I've given him the impression that I'm not nice at all?"

"Oh, stop it, Whitney." Emily waved off the comment. "You're always too nice. The issue might be something that has nothing in the world to do with you."

"Taylor drives me crazy. He's my calculus tutor, and it's really obvious he doesn't like me."

"He's your tutor?" Emily looked surprised. "Wow. I knew he was super smart. I heard he's in the running for valedictorian. I also heard he got a perfect score on the SATs."

"Wow." I ran my fingers down the plastic chair arm. "He sure is super smart. Mr. Turner was right when he said Taylor was a genius."

"He's like the Albert Einstein of CHS." Emily swiped the last piece of popcorn from the bowl. "But I get the impression he doesn't have it easy. His mom works really late, and Taylor has a lot of pressure on him to take care of his sister, work, and also get good grades. I don't think his attitude is a reflection on you. He's just distracted."

"Distracted." I repeated the word and hoped she was right. The idea of helping Vanessa haunted me, and I couldn't let it go. I felt as if I was supposed to help her strive for her dream of making the CHS varsity cheerleading team. Somehow I would convince him to let me teach his sister how to be a cheerleader and help her prepare for tryouts.

chapter six

The following Tuesday I sat across from Taylor at the conference-room table while he examined and discussed the assignments I'd completed over the weekend.

"I think you're starting to get the hang of it." He looked up at me. "What's wrong? You're looking at me as if I'm speaking French. Am I going too fast? Have I lost you?"

"Why don't you like me?" The words sprang from my lips, and awkwardness surged through me. My shoulders tightened as I waited for his answer. For some inexplicable reason, I couldn't handle the thought of being rejected by this boy I barely knew.

"What?" Taylor shook his head. "You've lost me, Whitney. Why do you think I don't like you?"

"Isn't it obvious?" I gestured widely with my hands. "You act like you don't like me."

He paused and studied me. "Why do you worry about everyone liking you?" He regarded me with confusion, as if I were someone certifiably insane. "You're going to encounter people in life who don't like you, and there's nothing you can do about that."

"So that means you don't like me." The realization weighed heavily on my chest. I briefly considered packing up my books and leaving, but instead I was cemented in place, determined to figure out why this kid didn't like me.

"I only said that you shouldn't worry about what everyone thinks of you. I never said I didn't like you. You came to that conclusion on your own."

"You accused me of being a snob, and you won't let me spend time with your sister."

"You're still putting words in my mouth," he said with annoyance. "I never said you were a snob."

"Yes, you did." I tapped the table for emphasis. "You said I never noticed you at the peer mentoring meetings because you don't wear a varsity jacket, and you accused me of not having any friends in Great Oaks."

"I didn't mean it that way."

"So then how did you mean it, Taylor?"

He paused and folded his hands over his notebook. Agitation brewed in his eyes.

"You can't answer because you know it's the truth." I stood and packed up my books. "I gotta go." I picked up my phone from the table.

"Wait a minute." He leaned forward in his chair. "I don't have a problem with you spending time with my sister, but I don't want you to get her involved in cheerleading."

"Why?" I sank back into the chair and placed my phone on the table.

Taylor paused as if to choose the right words. "Look, I know the score around here. My sister is sweet and naïve. She mistakenly thinks everyone is genuine and wants to be her friend. I know she won't fit in with the cheerleader types, and I'd rather shield her from that pain."

"Why won't she fit in? I know I can train her. I've been helping cheerleaders since middle school, and have been leading camps since I was fifteen. I took gymnastics for years, and I even competed. You should see my shelves filled with gymnastics and cheering awards. I know I can help her. Even if she can't do a cartwheel, I can help her make the team if you let me."

"Don't act so naïve, Whitney." Taylor shook his head. "You and I both know it's not about ability."

"So, what is it?" I leveled my gaze with his as irritation nipped at me. "What are you afraid to tell me?"

"I'm not afraid to tell you I think she's not the cheerleader type. We all know there's a type. It may not be listed on the school's activity website, but if you take one look at the photos on the cheerleading page, you'll see that there's a type." He pointed at me. "You're it, and she's not."

Anger simmered inside me. "So you're saying that because she's not blonde and she's Hispanic, she won't fit in? You can take a look at the team and see we're not all Caucasian or blonde." I started counting off on my fingers. "Tiffany is Asian, Krystal is Filipino, Diana is African American, and, oh, Monica has dark hair. Besides that, we also have very different personalities." My voice shook. "I think you're the one with the problem, not me or my cheer team. You're the one who's prejudiced against my *type*."

I slung my purse and backpack over my shoulder. "I have to go." I bolted through the door and rushed down the hall toward my next class.

I was nearly fifteen minutes early for class, so I found a quiet corner in the hallway, slid onto the floor, and sat with my knees propped against my chest. My body still vibrated with a mixture of anger and hurt. Although I was beginning to believe Taylor and I could be friends, I found he was just as judgmental as Brett and Doug. Maybe it was a guy thing. Perhaps all guys were self-righteous and arrogant.

But his accusations still hurt. All I wanted to do was help his sister. Vanessa had seemed so determined to become a cheerleader, and I excelled at training. I'd taken freshmen who didn't know how to do cartwheels and taught them how to flip from the top of a pyramid. I had taught at the cheer camp three summers in a row. I knew I was capable of helping Vanessa, but Taylor refused to let me because of how he felt about "my type."

I considered his accusations. Maybe I was the problem. Perhaps I'd done something to offend Taylor over the years, but I couldn't imagine what it was. Had I somehow rebuffed him in middle school? I couldn't think of one negative incident that had occurred between us. But his words had stung me.

I was so confused and upset, afraid I'd cry and embarrass myself in front of the whole school. Why did Taylor Martinez's opinion of cheerleaders affect me so deeply?

I dropped my head into my hands, closed my eyes, and prayed.

God, *please help me in my relationship with Taylor. I want to help Vanessa, but I can't if Taylor doesn't trust me. Please help me figure out what I can do to fix this situation. Make Taylor realize I would never intentionally hurt him or his sister.*

I cleared my throat, pulled out one of the novels Taylor had recommended, and read until the bell rang to announce the next class.

"Where is my stupid phone?" I folded forward the backseat of my Jeep and searched for my iPhone later that evening. "I know I had it earlier."

"Why don't you try calling it, genius?" Logan held up the house phone while standing by the garage. "Want me to dial?"

"Yes, please." I threw my hands in the air and moaned in

frustration. I'd been searching my backpack and car ever since I realized it was missing during supper.

"It went straight to voice mail."

"Oh no." I buried my face in my hands and moaned again. "The battery was dying when I was in calculus, and I was thinking about going out to my Jeep and plugging it in after lunch, but I forgot." *And then I got totally distracted after tutoring ...* I scowled at the memory of the tutoring session.

"So get a new one." Logan shrugged as if it was the most reasonable solution.

"Dad will never let me buy a new iPhone, Logan. Do you have any idea how much those things cost?"

"You might catch him in the right mood. That's how I got a new skateboard last week." My brother winked at me.

"You do have a point."

"As Grandma always says, give everyone a chance to say no."

I grinned. "You know, you're very smart for an eleven-year-old."

"I try." He disappeared into the garage.

I folded the seats back correctly and locked the Jeep before heading into the house. I found my father sitting in his favorite recliner while watching the evening news.

"Hey, Daddy." I dropped onto the sofa across from him.

"Did you find your phone?" He looked over at me.

"Uh, no. I think it's long gone."

"I'm certain you'll find it." He turned his attention back to the television and changed the channel. "I imagine one of your friends found it and will give it to you tomorrow."

"But that's the thing, Dad. If someone found it, they would've called me. I already called Kristin and Tiffany, and neither of them have seen it. I'm sure if any of the guys had found it, they would've given the phone to Tiffany or Kristin or even called me themselves. I really think the phone is gone. I've searched my Jeep and my backpack nearly a dozen times. I even retraced my steps through the house and searched my room. It's nowhere to be found."

Dad gave me a sideways glance. "It's not the end of the world, Whitney. I would actually enjoy the silence if my phone or computer were lost. I'd get some peace for once."

I folded my hands and gnawed my lower lip while trying to think of a way to convince Dad that my missing phone was a huge deal. "Actually, I was wondering if I could go to the cellphone store and get a new one."

My father shot me a look of disbelief. "You can't be serious. You want me to give you permission to spend two hundred dollars to replace a phone you'll probably find tomorrow?"

"But it's gone, Daddy." My voice raised an octave as I begged.

"Whitney, I think you should wait at least forty-eight hours and confirm it's gone." He scowled. "You can survive a day or two without the phone."

"But Daddy—" My whining was interrupted by the doorbell. "I'll get it." I jumped up from the sofa and made my way to the front door. I pulled the door open and froze when I found Taylor standing on the front step. "Taylor. Hi." I stood up straight. "What are you doing here?"

"Are you missing something?" He held up my iPhone.

"My phone!" On impulse I launched myself into his arms. When I realized I'd hugged him, I stepped back as I took the phone from him. "Thanks, Taylor. I've been searching everywhere for it."

"Sure." He cleared his throat and rubbed the back of his neck. Then he quickly looked down and kicked a stone on the front step.

"Where did you find it?" I asked.

"You left it in the library. I tried to find you, but you took off in a hurry." Taylor jammed his hands into his jean pockets. "I couldn't call your house because your phone was locked, and I didn't know your password. I had to leave school early for work, and I didn't want to leave it on your Jeep. I was going to bring it to school tomorrow, but I ran into Emily. She told me where you live, so I thought I'd bring it by after work."

"Thank you so much." I pushed on the screen, and the phone didn't respond. "I was right. The battery is dead. I tried to call it earlier, but it went right to voice mail."

My dad appeared in the doorway and smirked. "I see you found your phone. It's a good thing I didn't let you go buy a new one."

"As always, you were right, Dad." I pointed between my father and Taylor. "Dad, this is my friend Taylor Martinez. Taylor, this is my dad."

"It's nice to meet you, sir." Taylor shook his hand.

"Nice to meet you too." Dad gestured behind him. "Would you like to come in? My wife made her famous sugar-free chocolate cake earlier. It's out of this world."

"Oh, no, thank you." Taylor pointed toward the driveway. "My mom is working late, and my sister is home alone. I need to get home."

"All right." Dad nodded.

"Whitney?" My mother's voice rang out from the kitchen. "Who's here, dear?"

"It's my friend Taylor, Mom." I looked at Taylor. "I'm sorry. You're going to meet the whole family."

He shrugged. "It's okay."

"Well, invite him in, dear." Mom waved from the kitchen.

I lowered my voice. "Do you mind stepping in for a minute? My mom prides herself on being the best hostess in Castleton."

"I have a couple of minutes." Taylor followed me through the family room to the kitchen doorway.

"Mom, this is Taylor Martinez. He's my calculus tutor." I touched Taylor's arm and realized it was the second time I'd touched him today. I hoped he didn't get the wrong idea. Even though I called him my friend, I was still offended by his comments earlier about cheerleaders.

"It's nice to meet you, dear." My mother came around the island and shook his hand.

"Hi, Mrs. Richards," Taylor said.

"So, you're Whitney's calculus tutor." My mother folded her arms over her collared shirt and assessed him with her eyes. "Whitney hadn't mentioned you."

Taylor shot me a sideways glance. I was certain I'd get a lecture from him later. It was more fuel for his "cheerleaders-are-all-snobs" attitude.

"Where do you live, dear?" Mom asked.

"Great Oaks," Taylor said.

"Just down the street from Emily," I chimed in.

"Oh, well, that's nice." Mom pointed toward the Tupperware cake saver. "Would you like a piece of sugar-free chocolate cake? I just baked it this morning."

"Oh no, thank you. I need to get home, but I appreciate the invitation." He looked around the kitchen. "You have a beautiful home."

"Why, thank you." My mom stood a little taller. "You need to visit again."

"I will. Thanks." Taylor turned to me. "I guess I'll see you tomorrow."

"I'll walk you out."

Taylor said good-bye to my parents on his way out to the porch. We fell into step on our way to his motorcycle waiting in the driveway. I shivered in the February air.

"Thanks for bringing my phone over." I hugged my arms to my middle. "I really appreciate it."

"You're welcome." Taylor paused. "Look, I wanted to talk to you about earlier. I'm really sorry." He reached under the bike seat and pulled out a small bag. "This is for you. It's sort of a peace offering."

"A peace offering?" I opened the bag and pulled out Ludwig Becker's new novel. "Taylor! Oh my goodness. How much do I owe you?" I squelched the urge to hug him yet again. What was with my wanting to hug this guy?

"Nothing." He studied me. "Actually, I do want something in return."

"Okay." I held my breath.

"I want you to let me explain myself." He leaned against the bike, making us almost eye level. "I'm really sorry about earlier, and I'm afraid you got the wrong idea about me. I'm not prejudiced against anyone. I just want to protect my sister. I wouldn't be able to handle it if my sister was hurt. She's faced enough heartache in her life, and school is difficult enough without being rejected by an exclusive group."

I hugged the book to my chest in an effort to stop shivering as I considered his words. "Why do you keep calling my friends exclusive?"

"Whitney, that's just how it is here." He folded his arms over his faded-green jacket. "Do you really think Brett or any of the rest of his jock friends would hang out with me? Would they invite me to any of their parties?"

I remembered Doug's cruel words when he called Taylor a loser and pointed out that Taylor didn't hang out with them. "You have a point. But would you even consider going if they did invite you?"

Taylor shook his head. "No, because I know I wouldn't fit

in. And I don't want Vanessa to face that. I don't want her to think she could be captain of the cheerleading squad, because she can't."

"You don't know that for sure. If you gave me a few months to work with her, she could out-cheer some of the current seniors we have on the team."

He grinned. "You're really confident, aren't you, Whitney?"

I shrugged. "I know what I'm good at. I'm good at cheering and school … except for calculus."

"You'll get calculus. Just give yourself some time." He stood, and his smile faded into a more sullen countenance. "I don't have anything against you. And I'm sorry if I gave you the impression that I don't like you. I'm just worried about my sister."

"But you really gave me the cold shoulder." I thought back to our most recent conversation. "You're complicated. One minute you're recommending books to me, and the next you're telling me that not everyone will like me. I can't figure you out."

"I'm sorry." His expression showed he truly was. "I guess it's a defense mechanism for me to be standoffish at first. You have to understand I've dealt with Brett Steele, Doug Moor, and the rest of their ignorant friends teasing me since elementary school. That's why I'm automatically defensive around kids from their clique."

"What do you mean they've teased you since elementary school? What did they say to you?" Alarm surged through me. I knew Brett and Doug talked about Taylor behind his back, but I never knew they teased him.

"They used to constantly remind me that I lived on the poor side of town, as if I didn't already know that. They made fun of my mom's car and what she does for a living." His eyes darkened. "I've built a wall around myself because of them, but I was dead wrong about you. You're not like them. You're different. You're warmer and you're thoughtful. I shouldn't have judged you so harshly, and I'm sorry."

Disappointment filled me as I thought of my friends. Why hadn't I realized they were so mean to kids outside our group? I shouldn't have been so blind. I suddenly felt even more alienated from my friends. "I guess I should be the one who's sorry for the way my friends have behaved. If I'd known they were giving you a hard time, I would've confronted them."

"You don't have to apologize for their actions. I realize now you're not like them." He paused. "But I did mean one thing I said earlier. You really shouldn't worry about people liking you. You seem to worry too much about what people think. You should just be yourself. If someone doesn't like you, then they are the ones who have the problem."

"If only I could figure that out," I muttered.

"What did you say?" he asked.

"Nothing." I suddenly felt as if Taylor was finally letting me see past his hard exterior. I was beginning to understand what made him tick, but I felt I needed to explain myself better. "Taylor, I feel like I need to clear the air on something between us."

"Okay." His expression became curious.

"I'm not perfect, and I never asked for the life I have." I pointed toward my house behind me. "My mother tells me how to dress, what functions to attend, and who my friends should be. It's not as easy to be me as you think is."

"I never said it was easy. I just said you have more opportunities than I do."

"That might be so, but I just wish I could make one decision myself. It's not that I don't appreciate my life. I'm thankful for what I have. But sometimes I wish I could decide who am, who

Whitney Jean Richards truly is." I paused and wondered if I was getting my point across, or if I was only making his opinion of me worse. "Do I sound crazy and spoiled?"

"No. That actually makes perfect sense. You're tired of being molded by her." He shook his head slowly as if he finally understood what I was trying to say. "I guess you're complicated too. You're much more than you seem."

"What do you mean by that?" I asked, feeling defensive.

"I just meant you're more than just one of the popular kids. I feel like I understand you better now. I should've given you a chance instead of blowing you off. I'm sorry about that." He paused for a moment and then looked hopeful. "So, are we friends now?"

"Yeah, I guess so."

"You guess?" Taylor seemed unconvinced. "Do you have to ask your boyfriend for permission first?"

"I don't have a boyfriend, and I wouldn't have to ask his permission if I did."

"I thought you and Brett were going out."

"Not anymore." My thoughts moved back to Vanessa. I was still trying to understand why Taylor was so determined to protect her. "I need to ask you something."

"Okay."

"Why are you so worried about Vanessa? What happened to her? Was someone mean to her at school? I remember middle school was rough."

Taylor thought for a moment while rubbing his chin. "I wish it was only school, but it's worse than that."

"Oh." I worried I'd crossed a line. "If it's too personal, then please don't tell me. I don't want you to share something that's too painful."

"No, it's okay. I'll tell you. I guess it really isn't a secret my dad isn't around. He left us when I was six."

"We were in first grade," I said softly.

"That's right. It was right before school started." He stared off behind me while scowling. "I can still remember that day. My parents were screaming at each other. Honestly, my only memories of my dad are of him yelling and my mom crying. But that day he left and never came back. Vanessa doesn't remember him, and she still insists he's going to come back someday and take care of us like he should."

Taylor looked at me with a wry expression. "She thinks he'll just ride in on his white horse and sweep us off our feet like Prince Charming in some Disney fairytale. But he's not coming back. We don't even know where he is, and he doesn't pay child support. Every time a court finds him and starts to garnish his wages, he quits the job and moves."

He paused. "Vanessa keeps insisting to me that Dad will show up one day out of the blue with hugs, kisses, and lots of money. She constantly searches the Internet, convinced she'll find him through one of those social-network pages. I try to tell her that if he cared, he'd be here, but she won't accept reality. She just can't understand why a father would walk away from his kids. I don't get it either, but I'm tired of making excuses for him. It's been twelve years. The man has moved on and forgotten us."

I searched for something to say. "Taylor, I'm so sorry."

"That's life." He nodded toward my house. "Some people have families with two parents who love them. But some of us only have one parent who works her fingers to the bone to keep food on the table and a roof over our heads. I'm just thankful for my family, as broken as it is. And I'm determined to protect both my mother and my sister."

"Taylor, please just hear me out." I raised my hands. "Maybe cheerleading can bring some joy to your sister's life.

If you let me train her, I guarantee you she'll blow away the judges at tryouts."

Taylor shook his head. "I don't think it's a good idea. I've been trying to talk her into trying band. I told her I'll even sell a few things to make enough money to buy her a used clarinet."

"Fine." My shoulders sagged with defeat. I knew it was time to drop it.

He pointed at the book. "Are you going to start reading it tonight?"

I looked down at the novel. "I have to finish the other one first, but I'm almost done with it. It's really good."

"I'm glad you like it." He picked up his helmet. "I better go."

"Thanks again for the book and for returning my phone."

"You're welcome." He straddled the motorcycle, and I couldn't help admiring how he looked on it. He lifted the helmet and then stopped. "I have a question."

"What?"

"When did you and Brett break up?"

"Valentine's Day."

"Yikes." Taylor grimaced. "Did you break up with him?"

"Not exactly." A breeze caught my hair, and I pushed it back from my face. "He initiated the breakup, and I agreed to it."

Taylor shook his head. "Nice guy. You know, you can live in a neighborhood like this, but it doesn't mean you have class. See you at school." He slipped the helmet on and then brought the motorcycle to life.

I waved as he sped down the driveway. As he drove away, I felt as if I finally knew Taylor at a deeper level. He had let me see past his hard exterior, and now I understood why he seemed to have a chip on his shoulder. I was getting to know the real Taylor Martinez, and I felt as if we were truly becoming friends. He listened to me, and I had a feeling he understood me.

Another cool breeze whipped through me, and I shivered as I headed back into the house. My mother was waiting for me in the foyer. She studied me, and I felt my body tense.

"You were outside with that Taylor boy for quite a while, Whitney." Her tone was accusing, and I wasn't in the mood to defend my every move to her.

"He brought me my phone. I'd left it in the library after our tutoring session." I held up the phone. "It's no big deal, Mom," I snapped. "We were just talking about school."

"What's that?" She pointed toward the bag.

"He brought me a book I was looking for. Turns out we like the same author." I opened the bag, and she examined the contents. "Like I said, it's no big deal, Mom."

"I thought he was your calculus tutor. Do you have a book club while you learn calculus?"

"No, Mom. He mentioned he works at the mall, and I asked him if he'd seen the new book by my favorite author. That's it." I couldn't admit I'd snuck out to the bookstore while I was grounded. If she knew the truth, I'd be grounded again.

"Hmm." Mom crossed her arms. "I don't like you spending time with that boy. He's not a good influence."

"Why?" I challenged her. "Is it because he lives in Great Oaks? I already told you Uncle Brad and Emily live down the street from him. They're still welcome here, right? What's the difference if Taylor visits?"

"Whitney, you know what I mean. He's not like your other friends."

"Don't compare him to Brett, Mom. Taylor's a better person than Brett. And he's smart. Emily told me she heard Taylor is in the running to be the valedictorian. He got a full scholarship to U. Doesn't that count for something?"

"You watch your tone, young lady. Did your new friend

teach you how to talk back to me?" My mother glowered. "I don't want you socializing with that boy. Do you understand?" She wagged a finger at me. "You don't need to get mixed up with a boy like that. You need to concentrate on your grades right now."

I angled my chin. "Fine. I'll only talk to Taylor when we're discussing calculus."

"Don't be sarcastic. Now go to your room and finish your homework." She pointed toward the stairs. "Go on."

I climbed the stairs and made my way down the hallway to my room. I sat on the bed and plugged my phone into the charger by the nightstand before pulling out the book Taylor had given me. I ran my hand over the cover while thinking about him. Taylor was a complicated guy. He was handsome, even better looking than Brett, but he also had depth. I considered everything I had learned about him tonight. He deeply loved his mother and sister and would go to the ends of the earth to protect them. This fascinated me. I really enjoyed talking to him and getting to know him better. It was refreshing to have a friend who wanted to talk about something other than fashion and the next party. I had a sneaking suspicion Taylor and I would have more deep conversations like that in the future, and I looked forward to talking to him again. For once, I felt as if I had a friend who was a boy and not a friend who seemed to be a potential boyfriend.

My mind conjured up the image of Taylor straddling his motorcycle while pulling on his helmet, and an excitement hummed through me. Was I developing a crush on Taylor Martinez? How could I possibly even consider dating him? Since he was convinced cheerleaders and athletes were elitist, he'd never consider me.

Suddenly an idea popped into my head like a humongous light bulb: dating Taylor Martinez would drive my mother to the brink of distraction. She'd never stand for the idea of her perfect daughter dating a boy from the other side of town. Pursuing Taylor Martinez was the perfect way to rebel against my mother and show her that she couldn't run my life.

chapter seven

Friday morning I walked down the school hallway flanked by Tiffany and Kristin as we discussed our weekend plans. When I spotted Taylor up ahead, I quickened my steps. "Taylor!"

"Whitney, what are you doing?" Tiffany hissed.

"Taylor!" I rushed toward him. "Taylor, wait!"

Taylor spun and faced me. "Hey. What's up?"

"I finished that book by Brantley Morgan last night. I was up until almost two reading. I couldn't put it down."

"And …?" He raised his eyebrows. "What did you think?"

"Oh my goodness." I clapped my hands together. "I was so surprised."

Taylor laughed. "That was a good mystery."

"Yes, it was." I glanced behind me and found my friends watching me. "I just wanted to thank you for recommending it."

"You're welcome. Are you going to start the Becker book today?"

"Yes. I can't wait."

"Awesome. Let me know if you like it."

"Okay." I waved. "I'll see you later."

"Okay." He nodded and then continued down the hall.

I moved to my friends, and they both stared at me as if I were crazy.

Tiffany wrinkled her nose. "What are you doing?"

"I was talking to Taylor." I shrugged. "What's the big deal? Aren't we allowed to talk to people at school?"

"You know that could ruin your reputation." Kristin's expression was serious. "Brett was asking about you yesterday in English class, and I think he still likes you. If he sees you talking to Taylor, you could jeopardize your chance of getting back together with him."

I folded my arms over my chest. "Please, Kristin. I'm not interested in Brett, and I can talk to whomever I choose. Taylor is nice, and he likes the same books I do. I don't mind talking to him. We have a lot in common. You'd be really surprised."

"I thought you were doing a project with him." Tiffany tilted her head. "Why are you talking about books and stuff if you're only doing a project with him?"

"I *am* doing a project with him, but we like to talk about other things too. We can talk about stuff other than projects. I've seen you talk to people in class before, and it wasn't only about schoolwork." I pointed toward the line of classrooms. "We have to go, or we're going to be late."

Tiffany reached her classroom and waved before entering it.

As Kristin and I continued toward our homeroom, she lowered her voice. "I'm worried about you, Whitney. You're not acting like yourself."

"Maybe I'm trying to figure out who I am."

She stopped walking and studied me. "What do you mean? We all know who you are. You're Whitney Richards. You're the captain of the cheerleading squad, you have a 4.0, and you're going to Kentwood University, one of the most prestigious schools on the East Coast."

I shook my head. "I don't have a 4.0 anymore, and I don't want to go to Kentwood. I'm tired of being told who I'm supposed to be."

Kristin took my arm and yanked me over into a corner away from the hallway traffic. "What are you saying?"

I knew it was time to tell Kristin the truth, the whole truth, about Taylor. "Taylor isn't my partner on a project. He's my calculus tutor."

"What?" Kristin started to laugh and then stopped. "You're serious."

"Yes. I got a D on a test, and my mom went ballistic. She called Mrs. Jenkins and insisted I get a tutor." I watched the other students scurry to class like lab rats in a maze.

"I'm sure you'll get an A by the end of the semester. Don't worry about it." Her expression clouded. "But don't forget, Taylor is only your tutor. Yes, he's hot, and yes, he drives a motorcycle. But he's not your type, Whitney. You belong with someone like Brett. Taylor is too quiet and socially backward. He's totally standoffish, and he seems angry all the time. It's like he doesn't want to be one of the crowd. He has major issues. I bet he's had abandonment issues since his dad left him. We talked about that in psychology class once."

I opened my mouth to protest, but she continued on.

"That's enough about Taylor. Let's talk about you. You'll do great at Kentwood," she continued. "I wish I could've gotten in there, but I didn't have the grades. I'm going to have to go to my backup, since I couldn't get into my number-one choice. You're so lucky!"

"No, I'm not." I shook my head. "My mom is pressuring me to go to Kentwood, but I'm not sure it's what I really want. The University has an awesome teaching program. I was looking it up the other day, and I saw that some of the teachers who have won state awards have gone there. I really think I want to be a teacher, so why wouldn't I go to University instead?"

Kristin's smile was condescending. "You just have senioritis. You're ready to graduate but scared to leave home. You'll be fine. You'll get to Kentwood and love it. It'll all work out."

The bell rang, and we both started down the hall. I contemplated her comments, and frustration surged through me. I had tried to open up to Kristin and share my honest feelings, and all she did was put down Taylor and then wave off my concerns by accusing me of having senioritis. It seemed as if Taylor was the only friend I had who would listen to me.

As I slipped into my desk chair, I scowled. I felt as if I was losing my friends, the ones I had called my best friends since elementary school. I felt as if I was floating all alone.

But I wasn't alone. I still had Taylor, and I felt as if he understood me better than my friends who'd known me most of my life. He had listened to me when I opened up to him, and he didn't wave off my worries and call them a bad case of senioritis.

"So, I was thinking ..." I began as I sat across from Taylor during our weekly tutoring session.

"Uh-oh." Taylor leaned back in his chair and eyed me with suspicion. "This can't be good."

"Gee, thanks for the vote of confidence." I ran my fingernail over the smooth wooden table, creating figure eights while I spoke. "I've been thinking about Vanessa." I paused, awaiting a protest, but he continued to watch me. "I was thinking maybe trying out for cheerleading would boost her confidence and help her deal with your father's rejection."

I held my breath, hoping he'd give me a chance to prove I

could make a positive impact in Vanessa's life. I'd prayed about Vanessa, and I kept coming up with the same answer—I could show Taylor that being a part of the cheerleading squad could be a positive experience for his sister.

"I don't know." He rested his elbows on the table and blew out a puff of air. "I have a bad feeling."

"Please? Please, Taylor? I promise I won't break your sister's heart." I gave him my best puppy-dog eyes.

To my surprise, Taylor laughed. "How can I possibly say no to that face?"

Though I didn't want to risk ending the good moment we were having, I couldn't help but ask, "What does your mom think about Vanessa's wanting to be on the cheerleading squad?"

"Mom feels bad she can't afford the recreation league. Vanessa has been begging to join the rec team for years."

"Oh. That's a shame."

"I know, but hey, that's life, right?" He drummed the table and glanced down at the homework assignment we'd been discussing.

"Why don't you tell your mom about my idea and ask her what she thinks? Then you can text me tonight and let me know. Does that sound good?"

He nodded. "Yeah, that's cool."

"Great." I held out my hand. "Where's your phone?"

"Why?"

"I need to program my number in so that you can text me, silly."

"Oh. Right." He unlocked his phone before handing it to me, and I programmed in my number.

"Now send me a text."

He pushed a few buttons and my phone chimed with a text that read "*Hi.*" I programmed his number.

"Now I expect you to talk to your mom and ask her if I can start training Vanessa tomorrow. If you don't text me, I will come over to your house and ask your mom myself."

"Somehow I know you'll keep your word."

"You bet I will. And remember—I know where you live." I tapped my fingers on the table. "You haven't asked me if I started the Becker book."

We launched into a conversation about the book, and soon the bell rang announcing the end of the period.

Taylor looked surprised. "You do realize we never finished talking about your homework."

"It's okay. I'm sure I'll get it." I packed up my books. "Talk to you later."

"Yeah. You will." He slung his backpack onto his shoulder and then followed me into the library.

We moved through the library side by side, and I couldn't stop smiling. Not only was I on the road to convincing Taylor I wasn't a snob, but I could possibly help his sister. And to make it even better, I was going to defy my mother along the way. Things were looking up!

As we stepped into the hallway, Taylor touched my arm. "I'll see you later. I have to work tonight, so it might be late when I text you."

"Sounds good." I grinned up at him. "Sell lots of books."

Taylor saluted me. "I'll try." He turned and almost walked right into Brett, who glared at him.

"Watch where you're going, Martinez." Brett nearly barked the words at Taylor, and I gritted my teeth.

"I think you should do the same," Taylor retorted and then continued down the hall.

"Whitney." Brett waved an arm at me. "Wait."

I swallowed a groan and quickened my steps. "I have to get to class."

"You have a few minutes." Brett caught up with me and grabbed my arm. "I want to talk to you."

"I have nothing to say to you." I yanked my arm back and kept walking.

"Come on, Whitney. You know I care about you."

I stopped in my tracks and spun toward him. "You've got to be kidding me, Brett." I lowered my voice in the hopes of not attracting attention. "You broke up with me on Valentine's Day. That was pretty cold."

"But you agreed we should break up!"

"That's not the point. I have nothing to say to you. It's over." I started down the hall and prayed Brett would disappear.

"I know you're only using Taylor to make me jealous." Brett yelled the words.

I cringed, wishing I could crawl into a hole to avoid the eyes staring at me. I marched over to Brett, grabbed his hand, and yanked him into a nearby corner. "Don't you ever embarrass me like that again. I'm not using Taylor, and I don't want to make you jealous. I just want you to leave me alone."

"No, you don't." Brett's smile was wry. "You want me back, and I want you back too. Go out with me, Whitney. I'll treat you better this time. I'll take you to romantic restaurants and buy you teddy bears and jewelry. That's what every girl wants, right? I was just too dense to realize it. I know better now."

I regarded him with disbelief. "Are you kidding me? It's too late, Brett. I'm not interested."

"Why?" Brett gestured widely, almost knocking over a freshman who walked by. "Is it because of that loser, Taylor Martinez?"

I moved closer to Brett. "Taylor isn't a loser. In fact, you couldn't hold a candle to him as a person."

"Oh, really?" Brett snorted. "We'll see about that. You'll want me back, Whitney. You'll see."

I waved off the comment. "Good-bye."

The second bell rang, and I gasped. *I'm late to class!* I rushed down the hallway and up the stairs to Spanish class.

When I entered the classroom, I found all eyes in the room focused on me.

"*Estás tarde*, Señorita Richards." Señora Zoch announced that I was late.

"*Lo siento*, Señora Zoch." I apologized and made my way to my desk.

During class I slumped in my seat, hoping my incident with Brett wouldn't be fodder for gossip. Yet at the same time, I didn't care what everyone thought. Brett was the one who tried to embarrass me and did a better job embarrassing himself. Taylor's words echoed through my ears and reminded me that it didn't matter what people thought of me. I should only be concerned about being myself, which was what I was trying to figure out.

Later that evening I was sitting on my bed in my pajamas reading the novel Taylor had bought for me, when my phone chimed. I retrieved it from the nightstand and found the text was from Kristin.

What happened w/ u and Brett 2day?? Everyone is saying u argued in the hall.

"Oh no," I said. I considered not answering, but then she would call.

I quickly texted: *Nothing. He asked me out and I said no.*

Kristin responded with: *Why?? He loves u!*

"Oh, please," I mumbled while typing: *No, he's just jealous that I'm friends w/ Taylor.* I wondered why Kristin didn't understand how I felt about Brett. Why couldn't my best friend see that Brett wasn't the greatest choice for me? Kristin and I used to understand each other, but now I felt as if we were almost strangers. The change between us bothered me.

Kristin then sent: *Are u dating Taylor?? U better tell the truth!!*

I responded with: *No. We're friends. That's it.*

She texted: *Are u sure?*

Yes. I gotta go. C U 2morrow. I was anxious to get back to reading my book.

Ok, Kristin wrote. *Night.*

I was back to studying when my phone chimed again. I was relieved to find it was Taylor and not another nosy friend asking about Brett.

Hi. It's Taylor.

I couldn't hold back my smile. I was actually excited to see his text message.

I texted back: *Hi. How r u?*

Fine. U?

Ok. How was work?

Taylor wrote: *Good. I talked 2 my mom ...*

And ... ?

Taylor wrote: *She said sí.*

I laughed. Did he forget I was a Spanish tutor? I responded with: *Muy bien.*

So u do really know Español.

I'm a tutor, remember?

Taylor texted: *Yes, I remember. Was just teasing u. Vanessa is so excited about this. She wants 2 know if you can start Thursday after school.*

Yes, I can.

He responded: *Cool.*

I studied the phone, wondering if he would respond again.

When the phone remained silent for a few minutes, I returned to reading but found myself checking the phone frequently. When the phone chimed again, I jumped with a start.

Taylor texted: *Vanessa is bouncing off the walls. U made my sister's day. Thx.*

I wrote back: *De nada.* You're welcome.

LOL. Buenas noches.

I laughed while texting: *Good night 2 u 2. C U 2morrow.*

I returned the phone to the nightstand and then stared down at the novel. I was excited about the possibility of helping Vanessa make it onto the cheerleading team next year. But at the same time, I also felt excited at the thought of getting to know Taylor better. Where could this friendship lead, and how would my mother react to it?

The questions swirled through my mind as I tried to read. I wondered if Taylor would be home when I arrived at his house on Thursday, and I also wondered if he'd heard about the argument Brett and I had at school.

A knock sounded on the door, and my mom stuck her head in. "I'm heading to bed, Whitney. Don't stay up too late, okay?"

"Okay." I yawned and stretched. "I'm going to read for a few more minutes and then go to sleep."

"All right. Good night, dear." Mom blew an air kiss. "Oh, I have a meeting at the club Thursday, so you'll probably be home before me."

"Oh. I'll be home late too." I grasped my book and tried to think of an excuse for being home late Thursday. I couldn't admit I was going to Taylor's house, but I didn't exactly want to lie either. "I have a meeting after school."

"Oh. Okay," Mom said. "Don't read too late. You need to get your sleep."

"Good night."

She disappeared through the door. I felt a twinge of guilt, but I knew in my heart I was teaching Vanessa for the right reasons. I wanted to bring some joy to her life. I just hoped somehow my mom would understand when she found out the truth.

chapter eight

Thursday afternoon I parked my Jeep in Taylor's driveway and then walked up to the front door. I didn't see the motorcycle out front, and I wondered if it was in the garage. I adjusted the tote bag on my shoulder, straightened my blouse, and touched my hair before knocking on the door. I briefly wondered why I worried so much about my appearance. Had I learned that habit from my friends, who seemed to care only about appearances, not about getting to know someone in depth? I knew my friends would never understand why I wanted to help Vanessa, but I actually had been looking forward to this all day long.

The door swung open, and Vanessa beamed. "Whitney! I'm so excited you're here. Please come in."

"Thanks." I stepped into the house.

I glanced around and found the floor plan mirrored my cousin's house across the street. The small family room was decorated with a fireplace, two sofas, a recliner, bookshelves packed with books and framed photographs, and a television. Beyond it was a hallway reaching back toward a modest kitchen and two bedrooms. I wondered if Vanessa shared a bedroom with her mother or if she had to share one with Taylor.

I stepped over to the fireplace, and my eyes focused on

a framed photo displayed among a collection of vases and figurines. The photograph showed Taylor, Vanessa, and a woman posing in front of a blue background. Taylor was smiling a genuine smile.

I examined Vanessa's image, smiling between Taylor and the woman. She too had a bright and sunny expression. The woman had the same dark hair and eyes as Vanessa and Taylor. However, her smile seemed less genuine, almost forced, and her eyes had a hint of sadness.

"That's my mom." Vanessa moved beside me. "We had that photo taken a couple of years ago at church."

"She's very pretty. You look like her."

Vanessa grinned. "Thanks."

My eyes were drawn back to Taylor. I studied him, taking in every line of his face. What was wrong with me? The last thing I needed was a crush on Taylor Martinez, but I felt it swelling inside me. I glanced at the bookshelves and spotted more family photos. I scanned them, finding photos of Taylor and Vanessa at different ages.

Vanessa grinned. "We look goofy, don't we?"

"The photos are nice. I love seeing old photos." I turned to her and saw she was dressed in sweatpants and a T-shirt. "I brought some clothes to change into."

"Okay." Vanessa motioned for me to follow her down the short hallway. "You can change in the bathroom." She pointed toward a small bathroom located off the hallway.

"Thank you." I slipped into the bathroom and changed from my skirt and blouse to yoga pants, a T-shirt, and a pullover sweatshirt. I pulled my hair up into a ponytail and then folded my clothes and placed them into my bag.

I stepped back into the hallway and glanced through an open door into a small bedroom, including an unmade bed with a dark-colored comforter, a desk peppered with papers and books, a desk chair with clothes draped over it, and piles of clothes on the floor. Posters and pictures of motorcycles, along with academic awards, clogged the walls and shelves.

The room told me so much about Taylor that I felt as if I was prying into his private life. It was obvious he wasn't good at staying organized, but the academic awards showed that he could keep it together well for school. And his love of motorcycles intrigued me. I wanted to know more about him. Why was he so driven when it came to school?

"That's my brother's room." Vanessa startled me as she approached. "My mom has given up trying to get him to straighten it. She says it's his choice if he wants to live in filth."

"I totally understand. I have a little brother."

Vanessa pointed to a room across the hallway containing a double bed and two dressers. "I share a room with my mom."

"Oh," I said. "That's nice."

Vanessa's smile seemed forced. "Yeah, it's okay."

"What does your mom do?" I asked as I followed her back to the family room.

"She's a housekeeper."

"Oh." I nodded. "I bet that's hard work."

"Yeah, it is. She's exhausted every night. Taylor and I do all we can to help her. She keeps lecturing us about doing our best in school so we can go to college and get a good job." Vanessa stood in front of the bookshelves. "Mom regrets dropping out of high school, but at the time she was blinded by love, as she says. She says my dad was really convincing, and he promised to always love her and take care of her. She tells me constantly that boys lie, and I shouldn't believe them when they say they love me. She says boys don't know what love is until they're over thirty. Mom says I should never depend on a man to take care of me. I need to go to college and get a good job so I can take care of myself."

"That's good advice." I suddenly wanted to meet Vanessa's mother. She was a woman who had overcome a lot of obstacles in life but was doing her best to care for her children and teach them to be self-sufficient. I couldn't help but wonder what would happen if my mom and Vanessa's mom ever met. Their life perspectives would definitely clash.

Vanessa pointed toward the kitchen. "Would you like a snack or anything?"

"Oh, no, thank you." I touched my stomach. "I had a big salad at lunch."

She raised her eyebrows. "A salad filled you up?"

"Lots of croutons."

She laughed. "You're funny. So, where should we start?"

"I think we should go outside. I don't think we want to do cartwheels in here and risk breaking something."

"Let's go out back." Vanessa led me through a side door off the kitchen and into the small backyard with a picnic table, a small shed, and an area outlined with railroad ties that I assumed was a garden in the springtime. "So, what's first?" She clapped her hands. "I'm so excited!"

"I thought I'd teach you the first cheer I teach when I train the rec league. It's pretty basic." I began to show her moves, and she caught on quickly to everything I showed her.

After nearly an hour, she'd mastered two cheers and was eager to learn some gymnastics techniques. Her enthusiasm was contagious, and I was really enjoying teaching her. I had forgotten how much fun it was to instruct brand-new cheerleaders.

"How about we start with a cartwheel?" I rubbed my hands together.

"That would be awesome!" Vanessa beamed. "I've always wanted to know how to do one."

"Here's what you do." I was in the middle of showing her how to do a cartwheel when I heard a motorcycle pull up into the driveway.

"My brother is home early." Vanessa turned toward the front of the house. "Oh well. Where were we? Would you show me again?"

I hesitated, suddenly self-conscious about Taylor seeing me do gymnastics, but I pushed the thought aside. I'd been performing gymnastics since I was three, and it was preposterous for me to suddenly worry about what someone thought of my execution of a cartwheel. I did two cartwheels in a row and then stopped when I heard someone clapping.

I turned and found Taylor watching from the edge of the yard.

"Impressive." Taylor clapped again. "I can see why you're captain of the cheerleading squad."

I bowed while catching my breath. I was a little out of shape, since football season had ended in December. "I'm glad to see you can recognize good talent."

"How's your training session going?" He leaned against the back of the house.

"Awesome! Want to see what I can do?" Vanessa turned to me. "Can we show him our cheers?"

"Go for it." I motioned toward her and then placed my hands on my hips.

She looked nervous. "Would you do the cheers with me?"

"You know I can't try out with you, Vanessa. You're going to have to get used to performing in front of a crowd." I pointed toward Taylor, who looked on with a smile. "He's your brother. He won't make fun of you."

"Want to make a bet?" Vanessa asked with her hands on her hips.

"Fine. Let's start with the first one I taught you. Ready?"

We went through both cheers.

Taylor grinned. "That's pretty good, but I want to see Whitney do another cartwheel."

"Why?" I regarded him with suspicion.

Vanessa bumped me with her elbow. "Because he thinks you're cute, and he wants to see you flip around again."

"Really?" I asked.

"I need to get inside." Taylor stared hard at his sister and then disappeared around the corner of the house.

"I think he likes you." Vanessa sang the words.

I shook my head. "I doubt that."

"No, I think he does." Vanessa put her hands on her hips again. "I heard him tell my mom you're pretty and you're smart. He also said you know how to stand up for yourself, but you think of other people's feelings too. He said you're different from the other popular kids. You have more depth."

"I have depth, huh?" I felt a glimmer of hope and then pushed it away. "I don't think I'm his type."

"My best friend, Maggie, always says opposites always attract."

"I think that happens sometimes but not all the time. My cousin and her boyfriend are both crazy about cars. They actually fell in love working on a car together."

"Are you talking about Emily across the street?"

I nodded. "Yup, she's the one."

"Does her boyfriend drive a Jeep?" Vanessa asked, and I nodded again. "Oh, I know who you mean. He's really cute. I've seen him visit her on weekends."

"Yeah, Zander is cute. He's really a good guy too. He's going to a motorsports technical college. They love talking about cars together. It's their life. So, in that instance, opposites didn't attract."

"Hmm." Vanessa tilted her head. "Maggie isn't usually wrong, but maybe the difference is more than just their interests."

I nodded, considering her words. Could Taylor possibly be "my type" too? It didn't seem likely. I glanced down at my watch. "Oh no! It's after five. I have to get to youth group. We're having a potluck tonight."

"That sounds fun."

We walked back to the house together.

"Do you want to come?" I asked. "It's a fun group. We have a really good time."

"Thanks. I'll have to ask."

We stepped into the kitchen, where Taylor was busy pulling items out of the refrigerator. A pack of chopped meat, tomato sauce, a package of garlic bread, and a bag of frozen vegetables were lined up on the counter. I watched him in awe, stunned the motorcycle rider could cook too. *What can't this kid do?*

Vanessa scooted up onto the counter beside the food items. "Can I go to youth group with Whitney tonight?"

Taylor turned toward her. "Is your homework done?"

Vanessa's shoulders hunched as her expression darkened. "No."

"Then I think you know the answer." He began pulling pots out of the cabinets. "And get off the countertop. If you can't fit in the dishwasher, then you don't belong on the counter, right?"

Vanessa hopped down. "You sound like Mom."

"That's because Mom is right about that." He opened a cabinet and began poking through spices.

I stifled a snicker and retrieved my bag from a kitchen chair.

"I'm going to go get changed." I slipped into the bathroom and quickly changed into my skirt and blouse. I then brushed out my hair.

I moved back down the hallway but stopped when I overheard Vanessa say my name. Although I knew it wasn't right, I stood against the wall and listened like a spy holding a glass to evesdrop.

"Whitney is so nice, Taylor." Vanessa spoke in a hushed tone I could clearly hear. "She taught me so much. Thank you for letting her help me."

"You're welcome. I knew you'd have fun."

"So, you've changed your mind about cheerleading?" Her voice was hopeful.

"I didn't say that. I just think it's a good idea for you to give it a try."

"Did Whitney change your mind?"

I held my breath, waiting for his response and hoping he'd say something positive about me.

"Yeah, I guess so." A pot banged and then water ran. "Would you grab the spaghetti from the pantry, please? Mom is going to be home soon."

I started for the doorway.

"You like her, don't you?" Vanessa's question came in a singsong voice, and I stopped dead in my tracks.

"Who?" Taylor asked.

"Whitney, silly!"

"Oh. Sure, I do. She's my friend."

"She's really pretty, and I think she likes you."

I swallowed a groan and silently kicked myself for not barging into the kitchen and stopping this conversation. We were now moving into dangerous territory, but at the same time, I also couldn't keep myself from listening.

"Vanessa, I think you need to worry about making spaghetti instead of trying to play matchmaker."

More noise of dinner preparation rang out from the kitchen, and I took a deep breath to prepare myself for walking in on their conversation about me.

I moved to the doorway and found Taylor at the counter making meatballs and Vanessa placing spaghetti in a large pot on the stove.

"Well, I better get going. I had fun today." I crossed the kitchen and kept my eyes focused on Vanessa even though I felt Taylor watching me.

"I did too." Vanessa rushed over from the stove and hugged me. "Thank you. Will you come again?"

I glanced at Taylor for permission, and he nodded in response.

"Yes, I will," I said. "How about the same time next week?"

"Awesome!" Vanessa jumped up and down. "I'm so excited. Thank you."

"You're welcome." I looked back at Taylor. "You're both welcome at my church's youth-group meetings by the way. Maybe you can come with me next week after our cheer lesson."

"Maybe we'll do that sometime. It all depends on my mom's schedule, though."

"Okay. Well, I better go." I pointed a thumb toward the front door. "Have a good night."

"Thanks again, Whitney!" Vanessa waved. "I'll practice the cheers and try to figure out how to do cartwheels."

"Sounds good." I turned toward the doorway. "Good night."

"Ness, please put the meatballs in the microwave. The recipe is on the counter by the oregano." Taylor appeared beside me, wiping off his hands with a paper towel. "Let me walk you out."

Taylor opened the front door and then followed me out to my Jeep. "My sister had a great time. Thank you."

"*De nada*. I had a lot of fun too. Helping her made me realize how much I truly love the sport." I grinned. "*Buenas noches.*"

"Good night," he echoed in English. "Drive safely."

As I drove toward church, I suddenly realized I'd forgotten to tell my mother about the potluck at youth group—I'd be home much later than she would expect as a result. I fetched my phone from my bag and dialed the house number. I quickly told my brother I was going straight to church from my meeting and would be home later, and I asked him to relay the message. I then rushed off to the grocery store to pick up something to share at the potluck.

Emily sat across from me at the youth-group meeting. "These fudge-stripe cookies are just what I needed."

"I'm glad you like them. I stopped at the grocery store on the way over here." I picked up a cookie and broke it in half. "Did you work today?"

"Yeah, I did. Then I came straight here. The money is good, but I'm worn out."

I bit into the cookie and thought about sharing my confusing feelings for Taylor. I'd been engrossed in my thoughts since I left his house. I couldn't stop myself from analyzing every comment, every glance, every smile … What was wrong with me? I used to know where I was supposed to be. I once dreamed of going to the prom with Kristin, Tiffany, and the rest of our group. We used to spend every weekend at each other's houses, and we talked about planning a joint graduation party with all of our friends and relatives. Now I found myself excited about coaching

Vanessa, wondering when I would see Taylor again, and avoiding my former friends. Who was I? Where did I belong?

"Are you okay?" Emily leaned closer to me. "You look preoccupied. Did something else happen with your mom?"

"No, it's not her. I'm just confused."

"About ...?" Emily waved her fingers as if trying to pull words out of me.

"I went over to Taylor's today and started training Vanessa for cheerleading tryouts."

"Really?" Emily looked impressed. "You convinced Taylor to let you train Vanessa? That's great. He seemed really adamantly against it when you offered at my house."

"I worked some magic."

"You did the puppy-dog eyes and begged?"

I laughed. "How did you know?"

"I've seen you use that to work your dad a few times." She picked up a cookie. "How did it go?"

"I had a really good time. In fact, now I'm thinking really seriously about becoming a teacher and being a cheer coach on the side, like Coach Lori at our school." I lifted another cookie from my plate and broke it in half as I considered my words. "But I'm worried I'm getting too attached."

Emily raised an eyebrow. "Are you getting too attached to Vanessa or Taylor?"

I shook my head. "I don't know."

"You like him. It's time you admit it."

"But I don't want to." I covered my face with my hands. "It's too complicated. I'm so confused. I feel like I don't know who I am anymore. Everything is changing around me."

Emily touched my arm. "You'll figure things out." She bit into a cookie and pointed the other half toward me. "As my mom used to say, don't eat the whole elephant at once."

"Where have you been?" My mother met me at the back door with her hands on her hips and her foot tapping. "I've been worried sick about you."

"Didn't you get my message? I called earlier and asked Logan to tell you I was going straight to youth group for a potluck." I moved past her into the house.

"I never got a message."

"Oops!" Logan appeared in the doorway leading to the family room. "Whitney called before Dad and I left for karate. I was supposed to tell you Whitney was going straight from her meeting to church. Sorry!" He then disappeared, and I resisted the urge to chase him down and shake him for forgetting to relay my message.

Mom continued to scowl. "Whitney, I was worried something had happened to you."

"But Logan just told you he messed up. Why are you angry with me when he forgot to relay the message?" I glanced down at my cell phone. "The phone works both ways, you know. Why didn't you call me to check on me?"

Mom held her head high. "I was waiting for you to call me."

I stared at her. "That doesn't make any sense."

"Yes, it does. It's the principle."

I shook my head. "I don't understand. I told you I had a meeting after school. And you know I always go to youth group on Thursdays. Why is it an issue today?"

"It's an issue because I expect you to tell me where you're going." She folded her arms over her silk robe. "Where were you earlier?"

"I told you." I placed my tote bag and backpack on a kitchen chair. "I had a meeting and then youth group."

"What meeting?" She eyed me with suspicion, and I wondered if she knew the truth. But how would she have found out I went to Taylor's?

"It was a cheer meeting." I knew I should tell the truth, but I didn't want another lecture.

"If it was a cheer meeting, then why did Kristin stop by on her way home to see you?"

"She did?" I squeezed the back of the chair. "She didn't call or text me. What did she want?"

Mom took a step closer to me. "What are you hiding from me, Whitney Jean?"

"Nothing."

"Then why can't you tell me where you were this afternoon?"

"Fine!" I threw my hands into the air. "I went over to Taylor's after school. His sister is going to be a freshman in high school next year, and she wants to be a cheerleader. It's like her dream. She asked me to train her, and I wanted to help her."

My mom shook her head. "Whitney, why didn't you tell me the truth?"

"I didn't want to get a lecture from you about how inappropriate it is for me to spend time with Taylor."

"It *is* inappropriate." Mom tapped the table for emphasis. "Your focus needs to be on keeping your grades up and participating in the right activities. It's not your job to help a girl get on the cheer squad. She can do that herself."

"Not everyone has the opportunity to be part of a rec team, Mom. Taylor's mother is a single parent. She can't afford extras like that."

"That's not your problem."

"Really?" My eyes widened. "Mom, I've been lucky enough to participate in gymnastics and recreational cheering since I was little. Shouldn't I be willing to help out someone else? Isn't that what we're taught at church?"

"You're twisting my words around, Whitney! That's not what I said. I said school is more important. You can help someone less fortunate after school is out and you've maintained your grades and appropriate extracurricular activities. You don't need to feel obligated to help that girl just because her brother is your peer mentor."

"That's not it, Mom. I feel like I'm supposed to help her. You should've seen the look on her face today when I taught her a cheer. It was magical, Mom. Can't you understand that?"

"Whitney, you're missing the point. Helping that girl isn't going to guarantee your entry into Kentwood."

"What if I don't want to go to Kentwood? What if I'd rather go to the University and get my teaching certificate? They have a great program there."

Mom shook her head. "Now you're just being silly, Whitney. You're just upset you got that one bad grade in calculus." She patted my shoulder as if I were five. "Everything will be fine, dear. You'll bring your grade up. Just work hard like you always do. You'll go to Kentwood and get your law degree or maybe even go into medicine. You know you'd starve on a teacher's salary, so don't even joke about going into teaching."

I gritted my teeth. I couldn't stand it when she patronized me. "Mom, you're not listening to me! I don't want to go to Kentwood. I want to go to U, and I want to be a teacher and a cheer coach, like Coach Lori."

Her expression hardened. "Don't tell me you want to go to University because of that boy, Whitney."

"No, it's not that. I just don't think I'll fit in at Kentwood. I don't want to be a doctor or a lawyer. I want to be a teacher, and U has a great teaching program. I've researched it already. I've been trying to tell you this, but you don't listen to me."

"Now you're really talking foolishly. You won't be certain what career you want to pursue until you get to Kentwood and see all that it has to offer. You need to be thankful for this opportunity and take advantage of it."

"But what if it's not the right choice for me?" I pointed toward my chest. "I'm not you, Mom."

"You're not looking at it from my perspective. You have to understand I only want what's best for you. I don't want you to struggle like I did when I was your age. I was only able to go to Kentwood on scholarships, loans, and grants. I struggled hard to pay back my loans. I met your father when he was just starting out in the banking industry, and he helped me pay them off. You don't need to worry about that, since we can afford it, and you have scholarships due to your grades. I want you to take advantage of every opportunity you can. You'll thank me later when you're successful like your father." She patted my shoulder again. "Now, that's enough discussion. Go on to your room and finish your homework. It's getting late."

I felt something inside me snap, and for once I couldn't hold back my frustration. "I'm so sick and tired of you patronizing me and treating me like I'm five instead of eighteen." My words were laced with fury. "I've been trying to tell you I want to go to U, but you won't listen. I also want to help Vanessa learn how to cheer, and I don't think there's anything wrong with following my heart. You need to stop giving me orders and listen to me for once. Do you think you can do that, Mom? Can you pretend I'm one of your country-club buddies and listen to me?"

Mom gasped. "Where is this disrespect coming from, Whitney? Is this how Taylor talks to his mother?"

"No, it's not Taylor. It's me, Whitney." I lifted my tote bag and backpack.

"You need to go to your room right now. I will not stand here and listen to you talk to me this way." She pointed toward the stairs. "Go on. This conversation is over."

"Fine." My hands shook with anger as I climbed the stairs. I decided I was going to continue doing what I felt was right, despite what my mother said. She thought she could force me into the future she wanted for me, but I was my own person. She wasn't going to control me any longer.

chapter nine

The following Thursday I sat with Vanessa at her kitchen table and ate grapes. We had practiced cheers and cart-wheels for nearly an hour, and then I changed my clothes before heading into the kitchen for a quick snack. I had called my mother earlier and told her I was going to see Emily after school. It wasn't really a lie, since I stopped to talk to Emily before coming over to Vanessa's house.

I picked another grape from the bunch. "You're really getting the hang of it. I don't think you'll have any problems trying out in the spring."

"You think so?" Vanessa's expression lit up with excitement. "Do you really think I'll make it, or are you just being nice?"

I chewed another grape. "I really mean it. If I thought you needed to practice more, I'd tell you."

"How long have you been cheering?"

I tilted my head and thought back. "Well, I started gymnastics when I was three, and I think I started doing cheer through the recreational league in fourth grade."

"Wow! You have a lot of experience. I hope I can be as good as you are someday." She chewed a grape.

"You will be. You just have to practice."

The phone rang, and Vanessa jumped up and ran for the

cordless receiver on the counter. "Hello? Oh, hi, Mom. How are you?" She listened for a minute and then nodded. "Great. I'll see you soon, then. Bye!" She returned to the table. "Mom is coming home early tonight. She told me not to cook. She wants us to make something together."

"That's nice." I swiped another grape. "I bet you're happy she's coming home early."

"I am. She works too hard. I worry about her sometimes, but she tells me to only worry about my grades. She said paying the bills is her job and getting good grades is mine."

"That makes sense."

"Taylor says he wants to make it so Mom doesn't have to work so hard. He wants to be a lawyer. He says he'll take care of Mom and me. He got a full scholarship to U, and he keeps telling me I have to get good grades so I can get one too." She popped another grape into her mouth.

"That's great. I bet he'll be a good lawyer. He definitely knows how to speak up for himself." I thought back to his conversation about my "exclusive" friends. Taylor had no problems telling me just how he felt without any regard for how much it irritated me. I wondered if my mom was right, and his outspokenness was rubbing off on me. This new Whitney could've been inspired by Taylor, but I was tired of her running my life. I felt justified in my defensiveness, despite the teeny spark of guilt that nipped at me.

"I think so too." She glanced at the clock on the wall. "Maybe you'll get to meet my mom."

"I'll have to head out soon, but I'd like to meet her if I can."

"She'll like you." Vanessa took another handful of grapes. "I think my brother likes you."

"I think he likes me as a friend." I reflected on how nice Taylor had been at tutoring on Tuesday. He was friendly and even funny, but I seriously doubted we could be more than friends. Although I was beginning to notice I talked to Taylor more than I talked to Kristin and Tiffany. In fact, I hadn't had a real conversation with them all week. I'd only nodded to them as we passed in the hallway.

Vanessa shook her head. "I think Taylor *likes* likes you."

"I doubt it."

"He was telling my mom about you again last night."

"What did he say?" Although I wanted to know what he'd said about me, I was also nervous I might not like what I might hear.

"They were talking about his tutoring sessions, and he looked happy while he was talking about you. I see a difference in him. He used to be so serious all the time, but he's cracking jokes now." Vanessa grinned. "Why don't you invite him again to your youth-group meeting tonight?"

I shrugged. "I don't know. I'm sure he's too busy."

"I bet my mom would love for him to go. She says he works and studies too much."

I hesitated. I wanted to ask him, but what if he rejected me? It would be awkward, and I'd still have to face him at our tutoring sessions.

Vanessa and I talked about school, and soon twenty minutes had passed. I heard Taylor's motorcycle thunder into the driveway, and I stood. "I should get going. I guess I'll see you next week?"

"Yeah." Vanessa picked up our paper plates littered with grape stems. "Thanks for coming over. I really had fun."

"I did too."

The garage door slid open with a loud scrape.

Vanessa pointed toward a door off the kitchen. "You can walk out this way." She pulled the door open, revealing a small, one-car garage clogged with shelves, a washer, a dryer, various pieces of lawn equipment, plastic storage containers, and tools.

Taylor guided the bike into the small, empty space at the center of the garage and placed his helmet on the seat. "Hey."

"Hi." I hefted my bag onto my shoulder.

"Mom is on her way home." Vanessa crossed the garage.

"Oh, good. I'm glad she got off work early." He leaned against the bike. "Did you two have fun?"

Vanessa nodded. "We had a blast."

"She's a natural. I don't think she'll have any problems trying out for the team." I walked through the garage and moved toward my Jeep. "Well, I hope you have a good evening. I'll see you tomorrow."

"Whitney. Wait," Vanessa called.

"What's up?" I faced her, hoping she wasn't going to embarrass me.

"Taylor, you should take Whitney to dinner and then go to her youth group with her."

"What?" Taylor looked at Vanessa and then me. "Is this a conspiracy?"

"No." I held up my hand in my defense. "This is all your sister's idea. She thinks you need to get out more and make more friends."

He gave a palms-up. "So, you're saying I'm a loser?"

"No, not a loser. You're a *loner*." Vanessa enunciated the word for emphasis. "You can't study and work all the time. You need to have fun too."

I couldn't stop my grin. "You're a smart girl, Vanessa."

Taylor shot me a feigned glare. "Don't encourage her." He turned back to his sister. "I appreciate your concern, but I have a ton of homework. Maybe we can both go with her to her youth-group meeting next week."

A car steered down the street.

"There's Mom." Vanessa punched Taylor's arm. "Let's ask her opinion."

"Oh no. Now three of you are going to gang up on me." Taylor seemed more amused than annoyed.

"Hey, I'm staying out of this," I said. "It's a family matter."

I watched an older-model Ford sedan pull into the driveway next to my Jeep. Vanessa and Taylor both moved to the car and grabbed grocery bags from the backseat.

I stepped over and held out my hand toward Taylor. "Give me a bag."

Taylor shook his head. "You don't need to help." He turned to Vanessa. "Let's carry these in for Mom."

"Hello." The woman climbed from the car, looking at me. "I'm Maria."

She was a few inches shorter than I was and wore jeans and a short-sleeved, tan shirt dotted with a few bleach stains. She seemed to be quite a bit younger than my parents, which intrigued me. I wondered how old she was when she had Taylor, but I knew it wasn't my business to ask.

"Hi." I shook her hand. "I'm Whitney Richards. It's nice to meet you, Mrs. Martinez."

"It's wonderful to meet you finally. I've heard such nice things about you from Taylor and Vanessa." Her smile was genuine. "Thank you for being so nice to my Vanessa. She's really enjoying your cheerleading training."

"You're welcome. I'm enjoying helping her. She's a sweet girl."

Maria nodded as we stood together by the car. "Yes, she is. Taylor is worried Vanessa may not fit in with the other cheerleaders."

"I completely disagree," I said. "If Vanessa is good enough to be on the team, then she deserves a spot. I think I know who is going to replace me as team captain, and she's a fair girl. She'll recognize Vanessa's talent."

"I'm glad to hear that." She paused. "I think she should at least try rather than spending her life wishing she had. I know I think about things I should've done every day." She pointed toward the house. "Would you like to stay for supper?"

"Oh, no, thank you. I'm going to go grab something and then head to church for a youth-group meeting." I fished my keys from my bag. "I appreciate the offer, though. It was very nice meeting you."

Maria nodded. "Yes, it was very nice meeting you too. I hope to see you again."

"Mom," Vanessa called, walking out of the garage. "I think Taylor should go with Whitney tonight."

Maria turned toward Taylor standing behind his sister. "Do you want to go with her?"

Taylor nodded. "Sure. I'd love to go, but you just got home. I need to help you make supper."

Maria crossed her arms over her chest. "So you don't think I'm capable of making supper?"

I was almost certain I spotted the hint of a blush on Taylor's cheeks. I bit my lip to prevent myself from laughing. His mom was cool!

"I know you can cook, Mom," he began, "but I just didn't know if you'd prefer it if I stayed home."

"Why would I want you home? I see you every day." She waved off the comment. "Go have some fun."

"I told you Mom would make you go." Vanessa lifted her chin in defiance of her brother. "You need to go out and have fun. Take Whitney out to dinner too."

"You two enjoy yourselves." Maria placed her hand on Vanessa's shoulder. "What time will you be home, Taylor?"

Taylor looked at me. "What time is youth group usually over?"

"We usually end by eight," I said.

"Sounds good. See you later." Maria gave Vanessa a gentle push as if to tell her to go into the house and mind her own business.

"Bye, Whitney!" Vanessa waved before disappearing into the house.

Taylor moved over to me and pushed his hands into the pockets of his pants. "Does going to dinner and then youth group sound like a plan? My treat."

I hoped my embarrassment didn't show on my face. "That's really not necessary. I can pay for my own dinner."

"I don't mind. I managed to get a few extra hours in last week." He looked down at his bookstore shirt and then motioned toward the house. "Just let me run in and change."

"Okay. I'll call my mom and let her know what's going on." Taylor disappeared through the garage, and I climbed into my Jeep and dialed the house.

My mother picked up on the second ring. "Hello?"

"Hey, Mom. How are you?"

"I'm fine, dear. How are you?"

"Fine, thanks. I just wanted to let you know I'm going to grab something to eat and then head to youth group. I'll be home by eight thirty."

"Okay, dear," she said. "Have fun. Thanks for letting me know."

"Thanks, Mom." *That was easy!*

I flipped down the sun visor and checked my hair and makeup, almost out of habit. I had brushed my hair out after having it in a ponytail during the training session with Vanessa, and I noticed the dark roots lining my part were becoming more pronounced. My mother insisted I looked better as a blonde, but I was so sick of the appointments. What if I just let it go back to its natural light-brown color? I realized I needed to stop checking my appearance so often. After all, if Taylor truly liked me, he wouldn't care if my makeup had faded or my hair wasn't perfectly styled.

I looked out the window just as Taylor reappeared. He had changed into light-blue jeans and a long-sleeved, blue shirt, unbuttoned, with a black T-shirt underneath it.

I rolled down the window. "Hop in."

"Oh." He pointed toward the garage. "Have you ever been on a motorcycle?"

"No, I haven't." I looked down at my legs. "I can't today because I'm wearing a skirt, but I'd love a rain check."

"That's a deal." Taylor climbed into the passenger's seat.

"Where to?" I asked.

He shrugged. "How about the diner?"

"Sounds good."

Thirty minutes later, I sat across from Taylor at the Cameronville Diner. The restaurant was bustling with the dinnertime crowd. Families crammed the booths and tables while servers weaved through the sea of chairs, delivering food. I inhaled the warm smell of our bacon cheeseburgers and fries.

"This is heaven." I plucked a fry from my plate.

Taylor lifted his glass of Coke. "Are you talking about our dinner or my company?"

"Both, of course." I ate another fry. "My mother would flip if she saw me eating this."

"Why?" He held his burger.

"My mother is always worried about my appearance, and

I usually can't risk eating fattening food, or my cheerleading uniform will be too snug." I picked up a fry and waved it around. "But cheerleading is over, so I can eat whatever I want."

"I don't think you need to worry about your appearance, Whitney. And you looked just fine in your cheerleading uniform the last time I spotted you wearing it at school." He set his burger on the plate and ate a fry.

"Thanks." I felt the tips of my ears heat, and I tried to think of something to change the subject. "Your mom is nice."

"Thanks." He lifted his burger and took a bite.

"Vanessa told me you want to be a lawyer."

He nodded while chewing.

"I think that's great. You definitely have the intelligence and personality to be one." I took a bite of my burger and wiped my mouth with the paper napkin.

"What do you mean by that?" He peered at me over his glass of Coke.

I wiped my mouth again. "You're super smart, and you're not afraid to speak your mind or stand up for what you believe in. Is there a particular field of law you're interested in?"

"I want to concentrate on family law and help single parents like my mom who are struggling to support their kids."

"That's awesome, Taylor. You'll do a great job." I took another bite of my burger while imagining Taylor dressed in a suit and sitting in a fancy office surrounded by law books.

"What do you want to do?"

"I'm pretty sure I want to be a teacher. I'd love to teach high school and also work as a cheerleading coach." I picked up a fry and tried not to cringe while I waited for his reaction.

"That's cool."

"My mom doesn't think so."

He tilted his head. "Why not?"

"Well, isn't it obvious?" I asked, and he shook his head. "Teachers don't make any money. It's not prestigious like being a lawyer, doctor, or banker is."

Taylor continued to look confused. "Is that all your mom worries about?"

"You have no idea." I leaned back in the seat. "She's pressuring me to go to Kentwood."

"You got into Kentwood?" He stopped eating and studied me. "Whitney, that's amazing."

I folded my arms over my chest. "With your grades, you could've gone there too."

"Not really. Money is a big factor. There's no way I could've gotten a full scholarship, and without that, I can't go anywhere." He picked up a fry. "Why don't you want to go? It's a great opportunity."

"I don't know." I glanced out the window at the traffic rushing by on Highway 29. "I guess I'm tired of being told what to do, what to wear, how to do my hair, what to eat. I don't have anything against the school, but I want it to be my choice, not hers. She just wants me to go there, join her former sorority, and walk around campus with her Greek letters emblazoned on my hoodie. It's like she's living her life again through me." I met his curious gaze. "Is making my own choices too much to ask, or do I sound like a spoiled brat who doesn't appreciate her opportunities?"

He rubbed his chin. "That's a tough one."

"You think I'm spoiled and ungrateful, don't you?" I picked up a fry and wished I'd kept my feelings to myself. Maybe he didn't understand me as well as I thought he did. "I guess I am. Here you are trying to figure out how to pay for college, and I'm whining that I don't want to go to the fancy school my mom picked for me. You must think I'm terrible."

He shook his head. "I don't think you're terrible at all. I also don't think it's my place to judge you."

"I'm certain you have an opinion, Taylor. You've been very outspoken with me about other things."

"Are you saying you want the truth?"

I nodded. "The whole truth and nothing but the truth."

Taylor popped another fry into his mouth. "I think your future is your decision, but you should weigh all of the options before you decide you don't want to go to Kentwood."

I sipped my soda while mulling over his words. Silence stretched between us as I ate a few more fries and then bit into the burger. I realized I was comfortable with Taylor, more comfortable than I'd ever been with Brett or my ex-boyfriend Chad Davis. With Taylor, I didn't feel compelled to fill the silence with meaningless conversation. It was as if we'd known each other our whole lives.

And then it occurred to me—we *had* known each other our whole lives. At least our whole school careers.

While running a french fry through the puddle of ketchup on my plate, I thought back to our time together in elementary school. "Do you remember sharing your dessert with me in fourth grade?"

He lifted his drink. "How could I forget begging my mother to make chocolate-chip cookies twice a week so I had some to share with you?"

"You had your mother make those cookies just for me?"

"I used to run into the lunchroom so I could sit across from you and be the first one to ask you to trade."

I studied him, wondering if his story was a joke. "You're kidding me."

"Nope, I'm not. I couldn't stand the celery or carrot sticks you offered me in exchange, but I made the sacrifice just to be able to share with you." Taylor picked up three fries and ran them through the ketchup on my plate. "I'm surprised my mother didn't ask you if you still like chocolate-chip cookies when she met you, but she probably didn't want to embarrass me."

I paused for a moment as his words sunk in. "You brought those cookies to school just for me?"

"Did I stutter? Yes, Whitney, I did it for you."

"Why would you do that?"

He gave me an "Are you serious?" expression. "Why do you think I did it?"

"You felt sorry for me because my mother wouldn't let me have sweets and would only let me bring in fruits and vegetables." I sipped my soda. "I told you she's always been obsessed with weight."

"Not even close. That's not why I did it at all."

"So what was it?"

He continued to study me with a look of disbelief on his face. "I think it's obvious I had a crush on you, Whitney."

"You did?" I waited for the punch line. I was certain at any second he'd laugh and say, "Just kidding." But the punch line never came.

"Yes, I did. But even in fourth grade, you were too busy with the Brett Steeles and Chad Davises of the world to notice me."

"That's not true. I liked you."

"No, you didn't. You only used me for my cookies."

"All right, you caught me. It was all about the cookies." I joked and then laughed while grabbing another fry.

"I still can't believe Brett broke up with you on Valentine's Day." He ran another fry through the lake of ketchup on my plate. "That's unreal. What a moron."

"Yeah, my friends got candy, stuffed animals, and jewelry from their boyfriends. I got a cheap box of candy and a speech that basically said, 'You're sweet and pretty, but I just don't like you that way.'"

"What a total moron," he muttered.

My heart swelled with admiration. I enjoyed having someone defend me. "So, tell me something. Why do you like motorcycles?"

He shrugged while chewing a fry. "Why not? They're cool."

"Yes, they're cool, but is it more than that? I saw all of the posters of bikes in your room, so it seems like more of an obsession."

"Yeah, I guess it is." He wiped his hands on a napkin. "I like the feeling of getting on my bike and just driving without a care in the world. I can be free of all of the stress in my life. It's just me and the open road. Well, as open as it can be in traffic. It's freeing and exhilarating all at once."

"That sounds amazing." I blew out a sigh while imagining that freedom.

"You'll have to try it sometime." He grabbed another fry and then glanced at his watch. "We don't have much time, do we?"

I shook my head.

"We'd better order our ice-cream sundaes now, then."

"Oh no." I touched my stomach. "I can't."

He lifted his chin and grinned. "I won't tell your mom if you don't."

I laughed. "It's a deal."

Later that evening, I pulled into Taylor's driveway. "I had a really nice time."

"I did too." He unbuckled his seat belt. "Thanks for the invitation."

I rested my arm on the steering wheel. "I can't take credit. It was your sister's idea."

"I really liked your church. What time is the service on Sunday?"

"It starts at ten. Do you think you might want to come?"

"Yeah, I do." He held on to the door handle. "My mom started a second job a while back, and she has to work most Sundays. We got out of the habit of going to church because of her work schedule, but we shouldn't have. We used to go to another church, but I really liked yours. I'd like to give it a try."

"Cool. I'd love to see you at church." I contemplated our dinner and suddenly felt guilty that he'd paid, since his mother had to work two jobs to keep them afloat. "I owe you dinner, though. You shouldn't have paid."

"Do you know what my sister would do to me if I'd let you pay? She'd be really upset. Just consider it a payment for helping my sister."

"How could I take a payment from you?" I asked. "If it wasn't for you, I never would've had dessert in elementary school."

We both chuckled, and I relished the warmth of his laugh. I wished we'd had more time together. The evening had gone too quickly.

"Well, I guess I should get going." He pushed the door open.

"Yeah. I actually still have some homework to do."

"Oh." He sounded disappointed. "I don't want to keep you. Have a good night."

"I'll see you tomorrow."

He sprinted around my Jeep and up to the front step, stopping to wave before disappearing into the house.

I thought about the evening as I drove through Great Oaks toward my neighborhood. Taylor and I had enjoyed burgers, fries, and hot-fudge sundaes at the diner before heading to church.

During the youth-group meeting, we'd divided up into

groups and played board games. Taylor and I stayed together and played a game in the back of the room. Emily arrived late and joined us. I spotted her smiling at me every time Taylor teased me or made me laugh. However, I also noticed a few of the other girls in the group giving me strange looks as if to ask why I'd brought him with me. It bugged me to see people react to Taylor that way, but it didn't change my opinion of him.

I merged onto the main road and gripped the steering wheel. I knew I was falling for Taylor, and it excited and frightened me all at the same time. I was flattered and surprised to hear he'd had a crush on me in elementary school, and I wondered how he felt about me now. Did he like me just as a friend, or could it be more? And if he did like me, would it even matter after we graduated in June?

As I turned into Castleton, I thought more about the youth-group meeting and Taylor. I knew I needed to put my faith in God, but I couldn't help but feel confused. I didn't know where I belonged. Did I belong at the University with Emily and Taylor, or was I supposed to go to Kentwood and make new friends?

I didn't know what my future held, but I knew one thing for certain—I had a major crush on Taylor Martinez.

Later that night I climbed into bed and had a long talk with God. For the first time I prayed because I needed to share my feelings, not because I was supposed to pray every night before I went to sleep. I poured out my heart, sharing my hopes, dreams, and fears. When I finished, I was exhausted and felt as if I had finally cleared my mind. I hadn't come any closer to figuring things out, but it felt good to share my feelings with God.

chapter ten

On Sunday I followed my parents and Logan into church.
After taking a bulletin from the usher, I made my way to
the back pew, where my friends were sitting. I spotted my cousin
on the end and waved as I walked over to her. She scooted in to
make room for me.

I said hello to the group and then sat beside Emily. "How
are you?"

"Fine." Emily leaned in close. "It looked like Taylor had fun
at youth group Thursday night. You two were awfully friendly."

I shrugged, trying my best to seem casual about the subject.
"I think he had fun. He said he wanted to try to come to church
today."

"That's amazing. You're good at getting people to come to
church."

"Thanks." I eyed the bulletin.

"Whitney." Emily poked me in the side. "Look."

I turned toward the sanctuary door and spotted Taylor and
Vanessa standing at the back of the church, glancing around.
"Taylor!" I called his name and waved.

He saw me and led his sister over to me. Emily instructed
everyone to slide down in the pew, and Taylor sat next to me
with his sister on the end.

"Hi." I smiled at them. "I'm so glad you made it."

"Thanks." Taylor pointed toward Vanessa. "She made certain I was up on time since my mom left for work early this morning."

Vanessa swatted his arm. "He likes to sleep in on Saturdays and Sundays when he doesn't have to work."

"Weekends are the only days I get to sleep." Taylor glanced down at the bulletin.

Pastor Keith walked up to the front of the church and welcomed everyone, and soon the service began. Everyone stood and began to sing, and I felt someone staring at me. I looked across the aisle and spotted my mother looking back at me with an odd expression. She quickly looked away, but not quick enough that I didn't notice. I was bothered that she was watching me.

I tried my best to concentrate on the service, but I was very aware of Taylor beside me. Since our row was packed with the youth-group members, he sat close to me with his leg brushing against mine throughout the service. He frequently glanced at me and smiled, and I hoped I didn't seem as nervous or self-conscious as I felt.

Once the service was over, we followed the crowd into the fellowship hall for snacks.

I held a small plate with pieces of apple and watermelon as I stood with Taylor and a few other members of the youth group. "So, what did you think?" I asked him.

"I think you need to try a cookie." He held out a chocolate-chip cookie.

I shook my head. "No, silly, I'm asking about the service. Did you like it?"

"Yes, I did." He nodded toward his sister, who was talking with two other girls her age. "I think Vanessa did too."

"She does look comfortable." I picked up a piece of apple.

"You should really try this cookie. It's almost as good as my mom's recipe." He put the cookie on my plate.

"My mom would flip if she saw me with sweets." I picked up the cookie and attempted to hand it back to him.

"Whitney." My mom sidled up to me, and I wondered if she'd appeared magically out of thin air. "I hope you're not eating cookies."

I gave Taylor an "I told you so" expression, and he raised his eyebrows.

"Hello, Taylor." Mom gave Taylor a quick once-over and then turned back to me. "Are you staying for the youth meeting, dear?"

"I was planning on it." I picked at the fruit on my plate. "Is that okay?"

"That's fine. I have a committee meeting." She looked at Taylor again and then walked away.

After she disappeared, I leaned in closer to Taylor. "See what I mean about the cookies?"

"You weren't kidding." He shook his head. "Your mom is the food referee, huh?"

"She has to control every aspect of my life. I'm thankful she doesn't pick out my clothes, but she does tell me when she disapproves of something." I ate a piece of apple.

Taylor's eyes moved down my dress. "You always look nice, Whitney. I can't imagine her criticizing your clothes."

"Oh, you'd be surprised. I hear about it if my shirts are wrinkled or my jeans are too faded. It's ridiculous. Sometimes I wish she had a career so she'd have something else to worry about besides me." I pointed toward my brother, who was talking to a friend on the other side of the room. "She never picks at Logan like she does me."

"That's because you're the girl." He bit into a cookie. "Your mom's busy talking now. I can sneak you a bite when she's not looking."

I glanced toward where my mother was talking to my uncle Brad. "Okay. But we have to make it quick."

Taylor broke up a little piece of cookie and handed it to me.

I quickly ate it and then laughed. "I feel so sneaky. You're a bad influence."

"That's my best quality." He grinned, and I laughed again.

"Can you stay for J2A?" I hoped I didn't sound clingy, but I really wanted him to stay. "It's a thing for high schoolers after church."

"Sounds good to me." He finished the last cookie and then placed his plate in the trash bin.

"Great." I realized I was really enjoying getting to know Taylor. It was refreshing to become acquainted with a boy instead of going out on a date with him before I really knew him well. I was certain I wouldn't have dated Brett if I had gotten to know him first. I studied Taylor's face while he talked about school, and I found myself wondering if he was falling for me too. *What if he doesn't like me as more than a friend?* I dismissed the thought and enjoyed my conversation with Taylor.

Once the coffee hour was over, I walked with Emily and Taylor to the high school Sunday school room, which was the same room that was used for the youth-group meeting. Vanessa and Logan disappeared into their respective grades' classrooms.

"This is J2A," I told Taylor as we sat with Emily in the back of the classroom.

"That's Journey to Adulthood," Emily chimed in. "It's like Sunday school for high school kids."

"Cool." Taylor rested his elbows on the table.

Jenna, the leader, stepped into the classroom. She was a

young, pretty woman with warm brown eyes and dark hair that fell past her shoulders. "Good morning." Her eyes fell on Taylor. "Taylor. It's so good to see you again. I'm so glad you're here today."

"Hi, Jenna." He nodded at her. "I thought I'd give the church a try. My mom works on Sundays, but my sister and I came today."

"That's great."

Jenna walked toward the front, stopping to say hello to kids on her way. "Good morning, everyone. I thought we'd do something different today. I know some of you are getting ready to leave for college. So I thought we'd look for some Scripture verses that can help us face the uncertainty of the future." She picked up a stack of papers. "I'm going to pass around a list of Scripture passages, but you're always welcome to look in the Bibles on the tables." She looked over at the clock. "We'll take about ten minutes and pick out the verses you like best, and then we'll share them. Sound good?"

A number of the kids nodded.

"Great. Let's get started." Jenna distributed the papers, and soon everyone was flipping through the pages and the Bibles.

I looked over at Taylor. "Do you know what verses you like?"

"I think so." He looked at me. "Do you know?"

I shook my head. How could I find a verse that gave me comfort when I felt so confused about my future? I had no idea how I was going to convince my parents to let me go to the school I wanted to go to. I was afraid my future would be miserable if I was going to be forced to follow a path that I didn't choose.

I began searching the list of verses Jenna had given us. I hoped I could find something that represented how I felt and also gave me comfort. I'd had a strong faith in God my whole life, so praying and reading the Bible were never hard for me. Still, I was worried and wondered what God wanted me to do. What if my mother was right about Kentwood when I didn't want that school forced on me? I wanted where I went to college to be my choice.

A few verses on the list sounded good. Then I found one that rang really true to me. I'd memorized the verse as a child and had tried to follow it my whole life: "In the same way, let your light shine before others, that they may see your good deeds and glorify your Father in heaven."

Taylor moved in close, his arm brushing against mine. "What did you choose?"

"This was always my favorite." I pointed toward the verse.

"I always liked that one too. It helps you remember what you're supposed to do with your life."

"Exactly. That's why I want to teach and be a cheerleading coach. My mom just doesn't understand."

"Okay." Jenna moved to the front of the classroom again. "Who wants to share their verse?"

Taylor raised his hand. "I'll go."

"Great, Taylor." Jenna sat on a table in the front of the room. "Go right ahead."

"Okay." Taylor cleared his throat and then looked down at the verse he'd circled: "By day the Lord directs his love, at night his song is with me— a prayer to the God of my life."

Intrigued, I studied him.

"Why that verse?" Jenna asked.

Taylor shrugged. "Well, to me it means that no matter what you do all day, whether you're studying, or you're at work, or you're at school, you need to remember you have to live your day for God. He directs your heart, and he should be the focus of your life."

"Wow." Jenna looked impressed. "So how does this give you comfort when you leave for college?"

Taylor paused for a moment. "I guess it just helps me remember that no matter what happens to me in college, I need to keep my focus on God."

"That's great. Thanks for sharing with us, Taylor." Jenna glanced around the room. "Who else has a verse?"

I gazed at Taylor. I never imagined he had such a deep faith in God. It's not that I didn't believe he was a Christian, but I had no idea how easy it was for him to talk about his faith. I wondered if he had long talks with God at night. Was praying second nature to him? Did he empty his heart and soul into his prayers just as I had done the other night?

I turned my attention to Jenna and tried to concentrate on what the other kids were saying, but my thoughts kept creeping back to Taylor and what he'd said about his faith. I knew at that moment I was in trouble because I was falling even harder for Taylor Martinez. I was doomed!

After J2A ended, Taylor and I met Vanessa in the hallway and walked out to the parking lot together. Vanessa talked about how much she had liked her class and how nice the other kids were as we made our way to Taylor's motorcycle.

I looked at Vanessa. "You rode on the back of the motorcycle in that pretty yellow dress?"

"I have shorts on underneath my dress." She pulled up her hem, and I spotted little black shorts.

"Good idea."

Vanessa shrugged. "I have years of experience. Taylor got his love of bikes from our uncle Rico. I've been riding them since I was little."

"That's so cool." I hoped I could get a ride sometime. I grinned at the thought of my mother's reaction to me on a motorcycle. She'd probably pass out!

Taylor handed Vanessa a helmet and then turned to me. "Are you free for lunch?"

"That would be great." I nodded.

"How about another ice-cream sundae at the diner?" Taylor grinned. "I can be a bad influence on you twice in one day."

"That sounds great, but you have to let me pay this time." I motioned toward my mother's SUV across the parking lot. "I could get my mother to take me home for my keys and then meet you both there."

"Whitney!" As if on cue, Mom came across the parking lot. "I was looking all over for you."

I wondered if she had a sixth sense about when I was considering eating something fattening. "Hey, Mom. We just got out of class. I'm going to go to lunch with Taylor and Vanessa, but I'll come home right after, okay?"

"No, I don't think that's a good idea today." She shook her head. "We have to get home, dear. We have chores we must finish today."

I couldn't believe it. Whatever chores she had for me certainly could wait until after lunch. She challenged my frustrated expression with a stern look, and I backed down. I knew picking an argument with her in front of Taylor and Vanessa would cause more problems for me later. If I were grounded, then I'd have to stop my cheerleading training with Vanessa, and I didn't want to disappoint her. In fact, I looked forward to our cheerleading lessons almost as much as my tutoring sessions with Taylor.

"Okay," I finally agreed with my mother and then turned to Taylor. "I'm sorry, but I can't do lunch today. I'll see you at school, though."

"Sounds good." Taylor picked up his helmet. "Enjoy the rest of your Sunday."

"Thanks." I touched Vanessa's arm. "See you soon."

Vanessa waved. "Bye, Whitney."

I walked with my mother toward her car. "I don't see how lunch would've interrupted our plans to organize closets and pick out clothes for your charity drive, Mom."

"Don't argue with me, Whitney." She fished her keys out of her designer purse. "I'm not in the mood for your attitude today."

I stopped and looked at her as Taylor's bike roared across the parking lot. "I'm not trying to talk back. I'm just trying to understand why I couldn't have lunch first with my friends. I wouldn't have taken all day. I just wanted to have a little fun. Pretty soon I'll be at college, and I won't be able to enjoy my Sundays with my church friends."

"I think you're getting too close to that Taylor boy, and you need to put some distance between you." She motioned toward the other side of the parking lot. "He's not your type."

"How do you know what my type is?" I jammed a hand on my hip.

"Because I know you, Whitney. You don't belong with a boy like that."

"You don't have the right to judge Taylor when you don't even know him," I snapped as frustration boiled inside me. "He's a really nice kid, and his sister and mom are nice too."

Mom's eyes narrowed. "I've noticed you've been talking back to me more frequently since you started spending time with him. Does he talk to his mother the way you talk to me?"

"No." I shook my head and crossed my arms over my chest.

"You need to watch your tone with me, young lady. I'm tired of you taking my head off every time I share my opinion with you or try to give you some good advice." Mom suddenly smiled. "I meant to tell you I spoke to Rhonda yesterday, and she said Brett was talking about you. He asked her advice on how he can apologize to you."

"Oh, please." I rubbed my temple where a headache brewed. "He's the last guy I'd want to date."

"Don't be silly, Whitney. Before you know it, you'll be picking out a prom dress, and you don't want to go alone. No one wants to be *that* girl." She started toward her SUV again.

"There's more to life than having a prom date." I fell into step with her. "I'd rather go alone than go with a boy who could change his mind and break up with me the day before prom. He already ruined my Valentine's Day, so it's entirely possible he'd ruin prom too."

"Don't be so negative. The boy made a mistake. We all make mistakes."

"No, it's not the same, Mom. Brett never considered my feelings. Besides, I wasn't even talking about Brett. You brought him up. I was talking about Taylor and Vanessa. They're nice, Mom. I only wanted to go to lunch with them. Since when is going to lunch a crime?" I met her at the driver's-side door and touched her arm. "I'm entitled to have friends. You can't choose them for me."

"Let's discuss this later, Whitney. I have things I want to get done today." She shooed me away like an annoying bug. "Get in the car. I want to clean out all of the closets so I can load up the bags for the charity drive."

I climbed into the passenger's seat and wondered how on earth I was going to ever make my own decisions with my mother running my life. I knew one thing for certain: I wasn't going to let her keep me from being friends with Vanessa and Taylor, even if I had to continue to see them behind her back.

chapter eleven

The following Sunday I was sitting in my usual spot in church when I spotted Taylor, Vanessa, and their mother walking in.

"Emily," I whispered. "Look."

I stood as Taylor, Vanessa, and their mother approached. "Good morning."

"Hey. My mom finally got a day off and wanted to join us today," Taylor said.

"I'm so glad you could come too, Mrs. Martinez." I shook her hand.

"Thank you. Taylor and Vanessa had such nice things to say about your church that I wanted to come to the service with them this week. It's been a long time since I've been to church."

"How are you?" I asked Vanessa.

"Great." Vanessa looped her arm through her mother's. "I'm happy we have the whole family here today."

I gestured toward the row behind me. "How about we all sit here?"

I moved into the pew, and Taylor sat beside me, followed by his mother and his sister. Although we had plenty of room, Taylor sat close to me, with his leg brushing mine.

"I have to leave and go straight to work after the service," he said. "I normally don't work on Sundays, but my boss called last night. We're having a big sale, and they need the extra help."

My hopes of having lunch with Taylor evaporated.

"I'll see if any of our favorite books are on sale," Taylor continued. "With my discount, I can get them for next to nothing."

"Oh." I picked up my purse from the pew beside me. "Can I give you some money?"

He shook his head. "Do you honestly think I'd offer to pick up a book for you and then ask for money?"

"I didn't know ... if ... you know," I stammered.

His mother leaned over him. "Taylor asked me to make you some chocolate-chip cookies last night."

"Mom ..." Taylor turned to his mother. "You weren't supposed to tell her."

"What?" His mother gave him an innocent expression. "You said you were going to bring her some cookies for old time's sake."

"That was supposed to be a surprise."

I tried to hide my smile by glancing down at the bulletin.

Pastor Keith began the service, and we all stood for the opening song. I was reaching for a hymnal when Taylor touched my hand.

"Share with me." His voice was soft and warm.

"Thanks."

As the service went on, I enjoyed sharing Taylor's hymnal and sitting close to him. I wished the service would never end.

During the last hymn, I glanced over at my parents and Logan across the aisle and met my mother's eyes. I smiled at her, and she sent a forced smile back to me. I hoped my mother would be pleasant when I introduced her to Taylor's family.

When the service ended, I reached past Taylor and touched

his mother's arm. "Mrs. Martinez, I'd like you to meet my family."

Maria nodded. "I would like that."

My parents and Logan stepped out into the aisle, and I motioned for them to join us.

"Mom, Dad, Logan, I'd like you to meet Taylor's family." I gestured toward them. "Mrs. Martinez and Vanessa, this is my mom and dad, Chuck and Darlene Richards, and my little brother, Logan. Mom, Dad, and Logan, this is Mrs. Martinez and Vanessa."

"Nice to meet you." My father shook Maria's hand and then nodded at Vanessa. One of the ushers called out Dad's name, and Dad excused himself before going to talk to him.

Logan asked Vanessa about middle school, and they fell into a conversation.

"It's a pleasure to meet you." My mom gave Maria her most phony smile. "Whitney has a lot of nice things to say about you."

"Thank you," Maria said. "Call me Maria. Whitney has been so very nice to my children. Vanessa is truly enjoying the cheerleading lessons. I could never afford to put Vanessa in the recreational league, so I can't tell you how much I appreciate her generosity. From what I hear, your Whitney is quite talented."

"Oh yes." Mom puffed up like a bird. "We put her in gymnastics when she was three, and then she moved on to cheerleading in elementary school. You should see all of the trophies and medals in her room."

"Mom …" I wished she'd stop bragging. I looked at Taylor, and he grinned.

"You must be so proud." Maria's expression was genuine, and I was relieved the bragging hadn't offended her.

"Whitney has mentioned you work long hours." Mom folded her arms over her expensive suit jacket.

"I do." Maria nodded.

"What do you do?"

"I'm a housekeeper. I work in a hotel and then do some side jobs when I can." Maria touched Taylor's shoulder. "You do what you can when it comes to your kids."

"Oh yes." My mother gave an emphatic nod. "You do your best and try to get them everything they need." She moved her eyes toward the hallway. "Oh, there's Lorraine. I need to catch her to discuss the next ladies' luncheon. It was a pleasure meeting you. You have a good day."

"Oh yes. You too." After Mom left, Maria turned to me. "Your parents are awfully nice."

"Thank you." I shifted my weight from one foot to the other, wondering if she was being sincere. I hoped she couldn't see right through my mother's phony exterior.

We followed the crowd out into the hallway beyond the sanctuary.

"Well, I need to run." Taylor said good-bye to his mother and sister and then touched my arm. "The mall opens soon, and I have to be there on time."

"Oh." I looked up at him. "I'll walk you out."

"That would be nice."

We walked together out to his motorcycle, which was waiting patiently at the front of the parking lot.

"I'm glad you came to church."

"Yeah. I am too. I'll see you later." He rubbed my arm. "I'll see if I can find us any books to share."

"Great." I studied his expression and suddenly hoped he would kiss me. I wondered if he had any of the same strong feelings for me, but I also wondered if I was just being foolish. "I hope it's not too busy at work."

"Oh, I don't mind busy days." He shrugged. "Being busy

132 • Amy Clipston

makes the time fly by. Maybe I'll get the chance to catch up with you later. I managed to finish all of my homework last night. Do you have a lot to do?"

"No, I don't." I shook my head. "I have a report due Tuesday, but I finished it Friday. I just have to proofread it one last time."

"Cool." He picked up his helmet and then pushed his curls back.

"Do you know how much some women pay for curls like those?" I asked. "Do you even appreciate your hair?"

He shook his head. "No, it's mostly a pain. If it gets too long, it looks like an out-of-control Afro."

"It seems the people who have naturally curly hair don't appreciate it, and the rest of us can only dream of having hair like that. Emily doesn't like her curls either." My thoughts turned to my mother. "My mom really embarrassed me earlier with the way she went on and on about me."

Taylor held the helmet in his hands and leaned back on the bike. "I think that's a typical parent thing. You should hear my mom when she goes off about my grades. She'll talk your ear off about my GPA and my scholarships."

"But those are real accomplishments."

He studied me for a minute. "Are you embarrassed by who you are, Whitney?"

"What do you mean?"

"Compared to my life, you've had a privileged life filled with opportunities Vanessa and I can't have, but that's okay. You can be yourself around me and my family, and we'll still like you. My mother and sister are enjoying getting to know you."

"Is that why you asked your mom to make her cookie recipe?"

He shook his head. "You're changing the subject."

"No, I just asked a question." I tried to look innocent.

"You're something else, Whitney Richards." He lifted his helmet. "I better run. Don't want to be late. See you later."

"Bye, Taylor. Ride safely." I silently admired his lanky body as he put on his helmet and then straddled the bike.

I studied him as he rode through the parking lot and wondered if I would ever feel that freedom of zooming off on the motorcycle sitting closely behind him and holding tightly onto him. I considered his words. *Maybe I shouldn't be embarrassed by my gymnastics and cheerleading awards, since they are such a deep part of who I am. I love cheerleading, and I've realized just how much it means to me since I started coaching Vanessa.* The thoughts echoed through me as he disappeared from sight.

"Whitney?" Emily sidled up to me. "Are you coming to J2A?"

I nodded.

"You got it bad for Taylor, huh?" She slung her arm around my shoulders.

"Is it that obvious?"

"Cuz, you're almost salivating." She steered me toward the door. "Has he asked you out yet?"

"Not officially. We've done a few things together, but I'm wondering if he only wants to be friends."

"I doubt that. He was sitting really close to you in church today, and there was plenty of room in the pew."

We moved through the crowded hallway toward the classrooms.

I turned toward her. "You noticed how close he was to me?"

"Oh yeah. And he even wanted you to share his hymnal, which was just another excuse to be close to you." She grinned. "I'd say he's just as smitten with you as you are with him. I think it's only a matter of time before he asks you out."

"I hope so."

Emily gave me a knowing smile. "I've been there. It's really frustrating, but it's worth the wait if it's right."

"I hope that's true." We stepped into the classroom and sat in the back.

Misty Strickland, sporting a CHS cheer Windbreaker over a sweater and skirt, sat in front of us and turned around. "Where's your boyfriend, Richards?"

"My boyfriend?" I asked, challenging her with a stare.

"Yeah, you know, your charity case, Taylor Martinez. I saw you sitting with him and his family in church today."

I felt my body stiffen in defense. "He had to get to work, and not that it's any of your business, but we're just friends."

"That's sad he had to go to work, but I guess his mom doesn't make much money cleaning toilets." Misty smirked. "I heard you're teaching his sister how to cheer. I guess we need to take some charity cases on our team after you graduate, huh? But if I'm made captain, I won't have to do what you say anymore. I won't have to let her on the team just because you tried to teach her how to do cartwheels."

My blood boiled, and I grasped the desk in front of me to try to stop from launching myself at her.

Emily narrowed her eyes. "You better watch your mouth, Misty. Just because your dad is a banker doesn't make you better than anyone else."

Misty's smile was full of sarcasm. "Of course, you would say that, Curtis. You live near Taylor, don't you? I have a dress that's worth more than your house."

"That's it." I stood up and rounded the desk toward Misty. "Who do you think you are?"

"Girls!" Jenna rushed over. "What's going on?"

"Misty is making fun of Taylor and Emily because of where they live," I said.

Emily jumped up. "She's just being a self-righteous snob, and Whitney and I have had it with her."

Jenna narrowed her eyes at Misty. "Do you think this is an appropriate way to act?"

Misty actually looked humble for the first time since I'd met her in middle school. "No, Jenna." Misty studied her lap.

"You need to apologize to Emily and Whitney, and I'm going to talk to your parents after J2A." Jenna touched Misty's shoulder. "I expected more from you." She walked up to the front of the room.

Misty glanced at Emily and me. "Sorry," she whispered under her breath.

I looked at Emily, who shook her head and mouthed, "No, she's not."

Jenna began reading a story, but I kept thinking about Misty's cruel words. I wondered if my other friends thought of Taylor as my charity case. She sounded just as bad as Chad and Brett. I realized Taylor had a reason for being so cold to me when we first started our tutoring sessions, since he'd been treated badly by people I'd always considered my friends.

I began to worry that Taylor was right about girls like Misty who would never accept Vanessa on the cheer team. I made a mental note to talk to our coach before graduation so that Vanessa would have a fair chance during tryouts.

After class Emily and I walked out to the parking lot together.

"Misty Strickland really gets under my skin," Emily seethed. "She thinks she's so much better than everyone just because her parents are rich. Oh, I can't stand people like that."

I shook my head and fingered my purse strap. "I'm just glad Taylor wasn't there to hear it."

"I thought the same thing." Emily lowered her voice. "Here comes Vanessa. We need to change the subject." She cleared her throat. "Hey, Vanessa. How are you, neighbor?"

"Hey, Emily." Vanessa stood beside me. "Do you two want to come for lunch? My mom is making her famous enchiladas."

"Oh, wow. That sounds great, but I have to go to the shop for a while. I told my dad I'd help him get caught up on some inventory paperwork." Emily pulled out her keys. "I'll see you all later."

"Talk to you soon." I waved as Emily walked to her car.

"How about you, Whitney?" Vanessa looked hopeful. "Can you come over for lunch? I promise I won't make you work on cheerleading moves. We can just hang out."

"That sounds nice." I looked toward the church doors. "I just need to tell my mom."

Vanessa nodded. "Okay. Meet us by my mom's car."

"I will." I found my parents talking to another couple in the hallway. I hoped catching her off guard would help my case for spending time with Taylor's mother and sister. "Mom. Vanessa and her mother invited me over for lunch. Can I go?"

My mom hesitated and then looked at my dad, who nodded. "Yes, you may go for a little while."

Go, Dad! "Thanks, Mom."

She shot me a warning glance. "But don't spend all afternoon there. You need to finish your homework. Isn't that report due this week?"

"Yes. I only need to proofread it once more. Thanks, Mom." I squeezed her hand and then rushed out to the parking lot before she could change her mind.

chapter twelve

I wiped my mouth after nearly stuffing myself at lunch. "These enchiladas are delicious, Mrs. Martinez. I need to get your recipe."

"Thank you." Maria pushed the serving plate of enchiladas toward me. "Would you like another?"

"Oh, no, thank you." I held up my hand. "I don't think I could eat another bite."

"I hope you saved room for dessert." Vanessa jumped up from the table and grabbed a plate filled with chocolate-chip cookies. "My brother made these for you last night."

I looked at Maria. "I thought you made them."

She shrugged. "He really made them. And they were just for you."

"Oh." I felt the tips of my ears heat. "He told me that when we were in fourth grade, he asked you to make them for me twice a week so he had something to share with me at lunch. He felt sorry for me because my mother never let me eat sweets."

Maria smiled. "He always liked you. I'm glad calculus brought you two back together after all these years so you could be friends."

Vanessa brought the cookies, vanilla ice cream, chocolate syrup, and whipped topping to the table. "Let's make chocolate-chip-cookie sundaes."

Maria stood and gathered up the dirty dishes and leftover food from lunch.

"Can I help you get the bowls and spoons?" I offered.

"Don't be silly," Maria said. "You're our guest."

"But you cooked," I said.

"We appreciate you, Whitney. You've helped my daughter train for free. We're very thankful for that."

I fingered a napkin and didn't feel worthy of her appreciation. "Thank you."

Maria and Vanessa sat down, and we made vanilla-and-chocolate-chip sundaes while talking about everything from the weather to television shows. We were finishing our sundaes when the house phone rang.

"I'll get it." Vanessa leaped for the cordless phone. "Hello? Oh, hi, Maggie. What's up?" She moved into the family room and disappeared from sight.

"Vanessa and Maggie have been friends since kindergarten." Maria scraped her spoon in her bowl.

"That's nice." I spooned more ice cream. "She's a really sweet girl."

"Thank you. I've tried to instill manners and good study habits in my kids. I don't want them to make the same mistakes I did." She shook her head.

I wondered what exactly she was referring to, but I didn't feel it was appropriate to ask.

"Do you know where you're going to school in the fall?" she asked.

I absently moved the remaining ice cream in my bowl around with my spoon. "I've been accepted to the schools where I applied, but I'm having a difficult time making a choice."

"Oh." She picked up a cookie from the plate. "I imagine it's overwhelming to think about how much your life is going to change, but I'm certain you'll do well. Taylor told me you're a straight-A student."

I snorted. "I was until I took calculus."

Maria laughed. "I guess that is a tough class. Taylor tried to explain it to me once, and I was lost after his second word."

"He's so smart. I'm amazed at how he explains math. If he decides not to go to law school, he would be a wonderful math teacher. I heard he might be our class's valedictorian." I took a cookie from the plate. "You must be so proud of him."

"Thank you. Yes, I'm very proud of him. I encouraged him to concentrate on school and not get tangled up with a bad crowd." She paused and ate a cookie. "I dropped out of school and got married at seventeen. I wish I had at least graduated, but I was certain I was in love and wanted to be married more than anything else. And then Taylor came along when I was eighteen."

"Oh, wow." I broke a cookie in half while trying to imagine how I'd feel to be a mother at my age. "That had to be so difficult for you."

"It was very difficult. Taylor's father could never keep a job. He always had some excuse to quit. He'd say the boss didn't like him, the pay wasn't good enough, or the hours were too long." She scowled. "I was too blinded by love to see he didn't want to work. He was just lazy. I thought things would get better after Vanessa was born. But it was more of the same, except we had another mouth to feed. One morning he left to go to work and never came back."

"I'm so sorry," I said softly. "You must've been devastated."

She paused to chew another cookie. "Yes, I was. My brothers would come over and help me as much as they could, since my mother was gone. She died very young from complications with diabetes."

140 • Amy Clipston

I remembered Vanessa mentioning her uncle Rico. "Is Rico your brother?"

Maria looked surprised. "Yes, he is. Did Taylor tell you Rico helped him build his motorcycle?"

"Vanessa mentioned that her uncle Rico got Taylor interested in motorcycles. Taylor did a great job on these cookies, by the way." I swiped another one.

"They are very good cookies. Yes, Rico has really been wonderful. He's been sort of a surrogate father to my kids." She paused as if to gather her words. "Their father has never been interested in them, but he's missing out on so much. He'd be proud to see who they've become."

"I'm sorry their father let them down. I can't imagine how difficult it's been for all of you." I ate the cookie while contemplating her words.

"I've bored you enough with my life story. Tell me about your college choices."

"I was accepted at University, State, and Kentwood University. I really want to go to U, but my mom is pressuring me to go to Kentwood."

Maria's eyes rounded. "You got into Kentwood?"

I nodded and hoped she wasn't going to give me the same lecture everyone else hit me over the head with. "It's my mom's alma mater. It's a status thing with her, like everything else. I'm supposed to go to her college and join her sorority so she can brag to her country-club friends."

"Oh." Maria's expression softened. "From the look on your face, I can tell you'd rather not go to please her."

"Is that wrong?" I really wanted to know her feelings. Maria seemed to be so knowledgeable about life. With all she'd endured, I had a feeling she could give me valuable advice.

"No, it's not wrong." She tilted her head as if contemplating my question with extreme care. "You should definitely pray about it and then listen to your heart. Just don't let your mother's pressure cause you to make the wrong decision. I mean, don't do the opposite of what she wants out of spite. If you decide not to go to Kentwood, it should be because you truly don't want to go there."

"That makes sense."

"Let me put it to you this way. I married Carlos partially out of spite. I was blinded by love, but I also was tired of my mother lecturing me about finishing high school. I thought I could show her I was smarter than she was by dropping out of school to get married." Maria looked around the kitchen. "I love my kids, but raising them alone hasn't been easy. My mother was right. I should've stayed in school and maybe even tried to get into college on a scholarship. Finding a good-paying job without even a high school diploma isn't easy."

"Have you thought about maybe getting your GED?" I hoped maybe I could offer her some good advice too.

"You're sweet to suggest it, but I don't have the time to study for the test. I'd love to do it someday, but right now I'm trying to keep my head above water."

"Oh." I fingered my napkin. "It must be a challenge for you to try to balance work, children, and school."

"Try next to impossible." Maria reached for the gallon of vanilla ice cream in the middle of the table. "Are you up for another sundae?"

I rubbed my abdomen. "No, I don't think I could eat another bite."

"I feel the same way."

Maria and I talked for more than an hour. Soon Vanessa rejoined us, and the three of us continued our conversation.

We were cleaning up the kitchen when the door leading to the garage opened, and Taylor came in.

"What are you three ladies up to?" Taylor asked as he shrugged off his faded-green army jacket and hung it over a kitchen chair.

"We're up to no good," Maria joked. "We've enjoyed enchiladas, and we made your delicious cookies into chocolate-chip-cookie sundaes."

"Oh." Taylor's eyes grew wide. "Did you save me any enchiladas and cookies?"

"Maybe a few." Vanessa shrugged, and I laughed.

"Yes, we did save you a little bit of food, but you missed out on a good time." Maria pulled the enchiladas from the refrigerator. "Want me to warm them up for you?"

"That sounds great." He walked toward the doorway. "I'll go wash up."

I found Maria a plate in the cabinet and she put three enchiladas on it. Maria stuck them in the microwave while I cleaned up a place for Taylor at the table.

When Taylor returned, I took the plate from Maria and set it, along with a glass of iced tea, at the table for him. "Wow, Whitney. I could get used to you serving me."

Vanessa laughed.

"Don't get used to it, Taylor," I said with feigned irritation.

Taylor began to eat, and I turned to Maria. "Can I help you clean up?"

"Oh, don't be silly." She waved off my offer. "Sit with Taylor. I'm sure he'd like to visit with you."

I sank into a chair beside him. "How was work?"

"Good." He snapped his fingers. "I got a few books for us to share."

I raised my eyebrows. "Really?"

"I told you I would." He cut up the enchilada. "How did you like that Becker book?"

"Oh, it was great. Do you want it back?"

"I'll borrow it, but you can keep it after I'm done."

"Thanks," I said.

While Taylor ate, we continued our conversation about books. I didn't immediately notice that his mother and sister had finished cleaning up and disappeared from the kitchen while we were talking.

Our conversation moved from books to school as Taylor finished eating the enchiladas and made himself a chocolate-chip-cookie sundae. His bowl was soon empty, and I helped him gather up the dirty dishes.

"How about I wash and you dry?" I asked while filling the sink with hot, sudsy water.

"You really don't have to help with the dishes, Whitney." He dropped the bowl and plate into the sink. "You're a guest."

"No, I'm not. I'm a friend." I picked up the brush and began scrubbing the plate. "I really had fun with your mom and sister. They're awesome."

"I'm glad to hear that." He stood close to me. "I was glad to see you were still here when I got home."

I looked up at him. "You knew I was going to come for lunch?"

"Vanessa told me she wanted to invite you. I was hoping you'd stay." He looked at me with an intense expression.

"Thanks for the cookies."

He touched my arm. "Mom wasn't supposed to tell you I made them."

"I'm glad she did."

Taylor moved closer, and my breath caught in my throat. His hand moved to my cheek, and I thought my heart would burst in my chest. He dipped his face down to mine, and the sudden chirp of my cell phone caused me to jump.

Taylor moved away. "You'd better get that."

"Okay," I muttered as I crossed to the kitchen table and searched my purse for my phone. I pulled it out, and my lips formed a thin line when I found it was my mom calling. *Leave it to her to ruin the moment!* "Hello?"

"Whitney!" My mother's voice blared through the phone. "Do you know what time it is?"

I glanced over at Taylor, who was shaking his head while washing the dishes. I was certain he'd heard my mother's booming voice.

"It's almost six," I said.

"I know! That's my point. You need to get home now, young lady. I'm planning a special dinner." Her tone told me there was no room for discussion.

"Okay. I'll see if Mrs. Martinez can bring me home."

"Fine. See you soon, dear." She disconnected before I could say good-bye.

"I can drive you." Taylor dried his hands on a dishtowel.

"I don't know if that would work out." I looked down at my dress.

"I happen to have both a motorcycle license and a regular driver's license." He hung the dishtowel on the oven handle. "Let me get my mom's keys."

He disappeared from the kitchen, and I took a deep, cleansing breath. I knew he was going to kiss me just before my mother called. I couldn't stop wondering what it would've felt like to kiss him. Would it have been as wonderful as I imagined? Could Taylor Martinez actually like me?

"Hey, Mom. Can I use your car to take Whitney home?" Taylor called from the next room.

"Oh, is Whitney leaving?" Maria asked.

I stepped into the doorway and found Maria watching the

evening news while Vanessa sat on the floor and wrote in a notebook on the coffee table. "Thank you for a wonderful afternoon. I really had a great time, and the food was amazing."

"I'm sorry you have to go." Maria stood and crossed the room.

"My mom just called. She's making dinner, and she wants me home now." I fingered my skirt. "You can't argue with her sometimes."

To my surprise, Maria hugged me. "You're welcome here anytime, Whitney. We enjoy having you over."

"Thank you." I felt overwhelmed by her kindness. "I love spending time here."

I felt a hand on my back and looked up at Taylor standing close behind me.

"We'd better go." He gestured toward the door with his free hand. "I could hear your mom's frustration from across the kitchen."

"You're right. She wants me home right away." I waved to Vanessa. "See you soon. Good-bye."

I followed Taylor through the garage, where he stopped and retrieved a bag of books from his bike seat.

He handed the bag to me. "Let me know which ones are good, and then I'll borrow them."

I peeked inside the bag and spotted four hardcover mysteries. "Thanks so much."

"You're welcome. I love the bargain book section. I always find some good deals at more than half off the cover price."

We moved to the car, and he opened the passenger door for me. As I climbed in, I admired his manners. I'd never had a boy open a car door for me. It was as if Taylor were from another era. I wondered if his uncle Rico had told him how he should treat girls.

We made small talk about the cool weather and homework as he drove me home. When we reached the driveway, my stomach tightened. I hoped he'd possibly try to kiss me again.

"I guess I'll see you around school." He tapped the steering wheel. "If I don't run into you tomorrow, I'll definitely see you Tuesday."

"Okay." I waited for a moment, hoping he'd lean over to me. However, Taylor continued to sit erect in the driver's seat. "Good night."

"Good night, Whitney."

I climbed from the car and waved before heading toward the back door. I was daydreaming about how amazing Taylor's kiss would've been when I stepped into the kitchen and found my family at the kitchen table.

I slipped into my seat and joined in as my father prayed aloud.

"Whitney," my mother said sharply after the prayer had ended. "Go wash up."

I dropped the bag of books and my purse in the family room and then quickly washed my hands at the kitchen sink. My father and brother talked about sports teams I couldn't have cared less about.

I returned to my seat and reached for the platter of chicken cordon bleu. "It smells delicious, Mom."

"Thank you, Whitney." She patted her mouth with a linen napkin and then eyed me. "I resent how much time you're spending with that family."

I added mixed vegetables and rice pilaf to my plate. "They're my friends. Taylor had to work today, and I spent the afternoon talking with Mrs. Martinez and Vanessa. We had a really nice time."

I sipped my iced tea to prevent myself from laughing at my mother's shocked expression.

"Whitney, you can't forget that you'll be leaving for college soon. We don't have much more time to spend together. I'd like to have some special girls' days with you before you leave."

"I promise we will spend time together, Mom. I'm not leaving for school just yet." I studied my plate, but I had absolutely no more room in my stomach for food. I felt queasy just looking at the meal. I took a few bites to avoid upsetting my mother even further.

Mom cut up her chicken cordon bleu. "Besides, I think you need to concentrate more on your studies. Once supper is over, you will do the dishes and then get right on your homework. No phone and no television. Understood?"

"Yes, Mom." I half listened to my brother and father talking more about sports, but I continued to daydream about Taylor. I couldn't shake the idea that he would've kissed me if my mother hadn't called. I wondered what it meant. Did he plan to ask me out?

"Whitney?" My father's voice rang through my thoughts. "Are you listening?"

"I'm sorry." I looked over at him. "What were you saying?"

"I was asking if you enjoyed your afternoon with your friends." He placed his utensils on his empty plate.

"Yes, I did. Thanks." I gathered up the dirty dishes and platters.

My mother stood. "Would anyone care for a piece of the sugar-free apple pie I bought today?"

"If we have ice cream with it," Logan said.

"I think I have some fat-free vanilla in the freezer. Let me go check."

I glanced back at my father and brother and spotted them rolling their eyes. I'd once heard my brother ask my father if they were going to stop for ice cream after karate, which was proof they cheated on Mom's healthy cooking outside of the house just like I did.

I began loading the dishwasher while my mother placed the pie and ice cream on the table.

"Whitney, would you like a piece?" Mom asked.

"No, thanks. I'm pretty full." I dropped utensils into the little plastic baskets as I avoided my mother's probing stare.

"You hardly ate anything at supper. Did you fill up on junk over at Taylor's house?" Mom fetched desert plates and utensils.

"No." I kept my eyes on the dirty dishes. "I'm just not hungry."

"Then you go on and get started on your homework. Logan can help clean up."

Logan groaned.

"No complaining, Logan. You can help out." Dad gave Logan a warning glance.

"Fine." Logan scowled.

"Thanks." I wiped my hands, retrieved my bag of books and my purse, and hurried up to my room where I sat at my desk and pulled out the report I'd printed last night.

I was proofreading it when my cell phone chimed, announcing a text message. I dug my phone out of my purse and was surprised to see the message was from Taylor.

He texted: *Hi. Hope you're not in trouble for getting home late.*

I couldn't help but grin. He was worried about me! I responded: *Mom isn't happy but it's ok. She told me to stay in my room and get homework done. No big deal.*

Taylor said: *Good. Need help with anything?*

I raised my eyebrows and then responded: *Want to proofread my history report?*

Taylor didn't text back right away, and I regretted being so bold. I hoped he knew it was a joke. I turned my attention to my report. When another text rang through the phone, I jumped.

He texted: *¡Me gustaria ayudarle en cualquiera manera que puedo!*

I laughed out loud as I translated it to mean, I would be happy to help you in whatever way I'm able to.

I texted back: *¡Estás loco!* (You're crazy!)

He responded: *Do u want my help or not?*

I typed: *Sure. What's your email address? I'll send the report.*

He texted his email address, and I sent him the report. I then stared at my computer screen and considered my college choices. I surfed the Kentwood, University, and State websites, thinking about my future and wondering where I belonged. Was I meant to be a teacher and cheerleading coach, or did God have other plans for me? And how would I know what those plans were supposed to be?

My thoughts turned to Taylor, and I wondered what he thought of my history paper. I was so thankful for his friendship, and even if I never dated him, I hoped our friendship would last a long time. Yet I still couldn't stop wondering what it would have been like to kiss him.

chapter thirteen

The next two weeks flew by quickly. I did my best to avoid my friends, but I spent as much time as I could with Taylor. It seemed he was the only person who really understood me. We enjoyed our Tuesday tutoring sessions, spending approximately fifteen minutes on calculus and the rest of the time talking about everything from school to God and family. I also talked to Taylor in the halls between classes. He texted me every night to say hello, and he wished me sweet dreams in Spanish. He still hadn't kissed me, but I wasn't giving up hope that it would happen.

I also kept my Thursday-afternoon dates with Vanessa, when we worked on cheerleading and also got to know each other better. I sat with Taylor and his family at church, despite my mother's disapproving glances.

Sunday afternoon, my mother insisted I come straight home from church to help clean up the house.

"What is the big deal, Mom?" I ran a duster over the curio cabinets filled with her most precious and expensive figurines. "Didn't the cleaning service come last week? I thought I remember you telling Dad that Happy Maids were coming on Thursday or something."

"Yes, they did come, but I just want to freshen up the house a bit." She pulled her box of silver from the hutch across the long room. "We're having company tonight. I'm making a special supper. Pheasant."

"Wait a minute." I spun and faced her while she added the crystal glasses and serving platters to her pile of fancy pieces that she only used when she entertained. "Who's coming for dinner?"

"The Steeles."

"What?" I dropped the duster and marched over to her. "Do you mean Brett Steele?"

"Yes, I do, dear." She pointed toward the curios. "You missed a spot over on the right. Look at it from my point of view."

"Please, Mom, can you understand my point of view? How could you invite Brett and his family over for dinner when you know he broke up with me?"

"Now, Whitney, this is just a friendly dinner. You know I'm good friends with Rhonda. We've been discussing getting the families together for quite some time. This is nothing more than a social gathering. I love to entertain." She pointed toward the cluster of fancy serving platters, glasses, and utensils. "Help me carry the glasses and serving platters into the kitchen." She gathered up the glasses in her hands.

"I can't believe you're doing this to me, Mom. The last thing I want to do is spend an evening with Brett." I lifted the serving platters and followed her. "It's so unfair."

"It's not about you, Whitney. It's about having friends over and having a good time. Brett is still your friend, right? You've known him a long time, and you move in the same circles." She placed the glasses on the counter.

"You're not listening to me, Mom. How would you like it if I invited one of your ex-boyfriends over for dinner? Wouldn't you be mortified?"

My mom looked at me as if I were a silly child. "That's preposterous. How could you invite one of my ex-boyfriends over? That would be impossible."

"That's not the point!" Irritation bubbled inside me. "Are you even listening to me?"

"Yes, I'm listening to you throw a tantrum like a child." She pointed toward the dining room. "Now go finish dusting and then pull out the vacuum cleaner. I need to start cooking. The Steeles will be here at five for hors d'oeuvres. Oh, and wear that short-sleeved, blue dress with those pearls your grandma gave you. You always look stunning in that."

"Wait a minute." I eyed her with suspicion. "This isn't a friendly dinner at all, is it?"

"What do you mean?"

"You and Mrs. Steele are trying to set Brett and me up again, aren't you?"

To my great surprise, Mom was speechless. I'd caught her!

"Don't do this to me, Mom." I shook my head, and anger swelled inside me. "I will not date Brett just because you want me to. You can't choose my friends."

"I'm not choosing your friends for you. I'm simply trying to keep your options open."

"You should really get to know Taylor and his family. They're good people with good values. They're hardworking and honest. And Taylor is nice to me. He treats me with respect. He's a good friend, Mom. You'd know that if you gave him and his family a chance."

"We can talk about them later. Right now we have work to do before our company arrives." She pointed toward the doorway. "Go finish dusting and start vacuuming."

"I can't stand it when you dismiss me, Mom." I raised my voice. "I won't do this. I'll go to my room and not come out. You can explain to Mrs. Steele why I'm not coming to dinner."

"You will not talk back to me, Whitney. You will do as I say, or I will take your car keys and your phone. Do you understand me? You'll find yourself taking the bus to school, and you'll be cut off from all of your friends."

I opened my mouth to shoot back another smart comment and then stopped. I couldn't bear the idea of going to bed at night without Taylor's nightly text messages. "Fine. I'll do it, but I will not date Brett. Your little scheme isn't going to work."

"We'll just see about that." She motioned toward the door. "Now get busy before I ground you. We have things to do."

I marched into the dining room and took deep breaths to try to calm myself. My mother had never done anything as manipulative as this, and I was furious. I knew I had to play the game or suffer the consequences of losing my car, my phone, and maybe even my freedom, but I wasn't going to agree to any relationship with Brett beyond being polite to him this evening.

My mother would not succeed at taking Taylor away from me. I would not allow it.

Later that afternoon I stood in front of the mirror in my bathroom and studied my reflection. I'd slipped into my blue dress and put on my pearls and matching earrings. My makeup was complete, and my hair was styled in one single french braid running the length of the back of my head and ending down near my collarbone.

I wondered what Taylor would think if he saw me like this. Would he be moved to kiss me and ask me to be his girlfriend? Or would he tell me I looked like a rich snob who wouldn't give him the time of day? Whatever, I still wished he and his family were the ones coming to dinner tonight.

My mom's heels clicked by the bathroom and headed for the stairs. "Hurry down, Whitney! The Steeles will be here soon."

I closed my eyes and begged God to help me get through the night.

I opened the bathroom door, and an idea sprang to mind. Dad had helped me in the past when Mom became too overbearing, and I needed his help again. I wondered if he could possibly give me some pointers on how to get through this evening.

I headed down the hall and found him standing in front of a mirror tying his tie in the master bedroom. I tapped on the doorframe. "Daddy? Do you have a minute?"

"Sure, pumpkin. What's going on?" He turned toward me. "You look lovely, Whitney."

"Thanks." I smoothed my hands over my dress. "You look really nice too." I'd always thought my father was handsome, especially when he wore a nice suit and tie.

"What do you want to talk about?" He fixed the tie and then began to smooth his hair.

"I'm really upset about this dinner tonight." I leaned against the doorframe. "Mom is trying to set me up with Brett again, and I don't want to date him. I'm really tired of Mom trying to make all of my decisions for me." My voice sounded thick, and I hoped I wouldn't cry. I didn't want my mascara to run and show how upset I was. I couldn't give Brett that advantage over me. I cleared my throat. "I don't like Brett, and I'd rather not be anywhere near him."

Dad glanced over at me. "I talked to your mom a few months ago and told her to back off. I guess she's at it again, huh?"

"She is. In full force."

"I'm sorry you feel like Mom is pushing you too hard. I know she expects a lot of you. I'll talk to her again."

"Thanks, Dad, but it's not that she's pushing me. She's trying to control me. She's already picked my activities in school, the college she wants me to go to, and the sorority she wants me to join. Now she's picking the boy she wants me to date. Will she pick my husband and name my kids too?"

He walked over to me. "I'm sorry you're upset." He placed his hands on my shoulders. "Your mom thinks she knows what's best for you, but I realize it would be better if she just gave you suggestions and then let you decide."

"Exactly. She doesn't like Taylor and his family, but he's the boy I like, Dad."

My dad smiled. "I know you two like each other. It's been pretty obvious in church."

"Really?" My heart fluttered.

"Why don't you go along with Mom's little plan tonight. Just be cordial to Brett and his family but don't make any promises to see Brett again after tonight." He touched my cheek. "After the company's gone and the dust settles, I'll talk to your mom and ask her to back off with Brett."

I hugged him. "Thank you, Daddy."

"You're welcome." He kissed the top of my head.

"Whitney Jean!" My mother's voice called from downstairs. "Logan Charles! Get down here immediately. I need some help!"

"You better go, Whitney. You know how your mom gets about these dinner parties." He winked at me before I hurried down the stairs.

I found my mother flittering around the kitchen while Logan grumpily set out a cheese tray.

"Whitney!" My mother issued orders while checking the oven. "Get out the crackers, please, dear."

"Yes, Mom." I was pulling out the fancy crackers and setting them on the trays when I heard the Steeles' car pull into the driveway. I felt my body stiffen, and then a hand settled on my shoulder.

"It will be fine," my father whispered in my ear. "Just relax. I promise the evening will be over soon."

I looked up at my dad, and he winked at me again.

The doorbell rang, and I hoped my mother wouldn't send me to answer it.

"I'll get it." My father moved to the door, and I was thankful.

I asked my mom what I could do, and she directed me toward more hors d'oeuvres that needed to be set out on the island in the middle of the large kitchen.

Voices and laughter floated in from the front of the house, and I gnawed my lower lip. I longed to run from the kitchen and cower in the safety of my room, where I could text Taylor and tell him what torture my mother had designed for me. I planned to sneak up there later.

"Hello!" Brett's mother waltzed into the kitchen with a cake in her hands. "How are you, Darlene?"

"Rhonda!" My mother rushed over and air-kissed her as if she hadn't seen her in years. "What a lovely cake."

"Oh, I made it myself." Rhonda joked, and my mother laughed.

I squelched the urge to roll my eyes.

My mother took the cake. "Oh, I love red velvet. Thank you."

"You're welcome. We stopped at the bakery on the way here." Rhonda paused and inhaled. "Oh, Darlene. It smells divine in here."

"Thank you." Mom gestured toward the kitchen table. "Have a seat. We'll start out with drinks and hors d'oeuvres."

Rhonda's eyes moved to me. "Whitney! Why you're as pretty as a picture."

"Thank you, Mrs. Steele." I stepped over and let her hug me. Her hug was so tight, I lost my breath for a moment. "It's nice to see you again."

"Oh yes, dear." Rhonda touched my arm. "We've missed you." Her sickeningly sweet perfume almost made me gag. "Brett has missed you too. He knows he made a mistake when he let you go."

"Really? I haven't gotten that impression from my conversations with him." I kept my expression innocent, but my mother shot me a warning glance from across the kitchen.

"Logan!" Rhonda moved on to my brother, and relief flooded me.

Brett and his father stepped into the kitchen with my father in tow. They both were dressed in suits and ties, which seemed ridiculous for a simple dinner. I longed for the warm and casual atmosphere of Taylor's house. Enchiladas and chocolate-chip-cookie sundaes sounded divine to me.

Brett's dad, Edward, waved and then turned his attention to Logan, who brought up a sports topic. Brett looked at me, and I glanced down at the stove.

"Mom," I called. "Is it time to take the birds out of the oven?"

"Not yet, dear." Mom looked annoyed. "I have it all timed perfectly. We have twenty minutes for hors d'oeuvres, and then we'll start with salad. Would you please pour drinks for you young people?"

"Of course." I was relieved to have something to do while my mother talked about mundane things with Rhonda and the men discussed sports. I handed Logan a Sprite and then brought a Coke to Brett.

"Thanks," Brett said, eyeing me. "You look nice."

I glared at him and then squared my shoulders and stood up taller. I knew I could survive this horrible dinner. Somehow.

chapter fourteen

Exactly twenty minutes later, the timer on the stove buzzed, and I was relieved to busy myself with readying the food for the table. Mom served the salads to the guests in the dining room while I prepared all of the serving trays.

I began carrying the food into the dining room, and my stomach churned when I found the only empty seat left for me was next to Brett. I dismissed the idea of sitting in the kitchen and continued to bring the platters to the table.

"Perfect!" My mom clapped her hands after everything was brought to the table. "Let's pray and then enjoy this lovely meal."

Soon hands began passing around the serving platters, and the sound of utensils scraping dishes filled the air. The mothers eventually fell into a conversation about upcoming events planned for their women's group, while the men continued talking about sports teams.

I glanced around the table and didn't spot my favorite Italian dressing. After excusing myself, I headed back into the kitchen and searched the refrigerator for the missing bottle of dressing.

"So, how have you been?" Brett asked from behind me.

I grabbed the dressing from the refrigerator and stood up straight. "I'm fine, thanks. You?"

"I've missed you. I know I've been a jerk, and I'm sorry." He gave me his best sad face, and I just had to laugh.

"Why are you laughing at me?" He looked annoyed.

"Brett, I'm certain you haven't even noticed we broke up, since you didn't notice me when we were dating." I pointed the bottle of dressing at him. "You were never interested in me. You only wanted to date the captain of the cheerleading squad so you could put it on your activities list for college."

"What? You're not making any sense, Whitney." He leaned against the island in the center of the kitchen. "You're different now. Even Kristin has noticed how you hardly talk to her or Tiffany. You don't hang out with them anymore. What's happened to you?"

"I don't know exactly." I shrugged. "I guess I'm just figuring out who I am. People change all the time, so now it's my turn."

"It's your new boyfriend, right? He's the reason you're changing." Brett's expression was sarcastic. "Is he more exciting than I was? Do you like to ride through the neighborhood on the back of his rat bike?"

I narrowed my eyes as animosity rushed through me. "If you're referring to Taylor Martinez, then I should inform you he's not my boyfriend. But yes, he's much more exciting than you. He's kinder, more thoughtful, and more supportive. Oh, and he's also better looking."

Brett's mouth fell open, and I gave myself a mental pat on the back. I'd finally gotten the big-shot captain of the football team to be quiet. *Score one point for Whitney Richards!*

I hurried past him into the dining room and slipped into my chair. I was sprinkling the dressing over my salad when Brett returned and sat beside me.

"Whitney." Rhonda called my name, and I sat up straight. "Have you gotten yourself a date for the prom yet?"

"No, I haven't, Mrs. Steele." I moved the lettuce around my plate.

Rhonda raised her eyebrows and looked at Brett. "Did you hear that, Brett? Whitney doesn't have a prom date, and neither do you."

I wiped my mouth. "It's a little early to be thinking about prom, though. I mean, we have time."

"Not really, dear." Mom shook her head. "It's April. Prom is just around the corner. Pretty soon we'll be out looking at dresses."

I pushed my salad bowl away and tried to think of something to say that would change the subject.

Rhonda kept her eyes on me as I filled my dinner plate. "Your mom tells me you're going to Kentwood."

"I was accepted, but I'm keeping my options open right now. I've been researching the academic programs at Kentwood, U, and State. I'm not really sure what I want yet." I kept my eyes on my plate and knew I was embarrassing Mom by not confirming my choice of the prestigious school, but I resented her for planning this dinner.

"Kentwood?" Edward chimed in. "Why, that's very impressive, Whitney."

"Thank you." I began cutting up my food. Out of the corner of my eye, I saw my father shift in his seat.

"So, Eddie, how are things going at your orthodontist practice? I heard you're doing some expanding?" Dad wiped his mouth and faced Brett's father.

I looked over at Dad and caught a smile that seemed to be aimed at me. *Thanks for saving me, Daddy!*

My mother asked Rhonda a question about one of their mutual friends, and soon the adults were deep in conversation. I focused on my meal and tried my best to eat, even though my appetite had evaporated the moment Brett walked into the house.

I kept my gaze on my plate for the rest of the meal, thankful that no one pulled me into a conversation. After everyone was finished with dinner, I helped my mom clear the table and began filling the dishwasher.

Rhonda stepped into the kitchen. "What can I do to help, girls?"

Mom pointed toward the coffeemaker. "Would you like to start coffee?"

"I'd love to." Rhonda began searching for the coffee in the cabinet. "Dinner was positively scrumptious, Darlene. You really outdid yourself."

"Why, thank you." Mom beamed.

"We should do this again soon." Rhonda found the coffee and filled the coffeemaker.

I finished filling the dishwasher and wiped my hands. "I'm going to run upstairs for a minute, okay?"

My mother eyed me. "Why, dear?"

"I need to use the restroom. I'd like a little privacy." I knew she couldn't argue with that excuse.

"Oh." My mom nodded quickly. "Of course, dear."

I made my way through the doorway and hurried toward the stairs and up to my room. I grabbed my phone from the dresser and found a text waiting from Taylor. I smiled my first genuine smile of the evening.

He said: *Hey. How r u?*

He'd sent the message twenty minutes ago, and I hoped he was still near his phone.

I sat on the edge of my bed and quickly typed: *Wish u were here.*

I glanced at my reflection in the mirror and prayed Taylor

would answer quickly. I was certain Mom would send Logan after me if I was gone more than a few minutes.

My phone chimed, and I nearly jumped out of my skin. I swallowed a squeal when I spotted Taylor's response: *What's up?*

I typed: *Suffering through a nightmare dinner right now. Wish I were at your place having enchiladas and sundaes instead.*

Taylor quickly sent: *Want me to come get u?*

I laughed to myself: *Do I ever!*

"Talking to your boyfriend?" a voice asked.

Surprised, I turned toward the door, where Brett stood in the doorway and smirked at me.

"Did I startle you?" He stepped into the room.

"No." I locked the phone so that my conversation wasn't visible.

"What's he saying to you?" Brett reached for the phone, and I held it away from him.

"I wasn't talking to Taylor." I slipped off the bed. "I was texting Kristin back. She wanted to see if we could study together, but I had to tell her I was busy."

"Oh, really?" Brett moved over to me.

The phone chimed again, and I tried to hide it behind my back. I hoped my mother would come looking for me. *I could really use your interference now, Mom!*

"Let me see that." Brett reached behind me and swiped the phone from my hand.

"Give it back!" I lunged for him, but he reached the other side of the room before I could get there. Frustration and anger surged through me. "That's personal!"

"Let's see." He studied the phone. "Taylor's text message says, 'Seriously. I can come get u. Tell me when.'" He clicked his tongue and shook his head. "You're a terrible liar, Whitney.

Just like when you told my mother you didn't have a date for the prom. I bet your loser boyfriend has already asked you."

I reached out and grabbed my phone. "He's not my boyfriend. And no, he hasn't asked me, but that's none of your business."

"He hasn't asked you? I bet I know why." Brett sneered at me. "He won't ask you because he doesn't have the money to pay for it. How can he afford to rent a limo, buy you a ticket and a corsage, and also get a tuxedo?"

I pointed toward the door. "You need to leave."

Brett's expression softened. "Look, let's stop arguing. We both know we belong together."

"You're kidding, right?" I snorted. "Please. Just go downstairs."

"I'm serious, Whitney." He stepped toward me. "I messed up when I broke up with you. I'm really sorry. Let's get back together."

"No." I shook my head and took a few steps back. "Leave now."

"Then let's be friends. We can still go to prom. We look good together."

"I wouldn't go to prom with you if you were the last man on earth, Brett. You can just forget it." Agitation boiled up in me.

"Now listen." Brett held a finger up as if to calm me. "If you go to prom with me, I'll do it right. I'll get a limo, and we can ride with our friends. We'll have a nice dinner, and then we'll—"

"Just stop it." I held up my trembling hand. "I'm not going to prom with you, so just drop it."

"But, Whitney." He stepped closer to me, and I backed up until I hit my dresser, square in my lower back. "You know I care about you."

"No, Brett, you only care about one person, and that's yourself."

"Oh, please." He touched my arm. "You know I'm crazy about you. It just took breaking up with you to realize how much you mean to me."

"No." I shook my head. "You're jealous that I like Taylor more than you. You can't stand knowing you've been beat. And it makes you even angrier I picked a guy you don't like."

"Yes, I am angry you like Taylor, but I can show you how much better I am. Just give me a chance." He cupped his hand to my cheek, and my skin crawled. "You only need to just let me work my magic, and then you'll remember why we were good together. We're meant to be together. You're the captain of the cheerleading squad, and I'm the captain of the football team. We're going to be prom king and queen."

"No, we're not. You better get your hands off me, or I'm going to scream. My father won't be happy when he comes up here and sees you touching me." My heart pounded. I needed to get away from him. I tried to push him back and dropped my phone on the floor behind me in the process.

"Your problem is that you need to relax." He gripped my arms hard and then dipped his face toward mine.

"Whitney!" My mother's voice boomed from the doorway. "What's going on in here?"

Thank you, Mom! Brett finally let go, and I pushed past him toward the door. "I was just coming down."

"Well. That's good to know." Mom looked between us. "Coffee and cake are on the table. I'd like you both to join us now."

Brett followed me to the door. "We were just talking about prom."

"Oh?" Mom's eyebrow's lifted. "Is that so?"

"Unbelievable." I rushed toward the stairs and made a beeline for the dining room, where I found everyone passing out pieces of the red-velvet cake Rhonda had picked up at an expensive bakery downtown.

I sat next to my father and smoothed my dress over my legs. A shiver went through me as I imagined what could've happened if my mom hadn't interrupted Brett. I pushed that thought away.

"Is everything all right?" Dad whispered as he handed me a piece of cake on Mom's fancy china.

"Yeah." I took the plate. "I'll be all right."

Brett sat across from me, and my mother gave me a strange expression before sitting beside him.

My father poured a cup of coffee and handed it to me. "Here, Whitney. This should make you feel better."

"Thanks, Dad." I reached for the sweetener and then the cream and avoided Brett's stare as I stirred them into the coffee.

Conversations swirled around me while I ate cake and drank coffee. I realized I hadn't responded to Taylor's offer to come over and rescue me, and I considered excusing myself to sneak back upstairs and call him.

When I stabbed the last forkful of cake, my mother shook her head as if to tell me not to finish it because of the evil calories. With my eyes glued to her, I ate it, chewing slowly.

An engine boomed nearby, followed by headlights shining into the dining room windows.

"Who could that be?" Mom asked.

My pulse raced. Could Taylor have actually come to rescue me from the dinner party?

"I'll go see." I jumped up from the table and rushed to the front door. I stepped onto the front porch just as Taylor climbed the steps. "Taylor. What are you doing here?"

"I was worried about you." He wore tight jeans, a black T-shirt with a band name on it, and his jacket. His curls were matted to his head from wearing the helmet. And he looked great to me, so much better than Brett looked in his expensive suit.

"I'm okay." I shivered in the cool night air and hugged my arms to my chest.

His eyes moved down my body. "You look really nice."

"Thanks." I glanced back toward the door. "I can't stay out here long. My mom is watching me like a hawk tonight."

"Oh." He pointed toward the road. "I guess I sort of overreacted by coming out here, but I was worried when you didn't answer my last couple of texts."

"I'm sorry. I got interrupted when I was texting you back. I'll call you as soon as they leave." I turned toward the door again. "It's great to see you, but I really have to get back in there."

"You must have some pretty important guests in there." He stepped closer to me, his boots scraping the porch. "Should I be jealous?"

I couldn't help laughing. "No. I'd much rather be with you."

"Good." He caressed my arm, and I didn't recoil as I had when Brett touched me. I leaned toward Taylor, enjoying the warmth of his hand. "You're freezing, Whitney. You should go inside. Call me later."

The front door opened, and my mother poked her head out. "Whitney?" She glowered. "Oh. Hello, Taylor. This isn't a good time, dear. We have company now."

"I'm sorry for interrupting, Mrs. Richards." Taylor's expression was full of remorse. "I wasn't able to reach Whitney on her cell, and I had a quick question about our Spanish homework."

I shot Taylor a sideways glance, impressed with his quick thinking. From my viewpoint, the boy could talk his way out of any situation by the seat of his pants!

"Whitney answered my question, so I'll be on my way. I hope you enjoy the rest of your evening, ma'am."

"Oh. Well, thank you, dear." Mom turned to me. "I need you to come back inside, Whitney. It's rude to leave our guests waiting." She disappeared into the house and left the door ajar.

"As if they'd miss me," I muttered.

"I'd miss you." Taylor stepped closer to me.

I looked up at him. "Would you?"

"Yeah." Taylor touched my cheek. "I would. *Eres muy linda.*"

I blinked, wondering if I'd imagined him telling me I was very pretty. "*Gracias.*"

"You're welcome," he whispered. "I know I need to go, but I don't want to."

"Whitney." Brett stepped out onto the porch. "Did you want more cake? It's going pretty quickly."

Taylor's hand fell to his side, and his eyes darkened.

I spun and glared at Brett. "What do you want?"

"Oh, did I interrupt something? I'm sorry." Brett smirked at Taylor. "How are you, Martinez? I didn't realize you knew your way out to Castleton."

"Brett Steele. I'm amazed you can find your way off the football field." Taylor glanced at me. "I didn't realize I was interrupting a dinner party with your ex-boyfriend."

"I can explain." I reached for Taylor, but he backed away from me. "This wasn't my idea at all."

"Why don't you come join us, Martinez?" Brett gestured toward Taylor. "Oh, but you're not dressed for the occasion, are you?"

I turned my angry eyes on Brett. "Shut up and go back in the house now."

Brett threw his hands up in surrender. "I was only trying to be cordial, Whitney. I'll go back in now."

Taylor stalked down the porch steps and continued down the path for the driveway. I rushed after him, nearly slipping in my high heels.

"Taylor! Taylor, wait!" I stopped and kicked off my shoes and then continued toward the driveway trying to ignore the sensation of the cold cement under my feet. "Please, Taylor."

He reached his bike and then spun to face me. "I feel so stupid right now. Here I was worried about you, and you were having a formal dinner with your so-called ex-boyfriend." He raked his hands through his curls, his expression pained. "Whitney, I actually believed you liked me. Am I just a pawn for you to use to get your ex-boyfriend back?"

"No. That's not it at all." My voice was thick with emotion. "Taylor, I like you. I like you more than I ever liked Brett. You're real. You're kind and thoughtful. You treat me better than any guy I've ever known." I pointed toward the house. "This whole stupid party was my mom's idea. She and Brett's mom are trying to get us back together. I never wanted to be a part of this."

He stared at me, and his expression remained the same, unconvinced and hurt. I knew I had to bare my soul, as embarrassing as it might be.

"Look, I've spent the whole night wishing you were the one sitting next to me at dinner." I sniffed as a lump swelled in my throat. "I actually snuck up to my room earlier to text you because I couldn't stop thinking about you." A tear trickled down my cheek, and I wiped it away quickly. "I really like you, Taylor. I look forward to your text messages and to seeing you at school. I don't know what else I can say to convince you that you're the one I like, not that idiot Brett Steele."

Taylor opened his arms to me. "Come here."

I launched myself into his arms, and he pulled me close. I buried my face in his neck, trying to stop my tears from pouring from my eyes. I felt like a complete moron for crying, but the idea of losing Taylor's friendship was too much for me to handle.

"*Tú me gusta*," he whispered the words close to my ear, sending shivers rippling down my spine.

"I like you too." I stepped back from his embrace.

"And you don't like Brett." His words were more of a statement than a question.

"I can't stand the sight of him."

Taylor grinned. "Good. Keep it that way."

"Whitney." My brother's voice sounded from the far end of the driveway. "Oh, hey," he said to Taylor.

"Logan, you remember Taylor from church, right?" I said.

"Hey, Taylor. Cool bike," Logan said.

"Thanks man." Taylor nodded at him.

"Let me guess," I said, facing my brother. "Mom wants me?"

Logan nodded. "Yeah. Mom is getting really upset. You'd better come inside now."

"Go." Taylor squeezed my hand. "We'll talk later."

"Okay." I wiped my eyes again "I'll be right there, Logan."

My brother disappeared down the path toward the front door.

"*Buenas noches.*" Taylor grinned at me.

I watched him drive off and wished I were on the back of his bike, riding away from the suffocating dinner party in my dining room.

"Why did you tell Rhonda you're not sure if you're going to Kentwood?" My mom stood in the doorway to the dining room while I removed the tablecloth later that evening after our guests had finally gone home.

"I didn't say I wasn't going, but it's true that I'm still not certain I want to go." I rolled up the tablecloth. "I still can't decide which school is the right fit for me."

"You know Kentwood would give you the best opportunities, Whitney. I only want what's best for you. I want to give you and your brother the best options for your futures, so you can be successful like your father." She eyed me. "And why did you tell her you weren't certain about prom either?"

"Because I'm not. I don't have a date, and that's the truth. I may have to go alone." I couldn't tell her I was hoping Taylor would ask me. She'd have a heart attack at the thought of me in a gown on the back of Taylor's bike. I suppressed a grin at the thought.

"I imagine Brett will ask you to the prom." She looked amused. "You and Brett were getting cozy in your room earlier."

"No, we weren't. He was getting aggressive with me. You actually walked in at the right time."

"Oh." She paused for a moment, and her expression clouded. "Are you okay?"

"Yeah, I'm fine." I hugged the tablecloth to my chest as the memories of his sleazy hands flashed through my mind.

"Do you want me to talk to Rhonda about it?" Mom continued to look concerned.

"No, I'm fine, but thanks. He surprised me, but he didn't hurt me. I think he was trying to convince me to go out with him again. He acted as if I would fall madly in love with him if he kissed me." I set the tablecloth on the hutch. "He asked me to the prom, but I told him no."

"Have you thought about giving him a chance? Maybe he realized he'd been awful to you, and he really has changed. People can change if they really want to."

"I doubt he's changed." I pointed toward the tablecloth. "You'll have to take this to the dry cleaners. I don't think we should put it in our washer."

"That's a good idea." Mom turned toward the kitchen. "It's

getting late, so we'd better head to bed. I'll finish cleaning up tomorrow. Good night, dear."

"Good night." I yawned as I made my way up the stairs and down the hallway to my bedroom. I changed into my pajamas and then picked up my phone from the floor. When I unlocked it, I found four text messages from Taylor.

I flopped onto my back on my bed and read them:

Are u okay?

Whitney, what's going on?

I'm heading over there to check on u.

It was really good seeing u tonight. Heading to bed. Hope u sleep well. Sweet dreams. See u tomorrow.

I placed my cell phone on my nightstand, and then I turned toward my digital clock, which read 12:15. My mind raced with flashbacks of the evening, from my talk with my father to Brett's awful behavior and Taylor's heart-pounding hug. I found myself spiraling into a black hole of confusion. Why was I falling in love with a guy my mother would never embrace as part of our family? I never imagined I would face a problem like this. I wasn't the same person I used to be, and I wondered if I even fit in with my family anymore.

I closed my eyes and opened up my heart, giving all of my worries over to God:

God, please guide me. I'm trying hard, but my mother still isn't listening to how I feel or what I want. I want to be my own person, not some carbon copy of her. I want to make friends who don't attend the country club, and most of all, I want to date Taylor. I'm falling in love with him, and I never imagined I could feel this way. God, help me know what to do.

I covered my face with my hands as tears filled my eyes. Soon I fell into a deep sleep.

chapter fifteen

On Monday after school, I sat on a desk at the front of the classroom and read an events list off to my cheer team.

"So, pretty much we're just going to support the baseball team and attend their games until graduation," I said. "We don't have any official squad events or duties for the rest of the year. Of course, we're going to attend tryouts later on in the spring and vote on the girls who try out for next year."

"What about prom?" Monica Barnes' voice rang out from the back of the classroom.

"What about it?" I rested my elbow on the clipboard.

"Shouldn't we do something to recognize our squad at prom? After all, many of us are seniors." Monica hooted, and Tiffany gave her a high five.

"I don't think clubs and athletes are usually recognized at prom." I looked at Kristin in the front row, hoping she'd chime in.

Kristin spun and faced Monica. "We'll be recognized when Whitney is crowned prom queen, and Brett Steele is prom king."

The team cheered, and impatience swelled inside me. "I don't think that's going to happen. Let's move on."

"Why?" Misty Strickland called from the back row. "What do you mean you don't think it's going to happen, Whitney?"

"Oh, of course it will!" Kristin waved off the comment. "You're a shoo-in for queen, Whitney, and everyone wants Brett as king."

"Oh yeah." Tiffany said from beside Kristin. "You're like the royal couple of CHS!"

"Is there something you're not telling us, Whitney?" Misty's expression changed to a mean smile. "Are you not going to prom with Brett? Are you going with your new boyfriend instead?"

I glared at Misty. I was certain she was using any opportunity to single me out and do her best to embarrass me after what had happened at J2A two weeks ago. Misty crossed her arms over her hoodie, slumped back in the chair, and smirked at me.

"You have a new boyfriend?" Monica asked.

Questions rang out throughout the room, and I spotted Tiffany and Kristin exchanging surprised expressions.

Kristin held her hand up to silence the room. "But I thought Brett came over to your house for supper last night. He said he was planning to ask you to prom."

"He did ask me." My pleasant mood transformed into agitation as their eyes bored into me as if I were on trial.

"And ...?" Kristin threw her hands up. "What did you tell him?"

"I don't think that's any of your business." I couldn't stop my biting response, but I started to feel a twinge of guilt when Kristin blanched as if I'd slapped her.

"You don't have to talk to me that way." Kristin's voice was soft and meek, like a child. "I don't know who you are anymore, Whitney. You ignore us, and then you snap at us when we talk to you."

I opened my mouth to apologize, but Tiffany interrupted me before I could speak.

"So what did you say when he asked you?" Tiffany's eyes were wide with anticipation. "Did you say yes?"

"I told him no." I shrugged as if it were no big deal, even though my cheeks were on fire.

"Why would you tell Brett Steele no?" Tiffany asked.

"That's just stupid," Monica chimed in. "But maybe now he'll ask me."

"Did you get back together with Chad?" another girl asked.

"No, I'm not going with Chad. Let's drop it. I think you all need to be more concerned about your own lives rather than mine. This meeting is about our team, not my personal life." I looked down at the clipboard. "Can we get back to the schedule for the rest of the year? I have other things to do this afternoon." I knew my tone was biting, but their attitudes and nosiness were exasperating.

"Why are you avoiding the questions, Whitney?" Misty's voice rang out loud and clear above the curious murmurs. "Don't you want to tell the team who your new boyfriend is? Or should I tell them?"

I shot her an angry glance. "As I said earlier, my life isn't your business."

"You have a boyfriend, and you haven't told me." Kristin's expression was full of hurt. "I thought you were my best friend, Whitney. What's happened to you?"

The rest of the girls chimed in, asking who it was and shouting out a laundry list of football players. I held on to the edge of the desk to prevent myself from running from their questions.

"If you're too embarrassed to tell them, then I'll tell them." Misty stood and nearly shouted over the crowd.

I stood and squared my shoulders. I wasn't afraid to admit that Taylor was my friend, but I also wasn't about to give Misty the power to tease me in front of my squad. "I'm not embarrassed, Misty, and I know why you're acting this way.

You're angry I got you in trouble at J2A because you were mean to my cousin."

Misty shook her head. "I'm not getting revenge. I'm just telling the truth. I think the team has a right to know you're dating a loser. After all, you're our captain."

Kristin threw her hands in the air with frustration apparent on her face. "What is she talking about?"

"She's not talking about anything." I shook my head. "She's just trying to embarrass me."

"You're blushing, Whitney." Monica shrugged. "And you must have something to hide, since you won't tell us who this mystery guy is."

I scanned the room and found my team staring at me with wide eyes. I'd never felt like a stranger instead of part of the team until that moment.

"Just tell us," Tiffany said.

"Whitney is in love with Taylor Martinez," Misty said. "And she loves him so much that she's helping his sister train for tryouts."

"What?" Monica looked shocked. "Why him?"

"You picked him over Brett?" Kristin's expression was equally surprised.

"She's kidding, right?" Tiffany started to laugh and then stopped. "Oh no. Whitney's not denying it."

I glanced around the room again, taking in all of the curious and confused expressions. My eyes fell on Misty, and she blew me a kiss. I fought the urge to march back to her and smack that expression off her smug little face.

The room started to close in on me. I couldn't stand there anymore. Even Kristin, who had been my best friend since first grade, was looking at me as if I were crazy.

These people weren't my friends, and I didn't want to

associate with them any longer. I wanted to run, but I wasn't going to leave the room in tears. I was going to be strong, and I was going to hold my head high. After all, they were the ones who were acting like self-absorbed snobs.

I retrieved my backpack from the floor and then handed Kristin the clipboard. "I know you always wanted to be team captain, and you resented it when Coach Lori chose me. You're now the captain."

"What are you saying?" Kristin's eyes rounded. "You're quitting?"

The room suddenly fell silent as the other girls watched us.

"No." I shook my head. "I'm not quitting. I'm resigning."

Kristin held out the clipboard. "You can't do this, Whitney."

"I just did." I looked at the rest of the team. "Kristin is your new captain. I'm done here."

Kristin popped up from her seat, grabbed my arm, and pulled me into the hallway. "You can't resign, Whitney. You've worked so hard to become captain, and you earned it, fair and square."

"I'm resigning, and you can't stop me. I'll go talk to Coach Lori and tell her I recommend you for captain." I adjusted my backpack on my shoulder.

"This is crazy." Kristin's eyes studied my face. "You actually turned Brett down last night?"

I nodded. "I did."

"Why would you do that? I told him what to say and what to do. What did he do wrong?"

"You coached him?" My voice raised an octave, and I noticed that people passing by in the hallway were staring at us. "You knew how he hurt me, but you were still trying to help him get back with me?"

"Of course I was. I did it for you, Whitney. You belong with Brett."

"No, I don't belong with him. And if you truly were my best friend, you'd know that." A lump swelled in my throat, but I tried to stay strong. "You don't know me at all, Kristin."

"Apparently I don't. You haven't really talked to me in weeks. You're like a stranger. I don't understand you at all. I would never imagine you picking a nobody like Taylor over Brett. And I'd never let him come between cheering and me. Why would you do that?" Then her expression softened. "Look, everyone is just overreacting. Let's go back inside and talk this over."

"No. I think the team has already said enough. There's nothing else to say."

Kristin held her hands up as if to calm me. "Just listen to me, okay? You're going to regret walking away from this team. It's going to ruin your reputation. I don't understand why you're doing this, but I don't want to see you do this to yourself. I know we haven't talked, but I still care about you, Whitney. You're like a sister to me. I can't let you ruin your life like this."

"That's just it, Kristin. I don't think I'm ruining anything. In fact, I feel really good about this." I cleared my throat, hoping to sound more confident. "I don't belong here anymore."

"What?" Kristin shook her head as if in disbelief. "Of course you belong here. You're the best captain the team has had since we joined as freshmen. You're the most talented gymnast, and we've all improved so much because of you. This is our senior year, Whitney. Don't walk away from the team now. Everything will change next year. Don't walk away from all of us now."

"It's over for me, and you'll be a better captain. The girls respect you." I stepped away from her. "I have to go. I'll talk to you later." I started down the hallway.

"Whitney!" Kristin called after me. "Is he really worth this?"

"Yes, he is." I spun and hurried down the hall toward Lori Williams' classroom. Not only was Lori our cheerleading coach;

she was also one of the English teachers. I found her packing up her bag in her room.

She turned toward me. "Whitney. I was going to pop in at the team meeting."

"Oh, good." I wrung my hands. "I just wanted to let you know I stepped down as captain. I'm going to have to leave the team for the remainder of the year."

"Why?" Coach Lori tilted her head.

"I'm overwhelmed with school commitments, and my mom is really pressuring me to keep my grades up." I tried to smile, hoping to look comfortable with my decision. "Kristin will take over as captain in my place."

"Oh." Coach Lori looked unconvinced. "You know the rest of the year is really relaxed, Whitney. We'll just attend some sporting events, and we'll prepare for tryouts. We'll also help some girls who need any extra training. You can go at your own pace. You don't need to attend every event."

"I know." I shifted my weight from one foot to the other. "I'd just rather step down and concentrate on my grades. I don't want to lose any of my college acceptances."

"I hate to see you go. You're the best trainer I have." Lori looked troubled. "You're also the most talented, but don't tell the other girls I said that."

"Thanks. I appreciate the compliment, but it's really best if I step down." I started for the door. "I appreciate all you've done for the team, Coach. I'll see you around."

"Okay. Be certain to stop by to see me before graduation, Whitney." Coach nodded.

"I will." I started for the door and then turned back toward her. "Promise me that you'll make sure all of the incoming freshmen get a fair chance when they try out for the team."

She studied me with curiosity. "Of course I will. I always do."

"Great. Thanks." As I rushed out to the parking lot, I spotted Taylor standing by his bike talking to a few guys I recognized from honor society. I hurried toward them, and the boys gave me curious stares.

Taylor followed their gazes toward me and grinned. "Hey, Whitney. I was hoping to run into you today." His expression became serious. "What's wrong?"

"I didn't mean to interrupt, but I need to talk to you." I did my best to smile, but it felt more like a grimace.

The boys mumbled something and then waved before walking away. They looked back at us more than once as they crossed the parking lot.

"What's going on?" He reached for my hand, and I was thankful for his soothing touch.

I looked down at my jeans. "I was wondering if I could cash in that rain check. I could really use a motorcycle ride."

"Seriously?" His eyes widened.

I nodded. "Seriously."

"Wow. Cool." He lifted the helmet. "Let's see how this fits."

"Oh no. Then there's no helmet for you." I shook my head. "I'll be fine."

"No." I emphasized the word. "I can't stand to think about you getting hurt."

"All right." He rested the helmet on his hip. "What if we just go to the park? It's only a block away. I'll owe you a longer ride later when I have my extra helmet."

I paused.

"I'll go slow." His expression was full of hope.

I couldn't resist him. I just needed to be alone with him. "Okay."

Taylor slipped the helmet over my head and then fastened the strap. He glanced down at my Windbreaker. "You might want to zip that. It's colder on the bike than it is just standing here in the warm sun."

I zipped it up, and he grinned. "What's so funny?"

"I never thought I'd have a cheerleader on the back of my bike."

"I hate to break it to you, but as of a few minutes ago, I'm no longer a part of the team."

"What?"

"I promise I'll tell you when we get to the park. Right now I just want to get out of here and be with you."

"Your wish is my command." He climbed onto the bike, took my hand, and helped me on. "Just hold on to me. Don't worry about squeezing too tight. You can't hurt me. If you get scared, just pull on my jacket, okay?"

"Okay." I looped my arms around his waist and held on to him. He steered through the parking lot, and I held him close, breathing in the smell of his shampoo and resting my cheek on his shoulder.

I closed my eyes and let my thoughts go. The ride, though short, was exhilarating and refreshing, just as Taylor had said it was for him. I forgot my worries and just held on.

I wanted to hold on to him forever. It was comforting to feel his body close to mine. When I was with Taylor, I was free from the pressure of being Whitney Richards, perfect student and cheer captain. I was just Whitney Richards, high school senior and regular girl.

Taylor steered the motorcycle into the park and stopped at the far end of the parking lot. He climbed off the bike and then helped me down.

"What did you think?" He removed the helmet and locked it in place on the bike.

"It was amazing." I ran my hands through my hair. "I'd like a longer ride next time."

"I can arrange that." He took my hand in his. "Let's go find somewhere to talk."

We followed a path into a cluster of trees.

I looked up at him, enjoying the feel of my hand encircled in his. "Do you have to go to work today?"

"No. I'm off today." He squeezed my hand. "What happened with cheerleading?"

I led him toward an empty picnic table. "Let's sit here and talk." I climbed up on top of the table, and he sat beside me. "Do you know Misty Strickland?"

He shrugged. "I know who she is. Why?"

"She and I sort of got into an argument at J2A recently, and it came up again today." I paused, debating how much to tell Taylor. How could I admit she'd called him a loser?

"What is it, Whitney?" He moved closer to me. "Please tell me."

"Remember when you came to church a couple of weeks ago and then had to leave for work before J2A?"

"Yeah."

"She was there, and she teased me about being your girlfriend."

"Did that bother you?"

I ran my fingers over the worn wooden top of the table to avoid his eyes. "I didn't mind her saying you were my boyfriend, but I didn't like what she said about you."

"What did she say?"

I bit my lower lip and kept my eyes focused on the table. "She made fun of where you live."

"That's nothing new. I've heard that before." He placed a finger under my chin and angled my face so I was looking at him. "What does that have to do with quitting cheerleading?"

"She picked a fight with me in front of the whole team

today." I told him I thought she was trying to get back at me for getting her in trouble with Jenna. I explained how Misty said I was dating him and what the team said. I ended the story with my resignation and my conversation with Kristin in the hallway. By the time I finished my story, tears were flowing from my eyes, and I felt like a total moron for crying in front of him yet again. I couldn't help but bare my soul whenever I talked to him. I'd never felt so safe and comfortable with anyone.

"Hey. It's okay." Taylor wiped the tears from my cheeks with his fingertips. "Don't cry."

"I'm sorry." I cleared my throat. "They just really got to me."

"I'm sorry our friendship has caused you so much trouble."

"Don't say that." I touched his sleeve.

"But you've lost your friends because of me."

"No." I shook my head. "You're not the problem. They're the problem. If they can't see what I see in you, then they aren't my friends."

He studied me. "You mean that?"

"Yes, I mean it."

"But you lost cheerleading, something you love, because of me." His expression fell. "You may look back and regret that."

"No. I would regret losing you because of them."

Taylor's expression became intense, and my heart thumped in my chest. He reached out and cupped his hand to my cheek. He dipped his chin, and his lips brushed mine. I closed my eyes and lost myself in the sensation of his lips, wishing the kiss would last forever.

His cell phone began to ring from inside his jacket, and I pulled back.

"Should you get that?" I asked, my voice a little ragged with emotion.

"Oh. I didn't even hear it ringing." He fished out the phone.

"It's my mom." He pushed a button and then held the phone to his ear. "Hey, Mom. Oh. Okay. Sure, I'll be right there. All right. Bye." He put the phone back into his pocket. "I'm sorry, but I have to go."

He climbed down from the table, reached for my hand, and helped me down. We fell into step as we made our way back to the parking lot.

"Is everything all right?" I couldn't stop staring at his lips as I remembered the feeling of our kiss.

"Yeah. My mom has to stay late at work, and Vanessa left her house key and phone at home today. She thought she'd be home before Vanessa, but now she can't leave. I have to let Vanessa in." Taylor studied me. "Whitney, I care about you, but I don't want you to give up things that are important just for me. If you truly want to give up cheerleading, it needs to be for the right reasons."

"I gave it up because I don't belong there anymore."

"Are you certain?"

"Yes." I emphasized the word, and his expression softened.

He placed the helmet on my head and then helped me climb onto the bike. As we rode back to retrieve my Jeep, I held on to him and relived the kiss over and over in my mind.

I knew at that moment that I was in love with Taylor Martinez, and I prayed he loved me too.

chapter sixteen

Wednesday afternoon I was still floating. Taylor and I began spending more time together, and I longed to know how he really felt about me. We'd had lunch together in the courtyard, and we'd spent less than fifteen minutes of my tutoring session talking about calculus. The rest of the time we talked about everything from family to our hopes and dreams for the future. He hadn't mentioned the kiss or the significance of it, but I felt as if our relationship had risen to a new level. I wanted to know if he considered me his girlfriend, but I didn't want to ask and risk seeming desperate or needy.

I'd managed to avoid my former friends, and neither Kristin nor Tiffany had called or texted me. Although I was completely consumed with Taylor, I missed my friends and felt a little lost without them. I still couldn't figure out who I was or where I belonged at school or at home. My identity crisis was still in full swing, but I was thankful to have Taylor in my life.

When I reached the house, I steered my Jeep into the driveway and hurried in the back door.

"I'm home," I called before grabbing an apple and a bottle of water. I then hurried up the stairs to my room. I dropped my backpack on the floor, pulled my phone from my pocket, and sat at my desk, hoping to find a text from Taylor. He'd told me he had to go straight to work from school, but I'd hoped he'd texted me before he started working. I closed my eyes and tapped myself on the forehead, feeling silly for being so dependent on Taylor's text messages.

I placed the phone on my desk and bit into the apple while pulling my homework notebook from my backpack.

"Whitney?" My mother appeared in the doorway. "I didn't hear you come in."

"Oh, hey, Mom. How are you?"

"I'm a little concerned, dear." She crossed my room and sat on my bed. "Is there anything you want to tell me?"

"No. Why?"

"I spoke to Kristin's mother today."

"Oh." Alarm filled me. "What did you talk about?"

She studied me. "Why didn't you tell me you quit cheerleading?"

"I don't know. I guess I didn't think it was important." I was certain she could see through my lie. I hadn't told her because I knew she'd never understand. I'd hoped she'd never find out, but I realized the news would eventually get back to her.

"Whitney, you know this is important. You have to stick to your activities if you want to keep your college acceptances." She shook her head. "I don't understand why you would quit cheerleading. You've always loved it." She pointed toward my shelves filled with gymnastics and cheerleading ribbons, medals, and trophies. "Just look at your awards and all you've accomplished since you were a little girl. Why would you give that up?"

I shrugged. "It's no big deal, Mom. You know we don't really have any required activities in the spring. We just cheer on the baseball team from the stands and hang out. It's just a social thing. Colleges will understand that."

Mom stared at me, and I somehow knew what was coming.

"You're not telling me the truth, Whitney." Her tone was angry, reminding me of when my brother had thrown a ball in the house and broken one of her most precious Lladró figurines. "I want the truth, and I want it now."

I sat up straighter. "Something tells me you already know the truth, and you're only testing me to see if I'll say it out loud."

"I do know the truth. You quit cheering because of that boy."

"No. That's Kristin's version of the truth."

"So then, what's your version?"

"My version, which is the whole truth, is my so-called friends are pressuring me to end my friendship with Taylor." My voice was loud and shaky with resentment. "Misty Strickland has it in for me, and she deliberately tried to embarrass me in front of the team during our meeting on Monday. She told everyone Taylor Martinez was my boyfriend, and then the majority of the team weighed in on why I shouldn't even talk to him. If they can't accept my friendship with Taylor, then they aren't my friends."

"That's not true, Whitney. You've been best friends with Kristin since first grade. How can you possibly throw that friendship away? What kind of a person does that make you?"

"Did you hear what I just said? Kristin is one of the girls who put down Taylor. How is she my friend?"

"Shouldn't you be more concerned about keeping your lasting friendships with your girlfriends?" Mom pointed toward a framed photo of Kristin and me taken at a football game last year. We were in our uniforms, holding up our pom-poms and smiling as if life were completely and utterly perfect.

"Just look how happy you two were last year," she continued. "If you and Kristin work on your friendship, you'll be friends the rest of your lives. You know I've known Minnie Hancock since grade school, and we still talk all the time. We both dated boys throughout high school and college, but we never let a boy get between us. Just because you think you love that Martinez boy now doesn't mean you'll still care about him by the time graduation rolls around. Don't throw away a lifelong friendship for some boy who means something to you now but may mean nothing to you later."

"Are you listening to me, Mom? That's not my point!" I waved my hands wildly. "I found out Kristin was helping Brett to win me back. A true friend would see Brett isn't right for me. All Kristin cares about is seeing Brett and me crowned prom king and queen. Everyone says we should be together. Kristin keeps pushing me to go with Brett. I can't do it, Mom. I just can't."

Mom studied me. "You can't let that boy ruin your plans, Whitney."

"What do you mean? Which boy?"

"That Martinez boy. He's not worth your time."

"How would you even know if he's worth my time? You've never tried to get to know him."

"All I know is he very rudely interrupted our dinner Sunday night," Mom stated firmly. "That was enough information for me. He has no manners, and I blame his mother."

"You're wrong. His family has more manners and they are more thoughtful than any of the people you've ever invited for a dinner party. If you took the time to get to know them, you'd be impressed."

Mom twisted her face. "I don't know what's happened to you, Whitney, but I am tired of that boy poisoning your mind."

"He hasn't poisoned my mind, Mom." I pointed toward my chest. "This is who I am. I don't want to be a part of that cheer squad. You need to start respecting me for who I am. I have changed. I realize now what's important to me, and that's having friends who respect and understand me, the real me."

Mom shook her head. "I won't allow you to mess up your life. Your father and I are paying for your college, and we expect you to do your best. Dropping out of cheerleading in April of your senior year is not acceptable. You need to go talk to your coach and explain to her that you didn't mean it when you quit. Even if you have to grovel to get her to take you back."

I stood, trying to make a point. "No. I won't do it."

"Yes, you will." My mother moved in front of me and pointed at me. "Yes, you will go back to cheerleading, or I will take your phone and your car away from you until graduation."

"Fine." I shrugged. "Take my car and my phone, but I won't do it."

"Whitney. You don't mean this." She shook her head and reached for me. "What's happened to my sweet little girl who used to never give your father and me an ounce of trouble?"

"She's grown up." I grabbed my keys and my purse from my desk and rushed out the door while my mother called after me. I just had to get out of that house. I was tired of my mother not listening to me. I had to be free. I needed to be by myself.

No, I needed Taylor.

I jumped into my Jeep and drove toward the mall. I knew there would be serious consequences for my storming out of the house, but I couldn't take it anymore. This was the only way for me to get her attention. I was surprised my mother hadn't tried to call me, but then I realized I'd left my phone on my desk.

I held my raging emotions inside as I steered down Main Street and into the mall parking lot. I pulled into a space near the front and then crossed to the mall entrance.

I made my way to the bookstore, where I spotted Taylor ringing up a customer at the register. I stood near the entrance and watched him while he worked. He looked handsome in his blue shirt and khakis. He smiled as he took the customer's money.

I wondered if Taylor had any idea how good looking he was. Of course, I knew the answer: Taylor had no idea how his looks and demeanor affected me or any other girl, which was one of the main reasons why he was more attractive than Brett. Brett was good looking, but he knew it and thought he was the greatest thing since the invention of the iPhone. On the other hand, Taylor was humble and unassuming, and humility was much more appealing than conceit. I wondered why my mother couldn't see my point of view.

When the bookstore manager came toward me, I quickly moved to a stack of bargain books in the middle of the store to look busy. I was pretending to be interested in an autobiography written by an actress I'd never heard of when I felt a hand touch my arm.

I heard Taylor's voice behind me. "I think the book you're looking for is back by the science fiction section."

I raised my eyebrows at Taylor, and he winked at me. "Oh, right," I said. "I was looking for that new science fiction book by that author."

"Right." He nodded slowly. "Blake Bossert."

"Of course." I snapped my fingers for effect, hoping Taylor's boss would buy it.

"Follow me, miss." Taylor made a sweeping gesture toward the middle aisle, and I admired his acting ability. I wondered why he never auditioned for drama club.

Once we moved past the customer-service counter, Taylor reached back and took my hand in his. We walked all the way to the back of the store, and he pulled me close to him.

"It's so good to see you." His voice was soft and full of emotion. "How are you?" He touched my cheek with his free hand. "You look upset."

"I just had the worst argument with my mom." Tears filled my eyes. "I stormed out on her. I've never done that before."

He turned toward a door that said employees only. "Want to go in there?"

I shook my head. "I don't want to get you in trouble. I just had to see you."

"Tell me what happened."

While holding his hands, I explained my argument with my mother, leaving out her insults about Taylor and his family. I tried my best not to cry, but my shaky voice gave away my irritation and anger. "I'm so tired of her running my life, Taylor. I just want to be my own person. Why can't she understand I'm not going to follow the same path she did?"

Taylor shook his head, his eyes full of sympathy. "I know your mom drives you crazy, but she's still your mom. Maybe you should finish out the year in cheerleading but not participate in all of the activities."

"Honestly, it's pointless. All they're going to do is cheer on the baseball players from the stands."

He pursed his lips. "Do you think the baseball players are hot?"

"No. Why?"

"Good. Then I'm okay with you cheering for them."

"Taylor, I don't want to do it. I just want to graduate and move out." I cupped my hand to my forehead. "Why does my mom have to make my life so difficult?"

"That's what parents do. They drive you nuts and then send you to college." He pulled me closer. "My mom makes me crazy too sometimes, but I know she loves me."

"I just don't want to be a cliché anymore. I don't want to be Whitney Richards, perfect student and snobby cheerleader. I just want to be Whitney."

"You are Whitney. And you never were snobby."

I raised an eyebrow. "Oh, really? And what was it you said to me during the first tutoring session? You said I hadn't ever noticed you because you don't wear a varsity football jacket."

"I was wrong about you. You weren't the spoiled rich girl I thought you were." He dipped his face toward mine, and I closed my eyes, waiting for his lips.

A man cleared his throat loudly, and Taylor and I immediately jumped away from each other. I thought I might drown in my embarrassment when I spotted Taylor's manager studying us from the end of the aisle.

"Oh, hey, Kevin," Taylor said as if he hadn't just interrupted our private moment.

Kevin drummed his fingers on the bookshelf. "You need to say good-bye to your girlfriend and get back to work, Taylor."

"Yes, sir." Taylor nodded. "We were just saying good-bye."

Kevin disappeared around the corner.

"I'm so sorry," I whispered. "I didn't want to get you in trouble."

"It's fine." Taylor waved off the worry. "Kevin likes me."

"If he puts you on probation or anything, just blame it on me."

"No, I won't." He touched my hand. "I promise I'll call you later."

"I probably am going to lose my phone and all of my privileges now. I may not be able to call you back."

"Your mom can't take school away from you, so she can't stop you from seeing me during the week." He kissed the top of my head. "Just stay calm when you get home. Tell her you're sorry for storming out and then listen to her. You don't have to agree with her, but you have to respect her."

"I know." I squeezed his hand. "I don't want to go home."

"You have to, but I'll see you tomorrow." He lifted my hand and kissed it. "*Tú me gusta*."

"I like you too. I better go." I followed him toward the front of the store.

When we reached the customer-service counter, he slipped behind it and began ringing up a waiting customer. I glanced back at him once and found him watching me. With a little wave, I headed toward the mall exit.

I found both of my parents waiting for me at the kitchen table, and I wondered if my mother had called my father at work, told him it was an emergency, and instructed him to come home immediately.

"Where have you been, young lady?" My mother spat the words at me.

"I needed to cool down." I dropped my keys and purse on the counter and then faced them, trying to follow Taylor's advice and stay calm. "I'm sorry for storming out, Mom. I just needed to get away to collect my thoughts."

She lifted her chin while scowling. "Did you go to see that boy?"

I felt anger rise anew inside me. "I went to see *Taylor*. His name is Taylor, Mom."

"Whitney," my dad began, "please sit down."

I sank into the chair across from my parents and braced myself for a lecture on how terrible and disrespectful I was. I wished Taylor were sitting beside me and holding my hand, but I knew I had to face this alone.

Dad folded his hands on the table. "Whitney, your mother is upset about your behavior. You've been disrespectful to her."

"Disrespectful?" I looked from one to the other. "If you think I've been disrespectful, it's because Mom won't listen to me."

"I've been trying to listen to you, but you haven't been listening to me either," Mom said with a shake of her head. "I only want what's best for you, Whitney, but you treat me like a dictator."

"You act like a dictator," I said with my voice quavering. "I don't think you realize how much you've been pushing me away."

"All right." Dad held up his hands like a referee trying to stop a fight from breaking out on a ball field. "Let's calm down and discuss this like adults." He looked at me. "Whitney, I know you've been frustrated, and I've tried to ask your mother to back off a bit with you. I know you have a lot on your shoulders. I remember the stress of senior year. It's a fun time, but you also have a lot depending on your academic achievements. You worry about how much life is going to change after graduation."

"That's true." I nodded.

"But you need to keep in mind this is a stressful time for us as well. Our baby is going to graduate and move on with her life." Dad reached for my hand. "You'll always be our baby no matter how old you are."

"That's right," Mom chimed in. "I feel the same way. I don't think you realize how emotional it is for us to see you grow up. It seems like only yesterday you were going to kindergarten for the first time."

My eyes filled with tears.

Mom faced Dad. "However, the issues we have to deal with are that Whitney quit cheerleading, and it's going to reflect badly on her high school transcripts. I think she needs to talk to Coach Lori and get back onto the team, preferably as the cheer captain. The other issue is Whitney's punishment for her behavior earlier."

Dad studied me for a moment. "Why did you quit cheerleading?"

"I don't feel like a part of the group anymore." I tried to act as if it were no big deal, even though the idea of losing my best friends hurt my heart. "Besides, there aren't any official events left for the year, other than attending baseball games. I'd rather concentrate on my studies and hang out with my real friends."

"She's talking about Taylor Martinez," Mom chimed in again. "She's abandoning her friends for that boy."

My shoulders stiffened, and I gritted my teeth when she called him "that boy" again. "I'm tired of Mom running my life. I want to be my own person and have the right to choose my own friends."

"She does have a point, Darlene," Dad said. "You have to trust her intuition about her friends and let her make her own decisions when it comes to her personal life."

"I only want what's best for her, Chuck." Mom's expression remained stern. "I'm looking out for her well-being. She and Logan have so much more than Brad and I ever had when we were growing up. I was the first in my immediate family to go to college. I don't want Whitney to miss out on that opportunity by making the wrong choices."

Dad looked between us before his eyes settled on Mom. "I know you want what's best for our children. It was a huge accomplishment when you went to college, and I understand you want Whitney and Logan to follow the same path. However, I think you need to back off a bit, Darlene. Let Whitney choose her friends. She's a really smart young lady, and she'll do great at college. Just give her a chance to prove herself to you."

Mom was silent, and I bit back a grin. *Go, Dad!*

"What are you saying, Chuck? Are you insinuating I don't know how to raise our children?" She tapped the table. "I've always tried to do my best for our children."

"I know you have." Dad's voice sounded exasperated. "And

you've done an outstanding job. I just want you to take a step back and let Whitney make her own decisions. She's going to be on her own when she leaves for college. You can't guide her when she's living in the dorms. We both know she has a good head on her shoulders. Give her some space and trust her."

Mom paused and scowled. "Fine. I'll back off." She looked at me. "But you're grounded for a month because of the way you talked to me earlier. You need to watch your tongue. You've become disrespectful lately."

"A month?" My voice squeaked. "That's unreasonable."

"No, it's not." Mom rested her elbows on the table. I wondered if she realized she was breaking one of her etiquette rules. "You were totally out of line when you ran off earlier. I was still speaking to you. You didn't tell me where you were going or when you'd be back. In fact, I was worried you'd gotten in a wreck."

I glowered. Mom had a flare for the dramatic.

"I've also taken your phone." She pulled it out of her pocket. "You're not to use it for a month."

I slouched in my chair. How would I say good night to Taylor? "You can't do that."

"Yes, I can." Mom stuck out her chin and raised her head high. "I pay the bill."

I braced myself for her to ask me to hand her my keys, certain she was going to take my car next.

"Mom wanted to take your Jeep away, but I convinced her not to," Dad said. "But you're only to go to school and then come home. No social engagements at all."

"What about youth group and Vanessa's training sessions on Thursdays?" I asked.

"Forget them." Mom wagged a finger at me, while my dad took a deep breath. "That Martinez family is part of why you're in this trouble, so you need to distance yourself from them. That means Taylor too."

"Fine." Although I agreed to the punishment, I held on to the comfort of what Taylor said to me earlier—we still had school. "What about prom?"

My parents looked at each other, and then my father spoke. "I think you can go if you comply with your grounding."

"What does that mean?" I asked.

"I want to see your attitude toward me improve," Mom said.

"Okay." My voice was small and meek. I knew I'd been out of line and disrespectful to Mom, and guilt nipped at me like an anxious puppy. Yet at the same time, I hoped Mom heeded Dad's instructions about letting me choose my own friends.

"Now go to your room and finish your homework," Mom barked orders at me like a drill sergeant. "I need to start cooking. My schedule is behind because of your little dramatic episode."

I headed for the stairs wondering how my mom earned the right to call anyone else dramatic. My feet pounded up the stairs as if the weight of the world were on my shoulders. I hurried down the hallway to my room, flung myself onto my bed, and buried my face in the pillow. I wished Emily were still in the room down the hallway, and I could pour out my soul to her.

I rolled onto my side and wiped my wet eyes. I knew I had to get myself together. I wasn't going to let my mother run my life or keep Taylor from me. I had to find a way to get my mother to accept Taylor and his family. I wanted my relationship with Taylor to be real and constant, not just a passing conversation at school. I knew I couldn't make that happen on my own; I needed God's help.

I closed my eyes, took a deep breath, and began to pray: *Dear God, I need your help and your guidance. I'm changing, Lord, and I don't know who I am anymore. I feel like I don't fit in with friends I've known since elementary school. I miss Kristin and Tiffany, but I can't relate to them anymore. I'm going through some confusing identity crisis, and nothing makes sense anymore. Well, the only thing that makes sense is Taylor. He's become my strength and my comfort. I truly believe our friendship is a gift from you, and all things from you are good. Lord, I don't know how to make my mother see the good in Taylor and his family. How can I show her that Taylor and his family are a good influence in my life? She doesn't understand me, but I can't figure out how to tell her I've changed. I'm still her daughter, but I'm just not the same old Whitney. I'm so confused, God. Please guide me. In Jesus' name, Amen.*

The next afternoon I crossed over to the far end of the cafeteria, where Emily and her best friend, Chelsea Morris, were sitting.

"Hey, Whitney." Emily gestured for me to come to her table. "I'm not used to seeing you in our neck of the woods."

"Hi. I was wondering if I could join you today."

"Of course you can." Chelsea patted the seat beside her. "I thought I saw you eating in the courtyard with Taylor yesterday."

I sat on the bench next to her. "I did eat with him yesterday, but he had to help a kid study for an exam today. This was the only time he could fit it in."

"Oh," Emily said, "it looks like things are going well with Taylor."

"Yeah, you guys looked cozy yesterday." Chelsea bumped my shoulder. "He's hot."

I unpacked a bottle of flavored water, a sandwich, carrot

sticks, and low-fat string cheese. "He is hot. We've become really close friends."

"Just friends?" Emily raised her eyebrows while lifting her sandwich.

"So far. I'm hoping it will change to a more-than-friends status, but I'm sort of waiting to see." I glanced behind me and found Tiffany and Kristin watching me from their usual table, which was the table where I used to sit before I started questioning my friendship with them. Now I felt like a ship lost a sea. I had no idea where I belonged, but I felt comfortable with my cousin and Chelsea.

"What's going on, Whitney?" Emily picked up on my furtive look immediately.

"A lot is going on," I said as I picked up a carrot stick. "I was hoping to talk to you. Last night I was wishing you were still at my house."

Emily tilted her head. "You sound like you really need a friend."

"Yeah, I do." I took a deep breath and then told Emily and Chelsea all about my falling out with the cheer team and my mother.

Emily and Chelsea listened with their eyes wide throughout most of my story.

"Wow," Emily said when I was finished. "Your mom is really over the top. I knew she was controlling, but picking your friends goes beyond anything I've ever seen."

"I don't get what she has against Taylor." Chelsea picked up a fry from her tray. "He's such a nice kid, and his family is nice too. I'm certain your mom has met his mom at some point with all of the school events we've had through the years. Mrs. Martinez is a really cool lady."

"I know she is, and our moms have met at church. I've talked to her, and she was really sweet. In fact, she's easier to talk to than my mom." I studied my uneaten carrot sticks. "I really care about Taylor, and I don't want to lose him."

Chelsea touched my arm. "What if you gave your mom a few days to calm down and then tried to talk to her again? Do you think she'd listen if you both had some time to cool off?"

Emily shook her head. "No, Chels, she won't listen. Whitney's mom is really hard core when it comes to being controlling. When I lived there, she was always after me about my clothes, my hair, everything." She pointed a finger at me. "Whitney finally had to get her to back off."

"Yeah, and I had to practically hit her over the head with a brick." I gnawed my lower lip while considering my predicament.

"You said your dad seems to be more supportive, right?" Chelsea asked.

I nodded while chewing my sandwich. "He actually listens to me, and he usually understands my point of view. He actually told her to back off, and she said she would. But I'm still grounded, and I'm not sure if I can even go to the prom."

"Maybe you can let things calm down. Maybe she will back off, and maybe your dad will talk to her again." Chelsea gave me a sad look. "Don't give up hope. Things might get better after your mom has had a few days to think things through."

"Yeah, you're right. Maybe she will calm down after we've had a few days to let things cool off." I took another bite of my sandwich while thinking about what Chelsea had suggested. I hoped she was right.

I finished eating and said good-bye to Emily and Chelsea before crossing the cafeteria. Kristin looked up at me as I walked by, and I thought I caught a glimpse of regret in her eyes. My heart tugged at me, but I didn't stop walking. I couldn't stand to be around anyone who criticized my friendship with Taylor.

I rushed through the hallway to the library, hoping Taylor was still tutoring. I approached the small conference room and spotted Taylor talking to a boy, who was standing there holding his books.

Taylor's eyes met mine, and he motioned for me to come in. He opened the door. "Hey, Whitney. Did you need help with calculus?"

"Yes." I nodded. "I was wondering if you had time to talk."

"Sure, I do. Jared and I were just finishing up." Taylor looked at the student. "I hope you do well on that test. Let me know if you need more help."

"Thanks." Jared gave me a strange look and then left the conference room.

Taylor closed the door behind him, leaned back on it, and pulled me into his arms. "I've been looking for you all day."

I melted into his embrace and felt myself relax for the first time since I argued with my mother. I looped my arms around his neck and held on to him.

"Tell me what happened when you got home." He murmured the words into my hair.

With my eyes closed and my head on his chest I told him about the conversation I had with my parents. He rubbed my back as he listened.

"Like I told you last night, your parents can't take school away from you, so they won't keep us apart."

I looked up at him. "I know, but I feel so bad I can't train Vanessa anymore. She's going to be so disappointed."

"It's okay," he said. "You've already taught her so much. I'm certain she'll do great at tryouts."

"Would you tell her why I can't come over anymore?"

"Of course I will." He pushed a strand of my hair back behind my ear, and I wished I could hear his thoughts. I wanted to know how he felt about me. Was he as happy as I was to be standing here alone together in the library conference room? Did he love me?

I noticed a movement through the glass behind Taylor and saw a librarian glaring in at us. I quickly took a step back and dropped my backpack onto the table.

"So, about that calculus homework. I was wondering if you would look at my answers." I opened my backpack and fished through my notebook.

Taylor grinned at me. "You've learned quickly how to talk yourself out of any situation."

I looked up at him. "You're rubbing off on me, Taylor."

chapter seventeen

Two weeks later I sat down across from Taylor at the library conference-room table. "You do realize I don't need the tutoring session anymore, right?"

"I knew that a month ago, but I've been telling Mr. Turner you just don't get it."

I swatted his arm. "You told my math teacher I'm stupid?"

"No. I told him I needed more time with you."

"Oh." I rested my elbows on the table. "I miss our late-night texting chats."

"I do too." He took one of my hands in his. "It doesn't feel right when I can't tell you to have sweet dreams."

"How's Vanessa? I didn't get to talk to her much at church on Sunday."

"She's fine." He squeezed my hand. "How are things at home?"

"The same. Mom isn't saying much to me. I tried to talk to my dad about lifting my grounding, but he says he has to respect my mom. I know he sees how ridiculous Mom is being, but I guess he gets tired of arguing with her too. How's your mom?"

"She's fine." Taylor asked me about my classes, and we wound up discussing the upcoming unit test in calculus. Before I realized it, he was helping me study, and I was actually learning what I thought I'd already understood.

When the bell rang, I jumped. "Oh no. I was hoping we had more time." I packed up my books. "You need to start tutoring me in another subject so we have more time together."

He grinned. "How about Spanish?"

"That's a great idea." I laughed as I stood. "Well, I guess I'll see you tomorrow at lunch?"

"That sounds good."

I reached for the doorknob, and Taylor placed his hand on my shoulder.

"Whitney, wait. I wanted to ask you something."

My thoughts raced with anticipation as I looked back at him. "What's up?"

He paused and cupped his hand at the back of his neck. He looked either scared or nervous. "I was wondering," he began and then paused. "Would you consider going to prom with me?"

My eyes nearly popped out of my head. "I would love to."

"Cool." He crossed his arms over his chest. "The thing is, I don't want to go as friends."

My heart thumped in my chest. "What are you saying, Taylor?"

"Well, I'm sort of asking you to be my girlfriend."

I was almost certain he was blushing, and I loved it! "I thought you'd never ask," I said.

"Is that a yes?" His expression was hopeful.

"Yes."

"Good." He dipped his chin and kissed me.

The bell rang again, and I pulled away from him as my pulse leaped into hyper-speed. "I'm late for Spanish! See you later!"

I heard him laughing as I ran through the library toward class. I didn't even care that I was late for class. All that mattered was I was officially Taylor Martinez's girlfriend!

I was still floating on air after class when I stopped in the girls' restroom. I stood in front of the mirror and washed my hands while thinking about that last kiss. Oh, Taylor was so amazing! His kisses sent my heart soaring, and I'd never experienced anything remotely close to that when I kissed my ex-boyfriends, Brett or Chad. And Taylor asked me to prom! I was so excited I thought I might burst, but now I needed to come up with a plan to get my mother to let me go.

I grabbed a paper towel and dried my hands while looking at my reflection in the mirror. My eyes focused on the part in my hair, and I couldn't stop staring at my dark roots. I was born with nearly white-blonde hair that turned golden when I was a toddler. However, it slowly darkened over time to a light brown.

My mother had started encouraging me to highlight my hair in middle school, and I soon fell into a pattern of having my hair highlighted, and eventually dyed all over, every six to eight weeks. I was tired of the routine and also tired of being phony and worrying too much about my appearance. I wanted to just be comfortable in my own skin for once without worrying about keeping my hair blonde.

The bathroom door opened with a loud squeak, and Emily stepped in. "Hey, Cuz. Fancy meeting you here. What's up?"

"Hey." I tossed the paper towel into the trash bin. "What are you doing this afternoon?"

"Nothing. I actually got a day off from work. Why?"

"Can you come over?"

Emily eyed me with suspicion. "Would that be okay considering your mother?"

"It would be perfect. Mom loves you, and I need a favor."

Emily grinned. "This sounds sneaky."

"Oh, it is." I picked up my backpack from the floor. "I need to stop at the pharmacy, and then I need you to help me with something."

"All right." She handed me her camouflage colored bag. "Just give me a minute."

"Let's see." Emily sat on the edge of the counter in my bathroom an hour later while reading the back of the Nice 'n Easy hair-color box. "You're supposed to leave this on for ten minutes. After that, you rinse it out and then use the conditioner." She held up a tube.

"Okay." I sat on the edge of the garden tub and held a towel around my shoulders as the dye tickled my scalp. "Wait until my mom sees this towel." The peach bath towel, which matched the décor of the bathroom, was splattered with dark hair dye.

"No, wait until she sees your hair." Emily clicked her tongue. "I still can't believe you decided to dye your hair."

"Do you think Taylor will like me as a brunette?"

"I think he would like you bald." Emily studied me for a moment. "How are you going to convince your mom to let you go to the prom with him?"

"I haven't figured that out." I shifted my weight on the edge of the tub. "I assume you're going to prom with Zander?"

"Yes." Emily beamed. "I can't wait to see him in his tux. He looked so awesome last year at his senior prom."

"Yes, he did." I smiled, remembering Emily and Zander posing for photos in the driveway next door before they left for prom. "What color dress are you going to get?"

"I don't know." Emily shrugged. "I haven't talked to my dad about that yet. He wants me to save every cent of the money I'm making at the shop for college. I have to ask him if he'll get me a dress. If not, then I'll just wear the one I wore last year."

An idea popped into my head, and I snapped my fingers. "I've got it! What if I ask my mom to take you and me dress shopping? She'll be so thrilled the three of us are going out for a girls' day that she'll have to let me go to prom."

Emily frowned. "You know I hate being your mom's charity case."

"Please." I waved off the comment. "My mom enjoys spending money, especially on her family members."

"I'd love to go with you, but I'll pay for my own dress." She looked down at her watch. "It's almost time to rinse out."

"What if your dress is your graduation present?"

Emily looked up. "Seriously? A prom dress as a graduation gift? I doubt anyone spends that much on a graduation gift, Whitney."

"My mom would for you."

Emily glanced down at the instructions on the box. "Let's argue about this later. We need to finish your hair before your mom gets home from her country-club meeting."

I rinsed and conditioned my hair, and then Emily helped me dry it. When the process was complete, Emily and I stood next to each other staring at my reflection in the mirror. I looked completely different. And I liked it.

"Whitney." Emily squeezed my arm. "You look awesome!"

I chewed on my finger. "Do you think Taylor would like it?"

"I think so, but let's find out." Emily pulled out her phone, and I smiled as she took a picture. She then handed me the phone. "Send it to him."

My hands shook as I typed: *Hi Taylor! I'm on Emily's phone. What do you think of my new look?*

I hit Send, handed her the phone, and held my breath.

"Calm down." Emily hopped back up onto the counter. "He's going to love it."

A few minutes passed by, and then her phone beeped.

"What did he say?" I asked.

She glanced at the screen and laughed. "I have no idea. Does he think you're Hispanic?"

She gave me the phone, and I read: *Te vez muy bonita. Gracias por alumbrar mi día.* My heart swelled. "Thank you."

"Well?" Emily huffed. "What does that mean?"

"It means you look very pretty. Thank you for brightening my day."

"Aww!" Emily gushed. "That's so sweet, but why does he talk to you in Spanish?"

"It's kind of our thing, I guess." I texted: *Thank you. See u tomorrow.* I handed her the phone. "I'm so glad he likes it."

"Whitney, it's your hair. You're pretty no matter what." She stood. "I better get going before your mom comes home."

"Are you afraid of what she'll do when she sees me?" I picked up the dirty towel from the floor.

"I don't want to be here for the explosion." Emily retrieved her backpack from my room and then followed me down to the laundry room, where I tossed the towel in for a prewash. "I hope those stains come out."

"I doubt they will." Emily shook her head. "I helped my friend Megan try to dye her hair red back home, and the only thing that turned red was the towel. The stain never came out. The towel was demoted to rag status."

"Oh well." I poured the detergent into the slot. "It's just a towel."

"Will you walk me out?" Emily started for the door.

"Of course."

We walked through the family room, and Emily waved good-bye to Logan. He never looked twice at me, but I wasn't surprised. I always joked that Logan wouldn't notice an earthquake until it knocked his Xbox game system offline.

Emily and I walked out to her Honda, which was parked behind my Jeep. "Let me know how your mom reacts to your hair."

"Are you certain you don't want to stay for supper? Mom made lasagna." I leaned on the car. "You can call your dad and ask him to come here instead of cooking for him."

"No, thanks. I'll pass on eating here until the air clears." She opened the door just as my mother's SUV pulled into the driveway.

"It's show time." I waved as Mom climbed out of the SUV.

"You're crazy," Emily muttered before waving at my mother. "Hi, Aunt Darlene."

Mom's eyes focused on me, and her eyes widened. "Whitney Jean, what have you done with your hair?"

"Do you like it?" I tilted my head back and forth and then spun for effect. "Doesn't it look good?"

Mom stepped toward me. "Why on earth would you do that? We have an appointment to have Casey do our color on Saturday."

"I know." I wound a lock of hair around my finger. "I was just tired of having them lightened. It's a hassle, and this looks more natural. Besides, it would be a pain to have to travel home to get my hair done while I'm at college. This way, I just have to update the color myself if it gets dull."

My mom reached out and touched my hair as if it were a foreign object. "There are plenty of good salons near Kentwood, dear. We could figure a way to keep your hair blonde even while you're at school." She glanced at Emily as if only noticing her for the first time. "Oh, hello, dear. How are you? How's your dad?"

"We're fine, thanks." Emily gestured toward the car. "I need to go start supper for Dad. He'll be home soon, and I promised him homemade pizza. You know how he loves pizza."

I reached over and grabbed Emily's sleeve without taking my eyes off my mom. "Emily and I were just talking about prom. Would you like to take us prom dress shopping?"

"Oh." Mom's expression brightened. "I'd love to take you both prom dress shopping."

"Great." I glanced at Emily, who looked nervous. "How about Saturday, Em? Can you get time off work?"

Emily nodded. "My dad is the boss. I think I can get time off. He loves it when I spend time with you both."

"Great." I turned to my mom, who was still studying my hair. "What do you think about a girls' day on Saturday?"

Mom nodded. "That sounds nice."

"Okay." Emily pulled her sleeve out of my hand. "I better go. See you both Saturday."

"Good-bye, dear." My mom waved at her.

"Good luck," Emily muttered under her breath before climbing into the car and driving off.

Mom's expression hardened. "Why did you dye your hair?"

"I told you why." I pushed my hair off my shoulders. "I wanted a change."

"Does this have anything to do with that boy?"

"No. It has nothing to do with Taylor, Mom. I make my own decisions about my appearance."

Mom shook her head. "Somehow I get the impression you're doing this to spite me. You know the fund-raiser dinner at the country club is coming up in two weeks, and I need you to look your best."

"I think I look fine." I almost told her Emily and Taylor loved it, but I didn't want her to lecture me about how they have no taste. "I'm just experimenting, Mom. And I like it. It's my hair, not yours."

Mom pointed toward her trunk. "Would you help me carry

a few bags in? I had to stop at the craft store on the way home. Rhonda and Edward left for Europe today, and I have to pick up the slack with the fund-raiser. She won't be home until the day before the big event. I was teasing her yesterday that she planned this so I had to do everything."

"Rhonda and Edward?" I picked up two bags filled with ribbon, bows, LED lights, confetti, and candles. "You mean the Steeles?"

"Yes, dear. Brett's parents. They go to Europe every April to celebrate their anniversary." Mom took the other two bags and then slammed the trunk. "She was nervous about leaving, since graduation is coming up, but I told her not to worry. She'll be back for the prom and all of the parties."

"Right." I followed my mom into the house and placed the bags on the kitchen table.

"I guess Emily is going to the prom with Zander." Mom put her bags next to mine and then crossed to the refrigerator.

"Of course she is." I leaned against the table. "They're such a cute couple. I hope she buys a green dress. Green is her color."

"What about you?"

"I think I'd like a pink dress."

"No, Whitney." My mother's expression was suddenly grave. "That's not what I'm asking you. Who asked you to prom?"

"No one has. At least, no one has asked me yet." The lie slipped through my teeth before I could stop it.

"What?" Mom moved toward me. "No one has asked you?"

"No, but I'm sure someone will. I haven't given up hope just yet." Guilt rained down on me, but I knew this was the only way she'd let me go to the prom. I had to do it. Mom left me no other choice but to lie to her.

"Maybe Brett will ask you. Rhonda hasn't mentioned he had another date, so there's still hope."

"Maybe." I ran my finger over the back of a kitchen chair and felt myself sinking deeper and deeper into the lie as if it were quicksand. I knew it would break both my mom's and Taylor's hearts if they knew I was lying about my prom date, but I didn't see any other way.

"Oh." Mom clapped her hands together. "We'll go find you the perfect pink dress on Saturday. This will be so fun. I'll have to call Casey and make salon appointments for you and Emily. You and Emily can have your hair and nails done together the morning of the prom." She looked at me. "This will be so fun. Thank you for including me in your prom shopping, Whitney. Oh, I can't believe this is your senior prom. Time has flown by so quickly."

I nodded and listened as my mother prattled on about her wonderful prom memories. However, I only had one thought echoing through my head: *I'm a liar.*

Yet I couldn't bring myself to tell her the truth. All I wanted was to go to prom with my boyfriend, Taylor Martinez.

chapter eighteen

I love that color on you." My mother nodded her approval.
I swished back and forth in front of the dressing-room mirror while the big pink dress moved around my legs. We'd been trying on prom dresses all morning at my mother's favorite department store at the mall.

I met Emily's gaze in the mirror. "What do you think, Em?"

"I don't know." Emily was still wearing the green dress she'd gravitated toward as soon as we'd walked into the formal section of the store.

I spun and faced her. "Yes, you do know, and I want your opinion. What do you think?"

Emily pointed toward a lighter-pink, strapless dress hanging on the door to the dressing room. "I like that one better."

"Hmm." Mom tapped her chin and walked over to the dress. "I don't know, Whitney. If Brett asks you to the prom, then you'll have to see what color cummerbund and vest he decides to wear. That color might be difficult to match." She touched the hanging dress and then examined the price tag.

Emily hit my arm, and I turned to her. She mouthed the word *Brett* with horror on her face, and I shook my head, warning her not to say a word.

My mother examined the dress for a few more minutes, and I kept my eyes on her to avoid Emily's stares. "Well, you can always tell him just to wear basic black." Mom turned to Emily. "Is that the dress you want, dear?"

Emily held the tag in her hand. "I love it, but have you seen the price?" The hunter-green dress was plain but elegant. It was short-sleeved and came to her knees.

"Oh, don't be silly!" Mom waved off the question. "This is your senior prom. You should be able to have any dress you want. You look stunning, Emily. I can just imagine Zander's face when he sees you in it."

Emily looked at her reflection and touched one of her curls. "You think he'll like it?"

I laughed at her. "You're so modest, Emily. You're gorgeous."

Emily turned around. "Okay. It's settled."

"Fine." My mother moved toward the door. "You two get changed, and I'll be out here looking at the shoes." She disappeared through the dressing-room doorway, and Emily grabbed my arm with such force that I yelped.

"What were you thinking?" Emily eyed me with shock. "You didn't tell your mother you're going to the prom with Taylor?"

"Shh!" I took her arm and pulled her back into the dressing room, where I'd left my jeans and shirt. "I can't risk her hearing you," I whispered.

"Why did you lie?"

"I didn't lie. She backed me into a corner and asked me who I was going to the prom with, and I told her I didn't have a date yet. She's only assuming Brett will ask me, and I haven't corrected her. I haven't really lied. I've just not told her the whole truth."

"That's still lying, Whitney."

"I didn't have a choice. She'd never let me go with Taylor."

"But what if Brett finds out?"

"I never said I was going with Brett. Besides, his parents are in Europe for two weeks, so my mom won't have a chance to say anything to his mom. No one will know."

"But what if Taylor finds out? He'll be hurt if he knows you weren't brave enough to tell your mother you're going to the prom with him."

"How will Taylor know?"

Emily shook her head. "When you leave for the prom, silly!"

"Shh," I cautioned her. "We can all meet at your house."

"But your mom will want to take photos. This is a monumental occasion. She's going to figure it out."

"Hmm." I tapped my chin. "Let me think about this for a minute." I snapped my fingers. "I got it. I'll let my mom think I don't have a date, and then the night before the prom, I'll say that Taylor was able to get the night off work, and he asked me to go with him as a friend. She can't say no if I have the dress, shoes, and purse, can she?"

Emily slowly shook her head. "I don't know, Whitney."

"Hey, Mom lifted my grounding and gave me my phone back a week early." I pulled my phone from my purse. "She's so happy I want to go to the prom, even though I supposedly don't have a date. I made her happy, so I know I did the right thing."

"Your mom isn't stupid. She's going to figure it out."

"It will work out. Trust me." I turned so she could unzip my dress. "I know what I'm doing."

"I hope so." Emily's words were full of doubt.

Emily and I changed back into our jeans and shirts and then met my mother over by the shoes. We picked out shoes and purses that complemented our dresses, and then Mom paid.

We stowed our purchases in Mom's SUV and then ate Chinese food in the food court while we talked about everything from Mom's prom memories to graduation plans. I found myself glancing toward the bookstore at the end of the corridor and longing to go in and see Taylor. I just needed to find an excuse.

After finishing lunch, the three of us made our way down the corridor in the direction of the bookstore.

My mother stopped in front of the jewelry store and touched Emily's arm. "Do you know what jewelry you're going to wear with the dress?"

Emily touched her locket that Zander had given her for Valentine's Day. "I'm not certain. I was thinking about my mother's pearls."

Mom pointed toward the store. "May I buy you a pair of earrings to go with them?"

"Oh, no, Aunt Darlene. You've already spent too much." Emily shook her head. "I couldn't accept anything else from you."

"Don't be silly, dear. You're my niece." Mom took Emily's arm and tugged her toward the store.

I hung back as they walked away.

Mom turned to me. "Whitney? Are you coming with us?"

I shook my head and pointed toward the bookstore. "I was going to run into the bookstore. I'm looking for a new mystery to read. I promise I'll make it quick."

My mom hesitated and then nodded. "Fine, dear. We'll come find you when we're done."

Emily gave me a warning look before heading toward the store with my mom in tow.

I rushed into the bookstore and weaved through the aisles until I found Taylor stocking shelves in the back. I snuck up behind him and placed my hands over his eyes.

He stiffened, grabbed my hands, and spun, facing me. "Whitney?"

"Hey." I grinned. "I only have a couple of minutes."

"What are you doing here?" He studied me with confusion. "I mean, I'm thrilled to see you, but I'm surprised."

"My mom, Emily, and I are here shopping for prom dresses. We just finished lunch." I touched his hand. "I can't wait until you see my dress. I hope you like it."

"I'm certain I will."

"Guess what color it is."

He glanced down at my shirt. "Pink?"

"Am I that transparent?" I pulled my phone from my purse. "Look at what I got back this morning."

"That's awesome. I've missed our good-night text messages."

"Yeah. I have too."

He reached out and touched my hair. "Have I told you I love the color?"

I turned my face toward his hand. "You have, but I like hearing it."

His fingers moved down my cheekbone, and I smiled up at him. I was lost in the moment until I realized I was running out of time.

"Oh no." I took his hand in mine. "My mom and Emily are going to come looking for me. I'm supposed to be looking for a book."

"What book?"

"What are you stocking?" I glanced down and found a murder mystery by an author I'd heard was excellent. "How about this?"

"I heard it was pretty good, but I haven't read it."

"I'll take it." I moved up onto my tiptoes and brushed my lips against his. "I have to run. Text me later." I started down the aisle.

"You bet I will," he called after me.

I reached the cashier just as my mother and Emily were stepping into the store. I paid for the book and then headed out toward the exit with my mother and Emily. My cousin gave me a relieved expression.

I pointed toward the small bag she held with the jewelry store's logo on it. "What did you get?"

"Your mom insisted on buying me the most beautiful pearl earrings." She looked up at Mom. "I can't thank you enough."

"Oh, don't be silly, Emily." To my surprise, Mom moved between us and looped her arms around our shoulders. "I had a lovely time, girls. We must do this again."

"Thank you, Mom," I said.

"This was a blast," Emily said as we crossed the parking lot. "Shopping with my dad isn't half as fun as this."

We approached the SUV, and Mom unlocked the doors. "I'm glad I'm more fun than my brother."

"Oh, absolutely, Aunt Darlene. Hands down, you're more fun." Emily climbed into the backseat.

I hopped into the front passenger seat and closed my eyes as my smile deepened. I was so very happy. It seemed as if everything was working out. My mom was happy, I was going to the prom with Taylor, and I'd had a fun day with my cousin. I silently prayed life would stay this perfect. However, I couldn't get Emily's warning out of my head. What if Mom or Taylor found out I'd lied about prom?

I pushed the thought away. No one would find out. Only Emily and I would know the truth. After all, how would anyone find out?

chapter nineteen

Two weeks later I glanced up at the sky and noticed gray clouds gathering in the distance while I sat in the backseat of my father's SUV next to my brother as we drove to the children's charity benefit.

"It looks like it's going to rain." Dad steered onto Seven Kings Road and the brick Cameronville Country Club sign came into view.

"Don't say that." Mom sounded anxious.

She'd been in her high-stress mode all day while preparing for the benefit. I'd tried my best to help her, but she kept sending me away as if I was too young or too stupid to help her. She seemed completely tense, but I assumed it was due to the event. I hoped she got it out of her system and was back to normal tomorrow.

"It's not raining inside, sweetie." Dad gave Mom a sideways glance. "I'm certain it will be just fine." He patted her hand, and she glared at him.

Logan elbowed me in the side, and we both stifled laughs.

"Hey, look!" Logan pointed out the windshield. "The club has valet parking tonight. That's new."

"It's special for the benefit." Mom lowered the visor to check her reflection, and I realized I must've gotten that habit of checking my reflection all the time from her. "We wanted to do things right so people feel like donating generously to the benefit. If you have a valet park your car, then you feel wealthy. Wealthy people like to give to good causes."

Logan nodded. "I guess that makes sense."

Dad pulled the SUV up to the front entrance, and a young man in a vest walked over to the car.

Logan elbowed me again.

"Ouch!" I hissed. "Stop it."

Logan gestured outside the door. "Isn't that your friend?" He whispered the question into my ear.

I looked out the window and spotted Taylor wearing the same vest and dress shirt as the young man who was talking to Dad. I swallowed hard and nodded.

"Let me get out first." Logan pointed toward the sidewalk. "I'll try to keep Mom busy."

"Thank you."

Logan hopped out of the car and rushed around to where Mom was climbing out. "Hey, Mom. Can you show me what they're selling in the silent auction? I thought I heard you say something about Xbox games or something."

"Just a minute, Logan." Mom looked back toward where Dad was talking to the valet.

"Come on." Logan took her hand and started pulling her toward the door. "I want to see the games, Mom."

I climbed out onto the sidewalk and walked over to Taylor. "Hey." I touched his arm.

"Whitney." Taylor looked up from studying a clipboard, and his eyes widened. "You look stunning. I love your hair that way," he said, referring to the loose curls I spent over an hour trying to get perfect.

"Thanks. Mom insisted I get all dressed up. This is her big

night." I pushed an errant curl away from my face. "I didn't know you were working here tonight."

"My mom got me the gig. She's working here tonight too." He placed the clipboard on the podium beside him. "I was going to text you earlier, but it was sort of last minute. One of the guys didn't show up."

"Wow. That's amazing." I glanced toward the door and spotted Logan dragging Mom through it. I made a mental note to thank him later.

"Whitney." My dad called me. "We need to get inside."

"I have to go." I jerked my thumb toward the door. "I'll try to catch up with you later."

"Great," he said. "Have fun."

"You too." I waved and then met my father at the door.

Dad placed his hand on my shoulder. "You still really like that boy, don't you?"

I looked up at him and held my breath, hoping he wouldn't tell Mom the truth.

"Your secret is safe with me." He squeezed my shoulder.

"Thanks, Dad."

We walked into the ballroom, which was decorated with silver streamers and silver balloons. Each round table was elegantly decorated with mirrors topped with LED candles and confetti. The items being sold through the silent auction were on long tables around the perimeter of the room.

I spotted my brother over by a table filled with video games and game systems. Mom was on the other side of the room talking to a few of her women's-group friends.

I sidled up to Logan. "Thanks for distracting Mom outside."

"You're welcome." He held a game and studied the box.

I watched him while trying to figure out his motivation for helping me. "How did you know?" I couldn't bring myself to finish the question.

"How did I know you're not allowed to see or talk to Taylor?" Logan raised his eyebrows. "Are you serious, Whitney? Do you think I'm deaf or dumb? I've heard the arguments. I know Mom has been keeping you away from Taylor because she thinks he's a bad influence."

"So then why would you deliberately go against Mom to help me?"

"I think Taylor is really cool. I like his motorcycle, and he's super-nice. I think it stinks Mom won't let you see him." He raised one shoulder. "Maybe someday you'll return the favor." He spotted Dad and grinned. "I'm going to see if I can get Dad to bid on this game. See ya."

"See ya." I stared after my brother, wondering if he had somehow been replaced by a cool little brother when I wasn't looking.

"Whitney, dear!" My mom called me, and I walked over to her.

Rhonda Steele stood next to Mom. "You look lovely tonight, Whitney."

"Thank you." Anguish filled me when I thought about the prom. I hoped my plan would somehow stay together, and my mom would believe I was going alone. "How was your trip?"

"Oh, it was lovely." Rhonda touched my arm. "You'll have to see the photos sometime."

"I'd love to." I smiled through my worry.

"Whitney," my mother began, "would you please stand by the door and tell folks they're welcome to walk around the room and bid on the items along the wall? They may also sit wherever they'd like."

"I'd be happy to." I took a position by the door and began greeting and directing guests. I couldn't help but glance down the hallway toward the club entrance and wonder what Taylor was doing. I longed to slip away and go see him, but I didn't want to upset my mother or get him into trouble with his supervisor.

I was explaining the silent auction to a woman when Brett came up behind her.

The woman thanked me and then moved into the ballroom.

"Whitney." Brett held his head high. "I see your boyfriend is where he belongs—doing blue-collar work."

"You're a snob, Brett. I don't know what I ever saw in you."

"Likewise." He studied me. "I can't get over your hair. I guess your loser boyfriend prefers brunettes, huh?"

I gritted my teeth. "You're not even worth a response. Go away, Brett."

"I'd be glad to leave you here alone." He continued into the room.

After nearly an hour of standing by the door, my feet began to ache, and I wondered why I'd worn high heels.

"Welcome, everyone!" My mother's voice rang out over the public-address system. "My name is Darlene Richards, and on behalf of the Country Club's Women's Foundation, I'd like to welcome you to our sixth annual children's charity benefit."

Everyone began to clap, and I scanned the sea of faces for my family. I found my father and Logan sitting with Brett and his family, and my shoulders stiffened. I silently prayed for strength as I weaved through the throng toward the table.

"Tonight we're coming together for the children," Mom continued. "We ask you to please bid generously on the silent-auction items. You may also write checks directly to our charity. With your help, we'll be able to provide scholarships and job-training opportunities to inner-city students. So please give generously, and thank you for coming."

I reached the table and found the only two places left to sit were next to Rhonda or next to Brett. I took a deep breath and then sank into the chair next to Brett.

"Now," Mom continued, "I'd like to say a blessing, and then we may start with our salad." She closed her eyes. "Lord, we thank you for this wonderful opportunity to come together in the service of others. We ask you to please guide our hearts when we make our donations. Please help us to remember there are many people who don't enjoy the privileges we are used to here. Help us also to remember we are all created in your image, and it's our duty to love and take care of each other. Amen." She opened her eyes. "Let's eat!"

The room filled with the murmur of conversations and the tinkling of utensils against the dishes. I studied my mother as she made her way back to the table. I was impressed by the words she'd chosen for her prayer. I hoped she sincerely meant what she'd said.

Mom came to the table and sat beside Rhonda.

"That was lovely, Darlene," Rhonda said. "I couldn't have done it any better myself."

I turned my attention to my salad plate while my father, Brett's father, Logan, and Brett discussed the weather and then moved on to the news. I was relieved the focus wasn't on me while I thought about Taylor.

A flash drew my attention toward the large windows on the other side of the ballroom. Another flash lit up the golf course and was soon followed by booming thunder.

"Sounds like a bad storm is coming." Brett leaned toward me. "I guess your boyfriend is going to get wet."

I regarded him with disgust. "At least he knows how to work for a living."

Brett snickered, and I looked over at my mother, who was watching me.

The evening dragged on, and soon the main course of filet mignon, fresh vegetables, and baked potato was served. Since I wasn't a big fan of steak, I picked at my vegetables and sipped my iced tea. I soon became bored and excused myself.

After using the restroom, I stepped out into the hallway and spotted Taylor's mother walking toward me with an armful of bathroom tissue.

"Mrs. Martinez!" I rushed up to her, relieved to see a friendly face. "How are you?"

"Oh, Whitney," Maria said, "you look gorgeous, and I love your hair. Are you here for the benefit?"

"Yes, I am." I held out my arms. "May I help you?"

"Oh, no, don't be silly. How's your benefit going?"

I folded my hands over my dress. "I think it's going well. I noticed a lot of people were filling out the cards for the silent auction."

"That's nice."

"I was surprised to see Taylor working outside. That's really great that you could get him out here tonight." I motioned toward the door, where the rain was starting to fall harder.

"Yes. One of the boys called in sick at the last minute, so I talked my boss into letting him come," she continued with excitement. "You know, he's really thrilled you're going to prom with him. He was trying on his uncle's tuxedo earlier, and I think he may borrow his uncle's car. He wants to make everything really nice for you."

"Whitney." My mother's voice sounded behind me, and I froze.

"Oh, hello, Mrs. Richards." Maria focused her gaze behind me. "How are you this evening?"

"I'm fine, thank you." Mom laid her hand on my shoulder. "I was looking for you, Whitney."

"Yes, Mom." I forced a smile at Maria. "It was nice seeing you. Please tell Vanessa I said hello."

"Oh, I will." Maria continued. "We'll have to talk about the prom. I don't know if you kids want to take photos at our house before you leave or at yours. Just let me know when we get closer to the date. I can't tell you how excited I am. I never dreamed Taylor would go to his senior prom with such a wonderful girl. He's very blessed. Enjoy your evening."

Maria disappeared into the ladies' room, and dread seized me as I turned toward my mother.

Mom stared at me while shaking her head. I waited for her to say something, but a few awkward moments of silence passed between us. I couldn't take it. I needed her to say something or at least yell at me.

I finally held my hands up as if to surrender. "Mom, please let me explain."

Mom held up one finger to silence me. "Not now, Whitney. I will deal with you and your deceit later."

"Please, Mom. I want to explain. I didn't mean to lie. I just knew you would never let me go to the prom with Taylor. I was going to tell you at the last minute so you would have to let me go."

"You knew all along what you were doing. You've done everything you could to deceive me and upset me. I know that's why you started dating Taylor behind my back in the first place." She touched my hair. "That's also why you dyed your hair. You did everything simply to rebel against me. I guess this is how you try to forge your own independence.'"

"No, Mom. It only started out that way, but I do care about Taylor. In the beginning I mainly wanted to upset you, but I've really fallen for him, Mom. He's amazing. He's become my best friend. Can't you see I want to be with him?"

My mom shook her head. "All I see when I look at you is someone I don't know. My daughter never used to lie to me or sneak around behind my back. You're a stranger to me."

Tears filled my eyes. "Mom, that's not true. I'll always be your daughter."

"I don't have time for this now. We'll talk later." She turned and marched back toward the ballroom, her high heels clicking and her hair bobbing.

I thought I saw movement in my peripheral vision, but when I turned, no one was there. I wiped my eyes and looked toward the front door, where the rain was coming down in droves.

I slipped into the bathroom, with the excuse of checking my hair and makeup. After taking a deep breath, I made my way back to the table and did my best to ignore Brett's smug expressions for the remainder of the event.

When the benefit was over, I helped my mother pack up her things. She never spoke to me, and I found her silence was the worst punishment of all. I felt so guilty for lying to her and hurting her. I still loved her even though she drove me crazy. She was my mother, and I needed her.

After we had everything packed up, we headed out to the entrance, and I looked around for Taylor but didn't see him. I was going to ask one of the other valets where Taylor was, but I didn't want to upset my mother further.

I remained quiet in the backseat of the SUV while my parents discussed how successful the benefit had been. I couldn't stop thinking about the hurt in my mother's eyes when she told me I wasn't the daughter she once knew. I never imagined my little lie would be this hurtful.

When we reached the house, Dad parked the SUV in the garage. I climbed out of the car and faced my mother, waiting for her to tell me how I was going to be punished. Instead of speaking to me, she headed straight into the house.

I followed her into the kitchen, where she put down her tote bag and purse. "Mom?" I placed my hands on the island in the middle of the kitchen. "Mom, will you please talk to me?"

Mom looked at me with her eyes full of hurt and anger. "Whitney, I can't deal with you right now." She hurried through the kitchen, and soon the sound of her footsteps marched up the stairs.

I made my way up to my room, where I changed into my pajamas and hung up my dress. I pulled my phone from my purse and was disappointed to find no text messages waiting from Taylor.

I sent him a text that said: *Hey! Hope u had a nice night. Sweet dreams!*

I stared at the phone, waiting for a response, but none came. I also found myself glancing toward my doorway, waiting for my parents to appear and tell me I was grounded for the rest of my life. But they never came either.

After nearly thirty minutes, I padded down to my parents' room and knocked on the door.

"Come in!" Dad's voice sounded through the wall.

I pushed the door open and found my parents sitting on their bed watching the late-night news. "Hi. I was wondering if we could talk?"

Mom kept her eyes glued on the television screen.

"Sure, pumpkin." My dad patted the end of the bed beside him. "Come in."

I crossed the room and sat on the edge of the bed, wishing my mother would look at me. I took the television remote from my dad's nightstand and turned it off. "Mom, we need to talk."

She turned toward me.

"I'm sorry." My voice was thick with emotion, and my eyes filled with tears. "I shouldn't have lied to you about prom. I just knew you would never allow me to go with Taylor. I thought you'd let me go if you thought I was going alone. I was wrong to lie, but I'm tired of you controlling every aspect of my life." My tears were flowing now, rolling down my hot cheeks and splattering onto my pajamas.

Mom shook her head. "I don't know what to say to you, Whitney. No matter what I try to do for you, you resent it. You've lied to me so many times that I don't know if I can even trust you."

"Yes, you can trust me." I sniffed. "I didn't want to lie, but it just felt like you don't trust me to make my own decisions. I want to date Taylor, and I want to be able to choose my own college. It … it just feels like you're controlling what I'm supposed to do with my life."

That was the wrong thing to say, if my mom's eyes were any indication. "What am I supposed to do when you're so intent on throwing everything away? Not to mention the fact you made a complete fool out of me, Whitney. I took you and your cousin out for dresses and shoes and purses. I made an appointment for you both to have your hair done. It was all a ruse, since you were apparently waiting for someone to ask you to the prom."

"Mom, I never meant to hurt you. I just wanted to go to the prom with Taylor."

She scowled. "I can't trust you anymore, Whitney."

"So then ground me. Take away my car! Do something so we can get past this, Mom." I gestured wildly as I continued to cry. "Please, Mom. Punish me and forgive me."

Mom shook her head. "I don't know, Whitney."

I looked at my father, who had remained stoic and silent during our conversation. "Dad? Can you please help me?"

Dad rubbed his forehead. "I don't know what to say, Whitney. You really hurt your mother by lying to her. You know it's never all right to lie."

"But I'm your daughter. Can't you forgive me?" I felt small and alone, like a child leaving for school her first day at kindergarten.

"Of course she'll forgive you, but it might take time." Dad touched my hand. "You need to learn that your behavior hurts other people, pumpkin."

I looked from one to the other. "So am I punished? Am I grounded until graduation? Are you taking my car and my phone?"

Mom looked at Dad. "I don't know, Chuck. You decide. I can't deal with this anymore. I'm going to sleep." She rolled onto her side with her back to me, and my heart shattered with regret.

My father faced me. "You're grounded until graduation. No social gatherings."

"What about prom?" My voice was still small and unsure.

"Your mom and I will discuss it tomorrow, okay? It's late, and we're all tired. Go on to bed, Whitney." He patted my hand.

I stood and wished my mother would look at me. "Good night."

I walked slowly back to my room, wishing I could take back all of the hurt I'd caused my mother. I found my phone on my bed and prayed there was a message from Taylor. However, the screen was blank. I hoped he was okay, but an eerie feeling filled me.

I sent him one last message: *I miss you.*

And then I crawled into bed and poured my confusion and despair into my prayers until I fell asleep.

chapter twenty

❦ ❦ ❦

Monday morning I left calculus class, wove my way through the sea of students in the clogged hallway, and rushed toward Taylor's locker. I hadn't heard back from him since I texted him Saturday night, and I was anxious to see him, especially since my mom had relented and decided I could go to prom as long as I was "responsible." I held my calculus unit test in my hand and couldn't wait to tell him about my grade. When I spotted him fishing through his locker, I picked up speed.

"Taylor! Taylor!" I rushed over to him. "Look! I got a B-plus!" I held the test out in front of him so he could see the giant, red B-plus for himself.

"That's great, Whitney." He kept his eyes focused on his books. "I guess that means you don't need me anymore."

"What do you mean?"

"You got your B-plus. You're done with me and can move on to someone else now." He slammed his locker door with such force that I jumped. He then hefted his backpack onto his shoulder. "See you later." He started down the hallway.

"What's wrong?" I hurried after him. "Taylor, wait!"

When he kept walking, I grabbed his arm and yanked him back, causing him to stumble. "Talk to me, Taylor. Why are you treating me like I did something wrong?"

He glowered at me. "I heard your conversations Saturday night, Whitney."

"What conversations?" I studied his eyes, finding anger and hurt there.

"I heard everything you said at the country club when you were in the hallway talking to your mother."

I cupped my hand to my mouth. *Oh no!*

"You're ashamed to be seen with me. That's why you never told your mother you were going to prom with me." His voice rose, and a crowd of curious spectators gathered around us.

"No, no." My voice was thick and sounded strange to me. "That's not true."

"Oh, really?" He swiped the calculus test from my hand. "The way I see it is I'm only good enough to tutor you and help you get a B-plus on a test. I'll see you later." He turned away, and I grabbed his arm.

"No, that's not true!" I spun him, and he faced me again as the crowd of onlookers grew. "Taylor, please!" I touched his arm, and he yanked it away from me. "Please listen to me, Taylor. Let me explain."

"I have to get to class," he groused.

"Taylor, please. Give me a minute."

He studied me, and the hurt in his eyes broke my heart. "What, Whitney?"

"Taylor, I care about you. I'm not ashamed to be seen with you. I lied because I knew my mother would never have approved if I told her I was going to the prom with you. I was going to tell her the truth at the last minute so she didn't have time to forbid me to go. Everything would've been planned by then, and she would have just had to accept it." Tears spilled from my eyes. "Please, Taylor. You have to believe I care about you. You know more about me than anyone. I've bared my heart and soul to you. You're my best friend."

He shook his head. "If you truly cared about me and weren't ashamed to go to prom with me, then you would've stood up to your mother from the beginning. Hiding behind lies proves our relationship meant nothing to you."

"That's not true." I swiped my hand over my burning face. "You mean everything to me."

The bell rang.

"I have to go, Whitney. See you around." Taylor stalked down the hallway.

After he disappeared around the corner, I rushed into a nearby girls' room, locked myself in the last stall, and sobbed.

Thursday night I sat alone in the back of the classroom at church during the youth-group meeting. I hadn't seen Taylor at school, and he hadn't answered when I tried to call his cell phone or responded when I texted to apologize.

I'd been up late nearly every night pouring out my heart to God and begging him for an answer. I didn't know how to apologize to my mother or Taylor. I felt as if my world was crumbling around me, and I'd never felt so lost and alone. Although pouring my heart and soul out to God was cathartic, it didn't bring me any closer to a solution to my problems.

I'd considered not coming to youth group, but I needed to get out of the house. Although my mother wasn't talking to me, my father told me I could attend youth group tonight despite my grounding. He said I looked like I needed to venture out and go to church. I knew he was right. The silence from both my mother and Taylor was slowly suffocating me as I drowned in my loneliness.

At youth group Jenna dimmed the classroom lights and then started a movie. The smell of popcorn filled the air as bowls made their way down the row of tables.

Emily slipped into the room just after the movie started and sat beside me. "Hey."

"Hey." I kept my eyes fixed on the screen.

Emily leaned in close. "You look terrible."

"Thanks." I forced a smile.

"What's wrong?"

Someone near the front told us to be quiet.

Emily grabbed my hand and pulled me out into the hallway, closing the door behind us. "Whitney, what's wrong?"

"Everything is wrong." I cleared my throat, willing myself not to cry again. I'd cried so much during the past few nights, I was surprised my tear ducts weren't dry. "You were right."

"I was right?" Emily shook her head with confusion. "What are you talking about?"

"My plan for prom backfired."

"Oh no." Emily groaned. "Let's go talk."

We moved into an empty classroom, and I told her everything that had happened at the country club and then filled her in on my conversations with my mother and Taylor.

"So, in the end, I'm left all alone. I've lost my mother and my boyfriend." I ran my fingers over the cool table. "You were so right, and Taylor's right too. I should've stood up to my mother."

"No, it's not that simple." Emily touched my arm. "Your mother isn't as easy to deal with as other mothers are. You did what you thought was best."

"But it was a dumb plan." I rested my chin on my palm. "I don't know what to do. I love my mom and I also love Taylor. How do I get them back?"

"Girls?" Jenna stuck her head in the room. "Is everything all right?"

"We were just talking," Emily said. "Whitney is trying to figure out a problem."

"Can I help?" Jenna stood in the doorway.

"That would be great," I said. "I told a lie, and when my mother and my boyfriend found out the truth, they both were heartbroken. Now my mother won't speak to me, and my boyfriend broke up with me and won't speak to me either. I've tried to apologize, but neither of them will listen or forgive me."

"Hmm." Jenna sank into a chair beside me and tapped her finger against her chin. "That sounds like a really complicated situation."

"I've managed to create a real mess." I looked at Emily, who gave me a sad look. "I should've listened to my cousin. She told me it wouldn't work out well. But I was arrogant and stubborn. I thought I had it all under control."

Emily shook her head. "I'm not perfect, Whitney. You know I've messed up before. I've let my stubbornness and my pride come between Zander and me when we first met. But I realized my mistakes, and it all worked out." She touched my hand. "Remember you're not alone. You still have me."

"Thank you," I said softly. I was so grateful for her.

"God reminds us he's always with us, even when things are tough," Jenna said as she faced me. "Good things can still come of bad situations. Sometimes we learn important things when we go through rough times. Whatever happens, God still loves you and will be there for you."

Jenna thought for a minute. "This is really hard, Whitney. I know you're very upset, and with good reason. I think you need to pray about all that's happening in your life right now. Ask God to give you the words to talk to your mother and your boyfriend. Ask God to help them listen to you and understand what's going on with you."

"I know I'm not alone, but my life has become so complicated over the past couple of months." I sniffed and wiped my eyes. "I feel as if I've been going through an identity crisis. I don't relate to my friends like I used to. In fact, my best friends from elementary school feel like strangers, and I was dating someone who I never thought I would date. And through all of these changes, I've been talking to God more than ever. I don't just say the same prayer I used to say every night at bedtime when I was little. I've been talking to God, really talking to him. I've been sharing all of my thoughts and fears."

"That's great!" Emily squeezed my hand. "That's what you need to do."

"But I don't feel like I'm solving anything." Fresh tears pooled in my eyes. "Why isn't God giving me the answers I so desperately need?"

"Do you remember I had a hard time praying after my mom died?" Emily asked.

"I remember that," I said. "You forgot how to talk to God because you were struggling with your grief."

"Well, I learned the hard way that life is hard sometimes, and sometimes things don't work out the way we want them to. But God is always there for us. You may not see him or feel him right now, but he's here with you. You're never alone." Emily hugged me, and my tears began to sprinkle down my cheeks.

"She's right." Jenna rubbed my back. "You might feel alone right now, but you're not. God is guiding you, and he'll give you the answer you need soon. You just have to keep talking to him and listening for the answer."

"Okay." I sniffed and swiped the back of my hand over my cheeks.

"Things will work out for you, Whitney," Jenna said with emphasis. "I know it will. Your mom loves you, and she'll move past her anger. You just have to give her time."

"I hope so." I cleared my throat. "It's funny how I couldn't stand how she used to nag me, but I think her silence is even more painful for me."

Emily chuckled. "I never thought I'd hear you say that."

"I know it's none of my business, but I have to ask," Jenna began cautiously. "Is Taylor Martinez your boyfriend?"

"Yeah." My voice cracked, and I hoped I wouldn't cry again. I was so tired of crying, but I was also inundated with anguish.

Jenna touched my arm. "From what I've seen, I think he really cares about you. I would imagine if you try again to tell him how you feel, he'll listen."

"Thank you." I hugged Jenna.

"You're welcome, Whitney." Jenna stood. "I better get back to the movie. Let me know if you need anything else."

"Thanks, Jenna," Emily said as Jenna left the room. She then turned to me. "I think Jenna's right."

"Yeah, me too." I grabbed a box of tissues from the desk behind me and wiped my nose. "I'm so thankful for you."

"Are you still going to go to prom?" Emily asked.

"I don't know. I'd feel like a loser going by myself."

"No, don't say that," Emily insisted. "You're not a loser, and you can't miss your senior prom. You'll regret it for the rest of your life. Come with Zander and me."

I raised an eyebrow. "You can't be serious. Why would you want me to interfere with you and Zander?"

"You wouldn't be interfering. I want you there." She sat on the table, facing me. "We'll all ride together. You can sit with us at prom too, which also might make your parents feel better about you going. Just friends hanging out. It will be so much fun."

I imagined myself sitting in the car alone in the backseat while she and Zander held hands and gazed at each other. At the dance I'd sit alone and sip my drink while she and Zander slow-danced together on the crowded dance floor with all of the other happy couples in our senior class. How depressing would that be?

"I don't know." I grabbed another tissue and swiped it over my cheeks. "I think I'd rather stay home alone. Maybe I'll rent a movie and pop up some popcorn with Logan."

Emily suddenly smiled. "But what if you stay home, and Taylor comes to the prom?"

My heart skipped a beat. "Did he tell you he was coming?"

"No, but he might decide to come at the last minute. You should at least come for a little while. If you're totally miserable, then I'll ask Zander to take you home." She folded her hands as if to pray. "Please, Whitney? Please come? You look stunning in that dress."

I knew arguing was pointless. "Fine. I'll think about it, but I just hope I don't regret this."

"You won't." Emily said the words with emphasis. "Trust me."

Later that evening, I knocked on my parents' bedroom door and entered after my father told me to come in. My parents were both propped up in bed. Mom was reading a book, and Dad was watching the news.

I stood in the doorway, wishing my mother would look over at me. "I just wanted to say good night."

Dad muted the television and then looked at me. "Did you have a nice time at youth group?"

"Yeah, I did. Emily was there." I fingered the ribbon on my pajamas.

"That's nice," Dad said.

Mom glanced at me, her expression blank. Oh how I

longed for her to talk to me! It felt as if the silence between us had grown from a small crack to the Grand Canyon since Saturday night.

"Well, good night." I gave a little wave. "Love you."

"Good night, Whitney. Love you too." Dad winked at me.

As I stepped out into the hallway, I heard my mother's voice faintly say, "I love you, dear." The sound of her words gave me a glimmer of hope through my despair.

I hopped into bed, snuggled under my covers, and closed my eyes before taking Jenna's advice to open my heart up to God as I had the previous nights:

God, I hurt so much. I see now what a big mistake I made when I lied to my mother and Taylor. I know I should've been up front and honest with my mother about my feelings for Taylor. I believe Jenna when she says you're still with me, but God, I need your help. Please help me know what to say to Mom and Taylor. And please help them to be open to listening to me. Help them to understand. I'm so sorry I hurt them. I love them both.

The next morning I awoke with a sense of peace I hadn't felt since the fallouts with my mother and Taylor. Although I wasn't certain I'd found a solution, I felt as if I could handle the situation and find the strength to make it right. I just kept praying for the right words.

After school I was heading down the hallway when I heard someone call my name. I looked back and found Coach Lori waving to me from her classroom door.

"Whitney. Do you have a minute?" She beckoned me into her room.

"Sure." I stepped into the classroom. "What's going on?"

"We need to talk." Coach Lori closed the door behind me. "Have a seat."

I lowered myself into a desk in the front row. "Am I in trouble?"

She laughed. "No, you aren't in trouble. I just wanted to talk to you for a minute." She sat at a desk across from me. "I wanted to check on you. How are things going?"

"Fine." I hoped I sounded convincing.

"I had an interesting conversation with a couple of the cheer-team girls yesterday. I found out that schoolwork wasn't the reason you left the team." She folded her hands. "Do you want to tell me the truth?"

I hesitated, wondering how much I should share with her. How could I tell her the team didn't approve of my boyfriend? It sounded so childish.

"I know Misty Strickland and Monica Barnes weren't nice to you." Coach Lori said. "I've tried very hard to make my team not be the stereotypical mean-girl clique you see in high school movies. I'm starting to think I've failed."

"No, it's not your fault. I just didn't feel like a part of the team anymore. I've been going through some changes. I guess you could call it an identity crisis. I found myself not fitting in with the friends I've known since elementary and middle school."

Coach Lori sat back in the chair. "I remember going through that when I was your age. You're going to experience some big changes during the next few years. Where are you going to college?"

I hesitated. "I haven't figured that out yet. I've been accepted at three. My mom is pressuring me to go to her alma mater, but I really would like to go to University with my cousin." I almost said *and my boyfriend*, but I stopped when I realized

Taylor and I weren't even friends anymore. Now Emily and the superb teaching program were the only reasons I wanted to go to University.

"What's your mother's alma mater?"

"Kentwood University." I said the words as if they were cuss words.

"Really?" Coach Lori's eyes lit up. "I went there too! I loved it."

"You did?" I sat up straight.

"Yes, I did. I met my husband there. It's a wonderful school."

"It is?" I'd never imagined Coach Lori, my favorite teacher and the most amazing cheer coach, had gone to the same college my mother had. This completely surprised me.

"Why do you look so shocked, Whitney?"

"I just thought that since my mom wanted me to go there ..." My words trailed off. How could I tell Coach Lori I was simply turned off by Kentwood because my mom had gone there? The statement was so ridiculous and immature.

"Do you think Kentwood is uncool because your mother went there?"

"No." I thought for a moment. "It's not that it's uncool, but I'm tired of my mother controlling my life."

Coach Lori tapped on the desk. "My mother was the same way. She wasn't happy I decided to be a teacher."

"Really? How did you handle that?"

"I just told her I respected her opinion, but I wanted to live my life the way I saw fit. I'm very happy with my decisions." She pointed around the room. "I love what I do. I love teaching and I love coaching."

"And she respected that decision?"

"Yes, eventually." Coach Lori crossed her legs. "You know, sometimes you have to follow what feels right in your heart and not worry about what other people think."

"Yeah." I thought about Taylor. "I hurt someone who means a lot to me because I wasn't strong enough to stand up to my mother."

"What happened?"

"My mom didn't like my boyfriend." I studied the top of the desk to avoid her eyes. "I lied to her and told her I was going to prom alone because I was too chicken to tell her the truth. He found out, and he was hurt. He broke up with me, and I can't blame him. I really messed up. I should've stood up to my mom and not let him go."

"If he's a good guy, he'll give you another chance."

I looked up into her sympathetic eyes. "I hope so." I sat up straighter. "So, tell me more about Kentwood."

"Oh, I'd love to!" Coach Lori talked about the dorms, her friends, her sorority, and her favorite professors as I listened with interest. "Have you ever visited the campus?"

"I went once with my parents last spring. It's nice, but it's pretty far away."

"It's not that far away. You can make the trip home in one day." She leaned over to me. "And Kentwood is a good option if you really want to put a little bit of distance between yourself and your mom."

I paused for a moment, considering her words. "Do you think not finishing the year as cheer captain could reflect badly on my Kentwood application?"

Coach Lori smiled. "Not if I write you a glowing recommendation. After all, I did graduate magna cum laude from Kentwood."

"Would you do that for me?"

"Of course I would, Whitney." She stood. "Do you think you'll consider going to Kentwood now that you've heard about it from an alumnus who isn't your mother?"

I stood and lifted my backpack onto my shoulder. "I think I will consider it. I know it's a good school, and my guidance counselor told me earning a degree from Kentwood is similar to earning one from an Ivy League school."

"That's true." She walked me to the door. "It's an honor to be accepted there. You should be proud of yourself for getting in, and you should really consider the school as a good choice, not as your mother's alma mater."

"Thank you," I said. "I appreciate being able to talk to you."

"Anytime, Whitney. And don't give up on that boy."

"I won't." I headed down the hallway wondering what my parents would say if I told them I was seriously considering going to Kentwood.

chapter twenty-one

Saturday afternoon I was thinking about my conversation with Coach Lori and surfing Kentwood's website while sitting on my bed. Emily and Mom burst into my room, and I nearly jumped out of my skin.

"Whitney!" Emily gestured widely. "Why aren't you dressed? We need to leave for our salon appointments. Zander is going to be ready to head out to the prom at five."

I looked at my cousin and mom. "I wasn't planning on going."

Mom stepped into my walk-in closet and began poking through my clothes. "I bought you a gorgeous dress, shoes, and a purse. You're going to prom if I have to drive you there myself. Let's find you some jeans and a button-down shirt."

Emily grinned. "We're going to have the best time, Whitney! Oh, I can't wait. Zander looks so hot in a tuxedo." She fanned herself as if the temperature had shot up one hundred degrees.

I wondered what it would've been like if Taylor and I had double-dated with Zander and Emily tonight. Yes, it would've been perfect.

Mom tossed a pair of jeans and a yellow button-down shirt at me. "Get dressed, Whitney. We have to be there in twenty minutes. You know I don't like to be ..." She stopped speaking and stared at my laptop screen. "What are you looking at?"

"Kentwood's website." I watched her expression transform from frustration to delight.

"Really?" Mom crouched down and began pointing out buildings where she'd lived, had classes, and attended activities during her college career. She then studied me. "Why are you looking at this?"

"I was talking to Coach Lori yesterday, and she told me she went to school there."

"Oh." Mom's expression was hesitant. "Does your sudden interest mean you're considering it now?"

I closed my laptop screen and faced her. "Yes. I'm considering it."

"Well, that's good news." Mom pointed toward the clothes. "We need to head out. We only have fifteen minutes now."

"I'll be right down." I climbed off the bed.

Mom hurried through the door, but Emily lingered in the doorway. "We're going to have a magical night, Whitney. I'm positive."

"I hope so." I watched her disappear and shook my head before dressing.

Late that afternoon, Emily and I stood in the family room dressed for the prom. Emily looked stunning in her green dress, with her brown hair falling in curls past her shoulders. Her makeup perfectly accentuated her emerald eyes, and her nails were painted bright red. She wore her mother's pearl necklace along with the matching earrings my mother bought her. Uncle Brad couldn't stop grinning while he snapped photo after photo of Emily and me as we posed like runway models in front of the fireplace.

I checked my reflection in the mirror above the mantel. My light-brown hair, which was now highlighted with golden streaks thanks to Casey, was styled in a french twist, and I wore my mother's ruby necklace and matching earrings. I realized it didn't matter how I looked, since appearances were what had driven a wedge between Taylor and me. I knew I had to stop worrying about what people thought and just be true to myself.

Uncle Brad turned toward me. "You don't have anything to worry about, Whitney. You look beautiful."

"Thanks." I fingered my little silver purse that matched my shoes. I could only fit my phone and a tube of lipstick in it, but it was so cute that I had to have it.

"Okay, girls." Mom motioned to us. "One more photo before you go next door to Zander's house."

Emily and I stood together and gave our best cheesy smiles while Mom snapped another dozen photos. We then headed through the kitchen. Emily and Uncle Brad continued through the open sliding-glass door and out to the deck.

My father touched my arm and held me back. "Whitney. Don't go just yet." He rubbed my arm. "You look lovely. I just wanted to tell you I'm really proud of you. You've had a tremendous high school career, and I'm so in awe of all you've accomplished." He kissed my cheek. "This is a special night for you. Have a wonderful time."

"Thank you." I held my purse in my hand while overwhelming emotions flooded through me.

Logan nodded. "You look really pretty for an irritating big sister."

"Thanks, Logan. You're okay for an annoying little brother." I glanced at Mom, and I was certain her eyes were shimmering with tears. "I'm really sorry about everything, Mom. I never meant to hurt you, and I'm sorry for being so disrespectful. I appreciate all you do for me, and I know you've been pushing me because you love me and want what's best for me. I can't stand the silence between us anymore. I wish you would accept my apology." I paused and sniffed.

"Of course I forgive you, dear. You're my baby girl. I think I've been so hard on you because I've been afraid of losing you after you graduate. It's going to be difficult not having you around after you leave for college. I'm really going to miss you." My mom opened her arms, and I stepped into her embrace. "Now, don't cry, dear. If you do, then your makeup will run. You don't want to look like a clown at the prom."

I couldn't stop my laugh. Even during an emotional moment, Mom was most worried about my appearance. She handed me a napkin, and I dabbed it under my eyes.

"Go have fun, Whitney." Mom pointed toward the door. "If you don't hurry, Zander will leave without you. Take your time coming home. Your father and I will wait up for you, and you can tell us all about your evening."

The four of us headed out to where Emily and Zander were posing for photos in the driveway next to the brand-new BMW sedan Zander's father had bought.

"Whitney!" Zander opened his arms as I approached. "You look great."

"Thank you. You don't look so bad yourself." I stepped into his hug. "It's good to see you."

"Let me get some photos!" Mom immediately began directing us to stand together for another dozen photos.

"We'd better head out." Zander gestured toward his father's shiny sedan. "We don't want to miss the dinner."

"No, we don't." Emily gazed up at Zander.

I couldn't help but wish Taylor was here. I was certain he'd look just as handsome as Zander looked in his tuxedo. I hoped Emily was right, and somehow Taylor would be inspired to come to prom and give me another chance to explain myself and also apologize. I hoped he missed me as much as I missed him.

I said good-bye to Uncle Brad, my brother, my parents, and Zander's parents and then climbed into the backseat of the BMW. The scent of leather engulfed me as I buckled my seat belt and waited for Zander and Emily to join me.

After a few more minutes of talking to Zander's parents, Emily and Zander finally climbed into the front seat, exchanging a brief kiss before buckling themselves in. I felt out of place, like a fifth wheel. I wished I had insisted on driving by myself, but I knew Emily would never have agreed to it.

"I love this car." Emily glanced around. "I'd love to get under the hood and see what makes it tick."

Zander chuckled while steering out of the driveway. "Yeah, I would too, but Dad won't let me touch it."

Emily ran her fingers over the dashboard. "It's amazing. I hope I can afford something this nice someday. I'm surprised he let you drive it."

"I didn't think you two lovely ladies would want to climb into my Jeep Wrangler in your fancy gowns." Zander glanced at me in the rearview mirror.

"Thank you. I appreciate your thoughtfulness." I grinned at him. "Is Chelsea going to meet us there?"

"Yes. Her boyfriend had to work until three this afternoon, so they might be a little late." Emily checked her reflection in the mirror, and I smiled. I'd never known her to be so concerned about her makeup in the past, but she seemed to enjoy how she looked tonight.

Emily asked Zander a zillion questions about school as we drove toward the ritzy Cavalier Hotel downtown. I stared out the window and wondered what Taylor was doing. Could he possibly be getting ready to go to the prom?

I was lost in my thoughts when I heard my phone buzz. I pulled it out of my purse and gasped when I saw Taylor's number on the display.

"What's wrong?" Emily spun and looked at me.

"It's Taylor!" I said.

Emily grinned. "Answer it, silly."

"Hello?" I asked, my hand shaking as I held the phone to my ear.

"Hey." Taylor's voice was unsure.

"Hi." My voice was shaky. "How are you?"

"I've been better." He paused. "How are you?"

"Yeah, I'm about the same."

"Where are you?"

"I'm in the backseat of Zander's car. We're on our way to the prom. Why?" I held my breath.

"I've been doing a lot of soul searching, and I think we need to talk."

"That sounds like a good idea." Hope filled me at the possibility of working things out. "When do you want to talk?"

"Well, I just got off work. I took an extra shift so I could keep myself preoccupied after our argument. I was going crazy after our breakup. I can't stop thinking about you."

"I've been feeling the same way."

"I wanted to call you all day, but work was nonstop. We're having a big sale, and there were lines out the door. I can be at the hotel in a little while. I still need to get changed and take care of a few things. Maybe we can find someplace quiet to talk at the prom. Does that sound okay?"

"That sounds perfect." My heart turned over in my chest.

"All right. I'll see you in a little bit, okay?"

"I look forward to it." I disconnected the phone and blew out a deep sigh.

"Well?" Emily asked with anticipation.

"He said we need to talk. It sounds like he wants to work things out. He's going to meet me at the prom in a little while."

Emily squeezed my hand. "I told you not to give up hope. God heard your prayers, and he's answering them in his own time."

"You were right all along, Em. Thank you."

Zander pulled the car up to the entrance of the hotel, and a valet rushed out to meet him. After giving the man his keys, Zander moved around the car, opened the passenger door, took Emily's hand in his, and helped her out. I started to open my door, but Zander yelled for me to stop.

He then opened my door and held out his hand. "May I help you?"

I took his hand. "You're such a gentleman, Zander."

"I try my best." He helped me out of the car and then offered his arms to Emily and me. "I'm the coolest guy at the prom, since I have a beautiful date on each arm."

Emily and I laughed as he led us into the hotel. I glanced around the stunning lobby decorated with three enormous crystal chandeliers, a fountain, colorful paintings, large potted trees, and elegant leather furniture.

We followed the crowd of well-dressed teenagers down the hallway and into the ballroom, where loud music boomed through speakers and reverberated off the walls. Students were already moving on the dance floor, which was in the middle of a sea of round tables decorated with shimmering confetti, glasses featuring our school logo and year, and maroon, yellow, and white balloons.

Hoots and hollers drew my attention to the far side of the room, where Brett, Chad, Doug, Spencer, and a group of other football players were whistling and calling to Zander.

"Zander!" Chad hollered.

"Yo, Stewart!" Doug chimed in.

They motioned for Zander to join them, and he waved in response.

I dropped my hand from Zander's arm and slowed my steps as Zander and Emily headed off toward the group of football players and their dates. While he was in high school, Zander played one year of football until he injured his knee. Although he couldn't continue to play on the team, he remained good friends with the players. I understood why he wanted to visit with his friends, but I couldn't bear the thought of standing there and listening while Zander talked with them.

I glanced around the room and looked for someone to talk to while Emily and Zander stood with my former friends. Not finding anyone to visit with, I stood by a table and pretended to be absolutely fascinated with the flickering LED lights and the shimmering glitter on the table.

"Whitney?" A voice sounded above the blare of the music.

I looked behind me just as Chelsea rushed up to me dressed in the most amazing navy-blue gown I'd ever seen. "Chelsea, you look breathtaking!"

"Doesn't she?" Her boyfriend, Todd, placed his hand on her shoulder.

"Thanks, Whitney." Chelsea beamed. "I took an old dress from my mom and updated it a bit." She looked down and moved the shimmering skirt back and forth.

"You're so talented." I touched the dress.

"Thank you." Chelsea pointed at my dress. "You look gorgeous, Whitney. I love your hair. The highlights look really nice."

"Thanks. It needed to be brightened up a bit." I pointed toward Emily, who was standing next to Zander while he laughed with his friends. "Emily and Zander are over there."

Chelsea gestured toward the empty table. "Why don't we sit?"

"Good idea," I told her, raising my voice over the music.

The three of us sat down, and I studied the table settings while Chelsea and Todd talked to each other. A slow song rang out over the speakers. Todd took Chelsea's hand and led her to the dance floor.

I slumped back in my chair and contemplated my conversation with Taylor. I was so thankful he had called me, and I was anxious to see him. I hoped he wanted to work things out, but I feared he'd tell me he only wanted to be friends. I longed to be his girlfriend, but living without his friendship at all would be torture. At least being his friend would allow me to have a place in his life, which was better than having no contact with him at all.

I glanced across the ballroom to where Zander was high-fiving his friends as Emily began walking toward me. I hoped they would join me and not dance, even though I knew that was selfish.

They approached the table, and Emily sat next to me.

"Did you see Chelsea?" Emily asked, speaking loudly over the music.

"Yes." I pointed to where Chelsea and Todd were swaying together. "They took off for the dance floor when this song came on."

"Oh." Emily watched them dance. "She looks awesome."

"I know." I nodded.

Zander leaned over to me. "Chad tried to talk me into sitting at their table, but I couldn't do that to you. Emily told me how awful Brett's been to you. I'm going to give him a piece of my mind when I have a moment."

"Thanks, Zander." I tapped his arm. "I appreciate your offer, but it won't help. Nothing will change his attitude."

"I'll give it a try. I remember when he was a freshman and was struggling quite a bit on the football field. He wasn't so high and mighty then."

The slow song ended, and Chelsea and Todd weaved through the sea of tables to where we were sitting. Emily jumped up and hugged Chelsea while Zander and Todd shook hands.

Emily handed her phone to Zander. "Would you take a photo of Chels, Whitney, and me?"

"Of course." Zander held up the phone, and we posed for a few photos.

I dug into my little purse and handed him my phone, and he took a few more photos. We then sat at the table and made small talk while watching more of our classmates arrive. I couldn't stop myself from glancing at the doors, hoping to see Taylor appear in a tuxedo carrying a beautiful corsage for me.

Something drew my eyes to the other side of the room, and I found Kristin looking at me. I held her gaze for a moment and then looked down at my phone and examined the photos Zander had taken so I could avert my eyes from her probing stare. After studying all of the photos I'd taken since I bought my phone, I moved on to email, perusing all of the emails I'd received in the past week.

Several minutes later, I felt a tap on my shoulder.

"Hi." Kristin gave me a tentative expression. "Can we talk?"

"Sure." I left my purse and phone on the table and walked with Kristin toward the far end of the ballroom.

"You look really nice," she said as we walked.

"You do too." I pointed at her red, strapless dress, which fit her like a glove. A red-and-silver rhinestone necklace sparkled from around her neck. "Red is your color."

"Thanks." She touched her dress. "My mom wasn't happy I picked strapless, but I won."

We stopped in the far corner, and she faced me. "I want to apologize. I was a real jerk to you, and I'm sorry. I had no right to push you to get back together with Brett. It's none of my business who you decide to date."

"Thanks." I crossed my arms over my chest.

"You've been my best friend since first grade." She sniffed. "The truth is, I miss you, Whitney."

I hugged her. "I miss you too, Kristin."

Kristin gave a little laugh and wiped her eyes. "I told Coach Lori how awful we all were to you. She was really disappointed."

I snapped my fingers. "You were the one who told her the truth. I was wondering how she found out."

"Yeah." Kristin sniffed. "I couldn't live with the guilt anymore. She encouraged me to come and talk to you, but I was so angry with myself that I didn't know what to say. I realized the best way to handle it was to be honest and admit I was wrong."

"Thank you." I touched her hand.

"So, we're friends again?" She looked hopeful.

"Absolutely."

Kristin pointed toward my table. "Where's Taylor?"

"That's a long story. Basically I did something stupid, and he broke up with me."

"No!" Kristin cupped her hand to her mouth. "What happened?"

I told Kristin the abbreviated version of what transpired, and she shook her head with empathy.

I smiled at her authenticity. "He called me earlier and said he wanted to talk. He should be here soon. I'm just hoping he wants to work things out. It's been torture to not talk to him. I miss him so much."

She touched my shoulder. "If he really likes you, which I'm

certain he does, he'll give you another chance. I think Brett's been acting like such a jerk to you because he's jealous of you and Taylor. He can see how good you and Taylor are together."

"You're probably right, but nothing excuses Brett's behavior."

"Very true." She looped her arm around my shoulders. "I'm so glad we're friends again. I couldn't imagine graduating without having you as my best friend. Let's not fight again, okay?"

"Okay." I spotted the waitstaff bringing out the salads. "Hey, it looks like it's time to eat. We better get back to our tables."

She started toward her table. "I'll go tell Doug we're coming to sit with you."

"Wait!" I grabbed her arm and pulled her back. "I don't want Brett and Misty to come over."

"Don't worry. They're not invited." She hurried off toward her table.

I sat down next to Emily, and she moved close to me.

"It looks like you and Kristin worked things out," she said.

"Yes. She apologized and asked to be friends again. I'm so relieved. I missed her."

"That's wonderful news." Emily clapped her hands.

Kristin and Doug joined our table, with Kristin sitting beside me. Soon the waitstaff brought our salads, and we were all eating and talking over the loud music. I couldn't stop thinking about Taylor and wondering when he would arrive. The anticipation was eating me up inside.

I was listening while Zander shared a story about his automotive technical school when I spotted a flash out of the corner of my eye. I looked down at the table, and my iPhone was lit up, telling me I had a text message. I held up the phone, and when I found a message from Taylor, my heart skipped a beat.

I unlocked the phone and read the entire message, which said: *I'm looking for a good Spanish tutor. Do you know anyone who can translate this: Te extraño?*

He missed me! Tears filled my eyes as I typed back: *I might be able to help you. I think it means I miss you too.*

He quickly responded: *Is that so? How about this: Te vez linda en ese vestido rosado.*

My mouth gaped as I translated "You look pretty in that pink dress." I glanced around the room looking for Taylor but didn't spot him. *Where is he hiding?*

Emily touched my hand. "Is Taylor texting you?"

"Yes." I kept my eyes glued to the phone screen and typed: *U can see me, but I can't see u. That's not fair!*

My pulse quickened as I awaited a response. Where was he? Why wasn't he responding? A hand touched my shoulder, and I nearly jumped out of my skin. I looked up and found Taylor smiling down at me.

"Taylor!" I leaped from my chair and into his arms. "Oh, Taylor. I'm so glad you're finally here."

"You're the most beautiful girl in the room." His breath was warm against my neck as he whispered in my ear. "I've been going crazy without you. I've missed you so much."

"I've missed you too." I took a step back and studied him. I couldn't help but smile when I realized he was still taller than I was, even though I was wearing heels. Maybe we *were* meant to be together!

Not only was he tall, but he was handsome in his tuxedo. "You look amazing."

He held out a clear plastic box containing a wrist corsage with pink tea roses and baby's breath. "I was hoping I got the right shade of pink."

"Oh, I love it!" He put it on my wrist, and I held it next to my dress. "It's perfect."

"I have something else for you too." Taylor handed me a small pink gift bag. "It's a peace offering."

I fished past the pink tissue paper and found homemade chocolate-chip cookies. I laughed as I pulled one out. "Did you make these?"

He shook his head. "No, I can't take credit for that. My mom made them for me. I couldn't get off work early, so I knew I wouldn't have time to make them before I came tonight."

"Thank you so much." I hugged him again. "I'm so glad you're here."

He rested his chin on my head and rubbed my back. "I am too. I can barely hear myself think over the music. Can we go talk somewhere?"

"Yes." I placed the bag on the table and glanced at Kristin and Emily, who both gave me a thumbs-up. I then took Taylor's hand, and he led me out into the hallway.

chapter twenty-two

Taylor and I walked together toward the lobby.

"You look stunning, Whitney." He glanced down at my dress. "You actually took my breath away when I saw you. I mean that."

I blushed as I looked up at him. "Thank you. You're the hottest guy at the prom by the way. No one can wear a tux like you."

He laughed. "Thanks."

He led me toward a leather sofa on the far end of the lobby, and we sat together.

"I'm sorry for what I said to you at school." He held my hand while facing me. "I shouldn't have accused you of using me. I said all of that because I was hurt."

"I deserved it." My eyes filled with tears. "You were right when you said I should've stood up to my mom."

"No, I know it was more complicated than that."

"But it shouldn't be." I held his hand in both of mine. "I know now I have to stand up for what I believe in, despite what my mother thinks or what anyone else thinks. I need to be comfortable in my own skin and not worry about stereotypes. I am who I am, despite what everyone else thinks. You mean more to me than anyone else, and I'm ready to stand up for you."

"Thank you." He paused. "I guess what hurt me the most was when I heard you admit you had used me to rebel against your mother. I had thought your friendship was genuine from the start. I just felt foolish for believing you could like me."

"I always liked you." I emphasized the words. "I just wound up liking you a lot more than I ever imagined. I thought we'd be friends, but after I got to know you, I couldn't wait for you to ask me out. You've become my best friend. I've been able to share things with you that I've never told anyone. You bring out the best in me. You challenge me to think beyond myself, and I've learned so much from you. I've learned more than just enough calculus to get a B-plus. I've learned how to be a better person."

I squeezed his hand as I continued. "In the beginning I thought being your friend would be a great way to rebel against my mother, but I found I liked you more and more as we spent more time together. And I love your family. Your sister is a sweetheart, and your mom is easy to talk to. I truly fell for you and your family. I'm just sorry you had to hear my conversation with my mother. My mother couldn't understand how I could become close to you, but she's never taken the time to get to know you and your family. She's missing out on wonderful people who are genuine and work hard for a living."

"Wow," he said. "You've really figured things out."

"I have. There have been people like Emily and Jenna who've helped me along the way. I've also been talking to God a lot, and I feel like I have a deeper relationship with him. I realize now who I am as a person. I don't care what others think of me. I have to be true to myself. I can stand up to my mother for what I think is right, and I'm going to start doing that."

"I'm glad to hear that." He stared into my eyes. "I'm really sorry I broke up with you. I was wrong to not respond to your text messages or your calls, but I was trying to sort through all of my feelings. I was hurt, but I also missed you terribly. I couldn't stop thinking about you. I've never felt this way about anyone before."

"I haven't either. I felt like my heart was ripped out when you wouldn't talk to me."

Taylor ran his finger down my cheekbone and then rested his hand on my cheek. "I know part of my problem was I never felt like I was good enough for you. As much as I accused you of being a snob, I was just as guilty of not thinking we belonged together. When I realized I was falling for you, I got scared. I was afraid you didn't feel the same way about me that I felt about you. I was actually afraid to ask you out because I thought you would reject me. I thought you'd laugh at me and say that you only wanted to be friends."

"I would never laugh at you, Taylor. I thought it was obvious I was dying for you to ask me out."

"I think my low self-esteem got in the way. I was so convinced you would never consider me good enough to be your boyfriend that I sabotaged myself." He caressed my cheek with his hand. "I was so wrong about everything. I'm sorry for letting my pride get in the way. I never believed in myself. I never believed in us."

"You can believe in us now, Taylor." I turned my face and kissed his hand. "We do belong together."

"I know that now. And I plan to never let you go again."

"That sounds good to me."

He dipped his chin and kissed me. I lost myself in the warmth of his kiss, and I wanted the moment to last forever.

He looked down at me and touched my face. "I think we'd better get back into the ballroom before our friends eat our dinner."

"You're probably right. Zander looked pretty hungry."

Taylor stood and took my hand in his. He pulled me to my feet, and we started back toward the ballroom.

As we approached the door, I looked up at him. "What made you change your mind about me?"

He stopped and held my hand up to his chest. "You mean other than the fact that I couldn't stop thinking about you?"

I nodded. "Did you talk to someone who changed your mind?"

Taylor grinned. "Let's just say a neighbor spoke to me."

"A neighbor?" My eyes widened. "Emily?"

"Your cousin has a very good perspective on things, and she made me realize how much you and I care about each other. She and I had a long talk last night, and I was up most of the night thinking about what she said. She's very wise, and she also thinks a lot of you."

"It's mutual." I looked through the door and spotted Emily and Zander sitting close together talking to each other. I was so thankful for my cousin and our very special friendship.

The music transitioned from a loud, heavy rock beat to a slow song, and Taylor tugged on my arm, causing me to stumble forward.

"What are you doing?" I asked as I trailed him.

"You're going to dance with me, Whitney Richards." He grinned at me. "It's our senior prom, and we need some fun memories of making fools of ourselves on the dance floor."

"Speak for yourself! I took two years of tap and three of ballet."

"Along with the gymnastics?" He pulled me onto the dance floor.

"Yes. My mother was into running me around to different activities when I was younger." I wrapped my arms around his neck.

"You're something else, Whitney Richards." He looped his arms around my waist.

"That's why you like me." I grinned at him.

"No, I don't like you, Whitney." He shook his head and then leaned down. "*Te amo*." The words were like music to me.

"I love you too, Taylor." I closed my eyes and rested my head on his chest as happiness bubbled inside me.

The rest of the evening moved at lightning speed as we danced, ate, talked, and laughed with our friends. All too soon, the time passed midnight, and students were slowly starting to leave.

Emily yawned and placed her head on Zander's chest while we stood by our table. "I think I'm spent. I don't mean to be a killjoy, but I need to get home."

Zander glanced at me. "I assume you have a ride home, Whitney?"

"Well, that depends." I turned to Taylor. "Did you bring your motorcycle?"

"Nope." He placed his arm on my shoulder. "I brought my uncle's car."

"Really?" Emily's eyebrows shot up. "I think I want to ride home with you."

"Hey!" Zander feigned insult. "The Beamer isn't good enough for you?"

"You haven't seen Taylor's uncle's car." Emily bumped Zander with her elbow. "If you did, you'd leave the Beamer in the parking garage and ride home with Taylor too."

"What's the big secret?" I looked between Emily and Taylor while they smiled at each other. "What kind of car is it?"

Zander folded his arms over his chest. "I'm listening. If Emily is that impressed, then it has to be good."

"My uncle Rico restored a 1966 Mustang," Taylor said. "It's out of this world."

"And he let you borrow it tonight?" Zander asked.

"Yeah." Taylor puffed out his chest like a proud bird. "He trusts me."

"He obviously does." Zander pointed toward the door. "Let's go see this car. Maybe I'll let you take the Beamer, and I'll try out the Mustang."

Taylor shook his head. "I don't think so."

The four of us walked out to the lobby, and when we reached the entrance, the boys handed the valets their keys. While we waited for the cars, Zander and Taylor fell into a conversation about cars and motorcycles.

I moved closer to Emily. "You were right, Emily. Everything worked out perfectly. This evening has been magical."

"I know." She squeezed my hand. "I'm so happy for you and Taylor. I knew things would work out."

"Thank you. I owe part of it to you."

Emily shook her head. "No. He already knew you two belonged together. He just needed me to push him in the right direction."

"You're the best." I hugged her.

A roaring engine drew our attention to a shiny, candy-apple-red Mustang pulling up to the entrance of the hotel.

"Wow!" Zander's eyes looked as if they might pop out of his head. "Look at that."

"Isn't it awesome?" Emily ran her fingers over the hood.

"It's a gorgeous car." I stepped over to the passenger door.

Taylor moved ahead of me and opened the door. "Allow me."

"Why, thank you." I climbed in and smoothed my dress over my legs. I rolled down the window and waved to Emily and Zander. "Good night!"

"Have fun," Emily called.

Taylor jogged around the front of the car and then climbed in beside me.

"See you two later. We have to get together sometime." Zander pointed toward the car. "I want to drive it."

"I bet you do. Good night." Taylor revved the engine and pulled away from the curb. He steered through the parking lot and then rested his hand on mine. "Did you have a nice evening?"

"No." I teased him. "I had a wonderfully perfect evening."

"I did too." He squeezed my hand.

"I have a question for you." I angled my body toward him. "How would you feel if your girlfriend went to Kentwood instead of U?"

Taylor gave me a sideways glance. "I'd be super proud, and I'd look forward to visiting her often."

"Really?"

He laughed. "Yes, really. Why wouldn't I support you if you went to Kentwood? Just because we're a few hours away from each other doesn't mean our relationship has to end, Whitney. Don't let the fear of losing me crush your dreams. I'm not planning on going anywhere."

I nodded while considering his words.

He merged onto Main Street. "What made you change your mind about Kentwood?"

"I had a long talk with Coach Lori, and she shared that she went there. She told me how much she loved it, and she said something I'd heard before but hadn't really listened to." I stared through the windshield at the bright stars in the sky. "She said I shouldn't make my choice about a college just to rebel against my mother. I need to make my choices based on what I want to do with my life. I can respectfully tell my mother I want to follow my own path."

He squeezed my hand again. "Exactly."

"I was looking at Kentwood's website this morning, and

I started to get really excited about the idea of going there." I faced him. "I think that's where I want to go, but I don't want to lose you."

Taylor slowed at a stoplight and turned toward me. "Whitney, I will support whatever you want to do. Just don't forget me when you go off to your ritzy college."

"I won't. I'll look forward to your Spanish text messages every night."

He laughed and then accelerated through the intersection before turning into Castleton.

I glanced around the interior of the Mustang. "How did you get your uncle to loan you this amazing car?"

"It was actually Vanessa's idea." He turned onto my street.

"It was?" I ran my fingers over the dashboard.

"Yes. She said I had to take you in style, and Mom's old Ford wasn't pretty enough for you."

"That's sweet, but the Ford would've been fine with me."

He pulled into my driveway and parked behind my Jeep.

I unbuckled my seat belt and turned toward him. "Do you have a few minutes to come inside?"

Taylor raised his eyebrows. "Are you certain?"

"I'm absolutely positive. I want to formally introduce you as my boyfriend to my family." I pushed the door open.

"Wait. I need to live up to my sister's expectation of me by treating you like a lady."

I laughed as he jogged around the car, opened the door, and held out his hand. "You're so silly," I said as he closed the door behind me.

"No, I'm not silly. I'm a proper gentleman." He offered me his arm, and I latched on to it as we made our way to the back door of the house.

Taylor followed me into the kitchen, and I placed my purse

and the gift bag full of cookies on the counter. I heard the soft murmur of the television in the family room, and I motioned for Taylor to follow me.

I found my parents in their robes sitting together on the sofa. A late-night talk show featuring a man behind a desk talking to a lady holding a poodle was on the large flat-screen television.

"Hi." I took Taylor's hand in mine and tugged him forward as we stood in front of my parents. "I'm home."

"Whitney." Dad muted the television. "Did you have a nice time?"

I gazed up at Taylor. "I had a perfect evening." I turned back to my parents. "Mom and Dad, you remember my boyfriend, Taylor."

"Hi, Mr. and Mrs. Richards. It's great to see you again." Taylor held out his hand.

Dad got up from the sofa and shook Taylor's hand. "It's nice to see you again too, young man." Dad gave me a quick wink, and I smiled.

"Thank you. I think the world of your daughter." Taylor placed his hand on my back.

Mom stepped over to Taylor and shook his hand. "Hello, Taylor. You've really brought my daughter a lot of joy, and I'm thankful for that."

My heart warmed at my mother's kind words.

"Thank you," Taylor said. "She's been a wonderful inspiration to me and my family. She's taught my sister and me a lot. I'm really thankful she messed up in calculus so we had the chance to meet up again. It had been a long time since we last talked back in fourth grade."

I grinned up at him. "Thank goodness for calculus and Mr. Turner."

"I'm glad you helped her bring her calculus grade up to a

B-plus." Mom turned to me. "Whitney thinks a lot of you and your family. We'll have to have you all over for dinner one night before you leave for college."

"That would be great. I know my mom and sister would love that." Taylor looked at me. "Are you going to tell your parents your decision?"

I hesitated.

"What decision?" Mom studied me. "Is this about college?"

I nodded. "I want to go to Kentwood."

Mom clapped her hands. "Oh, I'm so very happy! Oh, Whitney." She hugged me.

"Now wait, Mom." I held up my finger. "Please listen to me."

She nodded. "I'm listening."

"I'm not going to promise you I'll join your sorority or any sorority at all. I'm going to Kentwood because it's my decision." I pointed to my chest. "I'll decide which clubs or activities I want to get involved in after I get there. Do you understand?"

"Yes, I do, dear," she said. "But you've made me very happy."

Dad hugged me. "As I said before, we're very proud of you, Whitney."

"Thanks, Daddy." I kissed his cheek.

"Well, it's after one." Dad took Mom's hand and led her toward the stairs. "We're going to head to bed."

"It was nice seeing you, Mr. and Mrs. Richards." Taylor waved to my parents.

"We'll talk soon about dinner, Taylor," Mom called as they disappeared up the stairs.

"Sounds good," Taylor said.

After they were gone, I hugged Taylor. "I'm so happy! My parents are finally okay about us being together, and we're agreeing about my college plans."

"I'm happy too." He squeezed me close. "I'm even invited to dinner."

I gazed up at him with my arms around his neck. "Yes. That means you've received my mother's approval."

"I'm so honored."

"I know we haven't worked out everything, but I feel like we're on the right track." I rested my head on his chest. "And Emily was right when she said that no matter what happens, God is always there."

"Yes, he is." Taylor's voice was warm and comforting. "I love you, Whitney."

"I love you too, Taylor." I looked up at him.

As he dipped his chin and kissed me, I closed my eyes and thanked God for leading me in the right direction.

Destination Unknown
discussion questions

1. When Whitney wasn't allowed to go to the prom with Taylor, she lied and told her mother that she didn't have a date. Just as Emily predicted, the plan fell apart, and Whitney lost Taylor and had a terrible argument with her mother. How do you think Whitney should have handled her desire to go to the prom with Taylor? If you were Whitney, would you have found a way to go with him without lying to your mother?

2. Whitney's friends try to pressure her to go out with her ex-boyfriend Brett because they think he and Whitney "belong together." Yet despite all of their pressure, Whitney doesn't give in, and she continues to pursue her friendship with Taylor. She refuses to believe she has to date a football player just because she's a cheerleader. Does anyone try to pressure you away from things you feel passionate about? How have you dealt with those types of moments?

3. Humiliated and lost after losing Taylor and arguing with her mother, Whitney was feeling pretty low. Thankfully she could talk to Emily, Jenna, and Coach Lori. Whom do you talk to when you're feeling low and why?

4. Whitney's friends don't understand why she likes Taylor, because he's not from their side of town or into sports. Whitney decides to quit cheerleading, a sport that she loves,

in order to get away from her prejudiced, elitist friends. Do you think Whitney made the right choice when she quit cheerleading? Have you ever faced a situation where your friends weren't supportive of a choice you made? If yes, explain.

5. Emily tries to offer Whitney advice and be a good cousin and friend to her while she's going through a difficult time in her life. If you were Whitney's friend, how would you try to help her cope?

6. Whitney believes God led her through this difficult time to build up her faith and figure out what she really wanted to do with her life. Do you ever feel that God is testing you? If so, what did you learn?

7. Taylor overhears Whitney admit she lied about going to the prom with Taylor, and that she used Taylor to rebel against her mother. Instead of confronting Whitney when he hears her conversations, Taylor avoids her until she confronts him at school. Do you think Taylor was right to avoid Whitney and not be up front with her? Have you ever been in a situation where you overheard something that upset you? If so, how did you handle the news?

8. Whitney's mother is constantly criticizing Whitney's choices and pressuring her to live her life a certain way. If you were in Whitney's shoes, how would you handle a controlling mother like Darlene?

9. Whitney uses prayer to help her find the words to apologize to her mother and Taylor. Do you pray regularly? What kinds of things do you discuss with God? How does prayer help you?

10. Whitney is unsure of which college to pick because her mother is pressuring her to go to her alma mater and join her sorority. If you were Whitney, how would you go about choosing a college? What do you want to do after high school?

Acknowledgments

As always, I'm thankful for my loving family, including my mother, Lola Goebelbecker; my husband, Joe; and my sons, Zac and Matt. Thank you, Mom, for always letting me bounce ideas off you. You're my best plotting partner!

I'm more grateful than words can express to my patient friends who critique my writing for me—Stacey Barbalace, Margaret Halpin, Janet Pecorella, Lauran Rodriguez, and, of course, my mother. I truly appreciate the time you take out of your busy lives to help me polish my books. Special thanks to Amy Lillard for your fantastic help with the little details that nearly drove me insane.

Thank you also to Christa Connelly for her assistance with the cheerleading research. Special thanks to Waleska Selles for her help translating text into Spanish.

Thank you to my wonderful church family at Morning Star Lutheran in Matthews, North Carolina, for your encouragement, prayers, love, and friendship. You all mean so much to my family and me.

To my agent, Mary Sue Seymour—I am grateful for your friendship, support, and guidance in my writing career. Thank you for all you do!

Thank you to my amazing editor—Jacque Alberta. I

appreciate your guidance and friendship. I'm grateful to each and every person at Zondervan who helped make this book a reality. I'm so blessed to be a part of the HarperCollins Christian Publishing family.

To my readers—thank you for choosing my novels. My books are a blessing in my life for many reasons, including the special friendships I've formed with my readers.

Thank you, most of all, to God for giving me the inspiration and the words to glorify you. I'm so grateful and humbled you've chosen this path for me.

Roadside Assistance

Amy Clipston

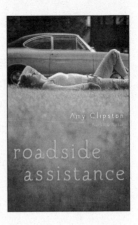

A very bumpy ride. Emily Curtis is used to dealing with her problems while under the hood of an old Chevy, but when her mom dies, Emily's world seems shaken beyond repair. Driven from home by hospital bills they can't pay, Emily and her dad move in with his wealthy sister, who intends to make her niece more feminine—in other words, just like Whitney, Emily's perfect cousin. But when Emily hears the engine of a 1970 Dodge Challenger, and sees the cute gearhead, Zander, next door, things seem to be looking up. But even working alongside Zander can't completely fix the hole in Emily's life. Ever since her mom died, Emily hasn't been able to pray, and no one—not even Zander—seems to understand. But sometimes the help you need can come from the person you least expect.

Available in stores and online!